# Tales from the Coast

More fascinating stories

From

## Askaroff

*Other titles by the same author*

Random Threads Volume I
Patches of Heaven
ISBN 0-9539410-4-3

Random Threads Volume II
Skylark Country
ISBN 0-9539410-2-7

Random Threads Volume III
High Streets & Hedgerows
ISBN 0-9539410-3-5

*Books published containing the author's work*
A Celebration of Childhood   Rivacre   Paperback
Natural Peace   Anchor Books   Paperback
Poetry of Kent   Millfield   Paperback
This Natural World   Arrival Press   Hardback
South East Poets   Arrival Press   Hardback
Let's do Lunch   Remus   new fiction   Paperback
Anchor Poets   Anchor Books   Hardback
This Vanishing World   Poetry Now   Hardback
Web of Thoughts   Anchor Books   Hardback
The Good Ol' Days   Arrival Press   Hardback
New Rhymes for   Arrival Press   Hardback
A Tapestry of Thoughts   Spotlight   Paperback
Mixed Musings   Poetry Now   Hardback
Special Occasions   Arrival Press   Hardback

## Contents

Author's note.............................9
Jaguar......................................17
Spies & Spitfires........................35
Touched by Fire.........................83
A Day of Stories.......................109
Nuria and the Clown.................123
Faith......................................127
The Driscoll Incident................129
Winter's End...........................137
Messerschmitt's & Blackboys......157
Evacuation for Flo....................179
Misty Mornings.......................193
The Witching Hour..................205
W.O.M.B.A.T.........................225
The Last Cockney....................285
Haunted House.......................299
Gone Fishing..........................317
Tears of a Child.......................325
Days end at Combe Hill............351
Wakes Week..........................353
Epilogue.................................379

148 WILLINGDON PARK DRIVE
EASTBOURNE
EAST SUSSEX
ENGLAND
BN22 0DG

Publications 2009

## *FIRST EDITION*

UK ISBN: 978-0-9539410-5-6

CIP library reference:

**Non-Fiction, Nostalgia, Local History.**

Printed and bound in Great Britain by
CPI Antony Rowe, Chippenham and Eastbourne

**First published in Great Britain in 2009**

**ALL RIGHTS RESERVED**

Without limiting the rights under copyright reserved above, no part of this publication may be reproduced or transmitted in any form, including photocopying, recording. No part of this publication may be stored on a retrieval system or be transmitted in any form or by any means without the copyright owner's permission.

The author asserts his moral and legal rights to be identified as the sole author of this work.

The greatest care has been taken in compiling this book. However, no responsibility can be accepted by the publishers or compilers for the accuracy of the information provided.

Although many events in this book are inspired by true incidents the names and places may have been changed for legal and personal reasons. I have visited many thousands of people. Although we are all human and similar in many ways it would be impossible to recognise any individual from the following pages unless so stated. Any similarities with any people living or dead are purely coincidental.

© ALEX I ASKAROFF 2009

Many thanks once again to Lin Hall for his tireless efforts (often wasted) to help my editing and improve my English. Also to Doreen Ramscar for her enthusiasm and guidance. And finally to Mandy Finch for the last read-through.

The **Random Threads Trilogy**, packed full of Alex's stories, available at all bookshops by quoting the details below.

1. PATCHES OF HEAVEN    ISBN 0-9539410-4-3

2. SKYLARK COUNTRY    ISBN 0-9539410-2-7

3. HIGH STREETS & HEDGEROWS    ISBN 0-9539410-3-5

## Crows Nest Publications

© ALEX I ASKAROFF 2009

**Front cover: Birling Gap at Dawn
by Alex Askaroff**

For more information on how to order our books visit our websites:

**http://www.sewalot.com**

**http://crowsnestpublications.com**

*'You may feel that you know Sussex but I will guarantee that Alex provokes you into wanting to look again. He will fill your minds with the happiest of thoughts which will be refreshed every time you turn a page.'*

**Frank Scutt OBE**

To my family and friends who help make this life a little sweeter.

**Alex Askaroff**

# Author's Note

Before we get going, I must tell you a little about myself—an introduction of sorts.

I was born in the latter half of the 1950s in the busy bomb-blitzed seaside town of Eastbourne on the South Coast of England. Rubble still lay about, in places, from the 11,000 or so buildings damaged by German bombs.

At Newhaven, along the coast a smidgen, the old fort still had empty shells and cartridges scattered around its gun emplacements. When fishing from the concrete pier was poor, our gang would explore the endless nests, lookouts and twisting tunnels of the derelict stronghold. The fort was heaven to a band of rebel boys protecting the shores of England.

As I grew, my playground was the soft green undulating hills of the glorious South Downs and as a wild-child I promised myself I would move only when the hills did! I was an Eastbourne lad, born and bred and, while I would wander far from home, I always left my heart at home.

For me there was no finer point in any journey than when I turned for home. Even when, in a Forest Gump moment, my brothers and I cycled from Eastbourne to the tip of Lands End in Cornwall before heading exhausted for the nearest railway station.

My father was a proud White Russian. A sword swirling Cossack, by his accounts, who had heard England's call after the terrible losses of the Second World War. Igor brought his young Austrian partner to England to make his fortune. He was handed a ten-bob note at customs and patted on the back and told to, "Go forth and prosper." That he did.

After a stint in the West Country, and then the smog-filled London streets, he headed for the clean seaside air of Eastbourne. There he raised six strapping lads who were the scourge of the neighbourhood. And so my life began. However, as I was to discover, my love for my country went far deeper than my birth in that sparkling south coast resort.

My grandmother turned out to have been a local girl too. She had run off to Vienna after a family squabble, married an Austrian and produced my mother. Where did granny run off from? Chislehurst in Kent! I had spent half my life thinking I was as foreign as a pot of coffee on a supermarket shelf. In fact I was only partly right for, if one were to read my label, it would say *product of more than one country*. That sums me up perfectly.

Through my veins runs the blood of not only a displaced Russian and beautiful Austrian girl, but Eton, Cambridge and cricket on the village green. To mix the pot, my paternal grandmother was French! I was a mongrel for sure.

The only thing that I excelled at during my schooling was scribbling. Maybe *excelled* is too strong a word—but I had an urge to write that stays with me to this day. Give me a blank sheet of paper and I am away like a sprinter from the blocks.

However I had to make a living to pay the bills. The wealth of my British relations, along with that of my Russian, French and Austrians, had long disappeared. Even good old Great Uncle Anton, Austria's most famous painter, forgot to leave a nugget or two for his distant relation in Eastbourne. Anton

Faistauer had gone to his early grave never knowing that a few decades down the line a chubby little lad would come into existence who wanted to write not work!

My maternal great grandparents lived at the Savoy Hotel in London after my Great Great Grandfather, Stanley Boulter, married its owner Helen D'Oyle Carte. I believe there is a lead planter, with an inscription, still in the hotel supporting a plant or two. They were mixed up with Gilbert & Sullivan and the D'Oyle Carte Opera Company. They owned the Savoy Hotel and the Savoy Theatre and were great friends with Sir Arthur Conan Doyle and Oscar Wilde.

James Robinson Planché, another grandfather-down-the-line, whose father was a Geneva watchmaker and a friend of King George III, was one of the Victorian Era's most prolific playwrights, his daughter, Matilda, wrote dozens of books, many still in print today.

With Matilda my family merges with Mackarness. My Great Grandmother's Uncle was the Bishop of Oxford, John Fielder Mackarness. He in turn was, by marriage, related to one of Britain's finest poets, Samuel Taylor Coleridge.

Did they think of me, their future cuckoo that needed wealth to support his dreams, his grand tour and scribbling? No.

Could I not collect oil paintings in Florence, marble statues in Rome? Was it possible that I had to work for a living? Could I not write poetry in country graveyards, paint in my manor and travel on dear papa's wealth? Another big **No**!

Just the opposite was true. All ancient wealth had disappeared, with just a few old photos and tales to keep us warm. As I grew from embryo to idiot it became clear that I was going to have to earn my crust like the rest of the world. How disappointing! The result was that Mum and Dad raised six hard-grafting lads. Worse was to follow. Of every penny we ever earned, half went to Mumsie. She would wait at the door with her apron held out as we drilled past. We would put half our paper-round money, half our Saturday-jobs wages, half of everything went to her. No pocket money for us. If we did not earn it we went without.

This made us lean and mean. We worked hard, before and after school. All summer, all winter. From the age that we could ride bikes we delivered papers, collected groceries and ran errands. At one time half of W H Smiths' entire paper rounds from Eastbourne Railway Station were delivered by us. Well under the legal age to work, we waited outside while the oldest stacked up our canvas paper bags with round after round.

In the summer we did odd-jobs. In winter drives were swept and carols sung. Anything to earn money. By the time we were teenagers we knew the true value of coin. It made us independent and self-assured. We could survive. Actually I survived really well because as soon as I left home all my money was mine. By leaving home I doubled my wages!

My parents were hard, as hard as people could become after surviving war, occupation, bombings, starvation and near-death. My dad had the unfortunate honour of being born during the October 1917 revolution in Moscow. The wrong place at the wrong time. He lived, but many of his family did not.

My European family lived through some of the most traumatic times in our history and just enough of them survived. Not only to pass on their genes but some amazing tales of struggle and hardship as well. My parents lived through the 1939–1945 war in occupied Vienna. My mother dug her stepfather's grave with a piece of broken wood when she was just 12.

However hard we think we have it today, we really have no idea. I have never discovered how my posh British granny could live in an occupied country and not be shot as a spy. I have never found out how my Russian dad survived in the same capital, when families were being rounded up daily and sent to their deaths.

Dad would tell me tales, mainly when he was in that strange stage of alcohol abuse between loose-lipped and paralytic, of the Black Market and the Resistance that were so closely intertwined during the war. He never got over his fears, sleeping with a weapon by his side till the day he died. These stories were electrifying and need to be repeated but they are stories for another rainy day.

Anyway, I digress, a habit of mine that you will get used to through this book. To me these stories probably energised me with my love for writing. And so, I needed to find a way to pay the bills and to write. The answer came by luck more than serious effort on my part. I managed to combine my work as a mobile engineer with my love for the ancient art. My books build slowly. The stories from my customers arrive like blue moons, rarely. I may go for weeks or months before a little gem drops before me. When they do, I am ready and waiting.

I love oral history. It is just so completely different from the stuffy old history books that were piled in front of our bored noses at school. Reading those kinds of books, with their endless details, I would fall asleep faster than Mr T from the A-Team after he was tranquillised for a flight. I will give you an example of my kind of history.

Today, as I write, I have been working all morning to earn a crust repairing sewing machines. This morning was nothing exceptional until I met Georgina—all 95 years of her.

Georgina was an unexpected present to her 46-year-old mum. Hated by her much older siblings, for the attention she stole from them. Born just before the Great War she grew up in Greenwich in south-east London. Her mother had been born in 1867. At 27, Georgina saw London burn in the Blitz. She sat out on Greenwich Hill night-after-night with her family and watched as German bombers tried to hit St Paul's Cathedral. She described to me the pounding guns and smoke, the flame, the crunching thuds of the bombs, the smell of a city on fire. She brought history to life… and there was more.

Her mother knew an old sailor who used to tell her tales at Greenwich, tales of his time in the navy. Tales of mutiny and war of cutlass, scurvy and blood. He told her about the Battle of the Nile and, later, Trafalgar where he, as a terrified teenager, was transferred to HMS Defiance. He told her how the ship was the fastest in the fleet and rammed into the French ships. How their guns laid waste to the French boarding party and how they cried like children when word of Nelson's death reached them. This is real history, the history I love.

As I left I shook her hand and knew that in a simple gesture I was touching an actual world. I was touching the hand that was brought up by the mother who had been told these tales. She in turn had known a man who had seen the victory of Trafalgar in all its bloody glory. In a second I was breaching over 200 years of living history.

I find these stories inspiring and, as I make my winding way through life, I try to scribble down as many of these tales as possible. I now combine my lifetime's dream of writing with working for a living. I make no promises as to the accuracy of my stories but they are written in the same spirit as they were told.

Now, as Book Four takes shape, I relive each moment as I write. To me some of the great pleasures of my life are the happy and fulfilling moments with friends. Chatting, reminiscing and exchanging stories, or just sitting alone in a quiet moment of reflection remembering times of long ago. Stories are our first window on the world, when the lucky ones among us fall asleep to fairytales and dream dreams of such colour and excitement.

And so we come to my next instalment of anecdotes, funny incidents, stories and life in general. Humour is also interwoven as I believe it is sometimes as important to us as the oxygen we breathe.

I write how I speak and, as I have said, I'm no literary master. Far from it. I write from the heart not from a dictionary. My life is woven between these pages.

*Enjoy!*

*Tales from the Coast*

# Jaguar

With many thanks to Sheila Russell who inspired this story.

I live an ordinary life, an ordinary life amongst ordinary people...

There is nothing really surprising about me or the people I meet. We are just the average throng of humanity, the countless many. Invisible to the entire world except to a close circle of family and friends. My life, our lives, mean little in the grand scheme of things.

Were there a report in the *Valparaiso Daily* of the unexpected death of a sewing machine engineer in Eastbourne, the only question that would be asked is, *why would anyone bother to print it?*

Basically I am no one, from nowhere. But—hang on a mo— is that the whole truth?

Every day I meet people, ordinary people—people like you and me who have made their journey through life as best as they could. They have struggled up and down the constant rolling hills of existence, survived all the battles, both external and internal. And the thing that I have come to understand is that we are not ordinary, not one single one of us.

We are all unique. Each and every human being. We live a life of events unique to us and our perceptions. They leave their marks, physical and emotional. Our bodies become the map of our uniqueness. Each scar, each wrinkle, each and every ache tells a story. Every tender muscle or swollen joint has a reason for being.

From the very second we are born and given our one-way, non-return ticket to life, we travel a unique path that only one person can really understand. That person is you.

No one else can feel your pain. It does not matter how close a person stands, they are a world apart. Your pain is personal and exclusive, as are your feelings.

Perhaps that human uniqueness is what intrigues me so much. Maybe that is why I get this urge that travels right down to my fingertips to put pen to paper. Sometimes my little fingers burn with excitement and I cannot wait to get back from my customers to start tapping away at the keyboard.

I fear I am no great writer but I am a great listener. I hear stories that have come from all over the world to end up on my doorstep and I love the challenge of writing them down. The inspiration with which I am filled is the source of my writing and my love for it.

I write down stories about many of the characters I meet because they are so fascinating. In my time as I write today, they are all real, and the one single thing that they all have in common is that they think that they are ordinary.

How funny, when that is the one thing that they, you or I can never be!

*****

"I just have to ask Sheila, why on earth is there a huge jaguar skin draped over the back of your settee? I have been dying to find out since I walked in the door."

The natural pattern was so beautiful, the pure gold coat looked like a child had added black finger-paint all over the skin in patches. It was an awesome sight.

"Aah," she said with a deep sigh, stroking the pelt, "I used to keep it hidden away in the loft but now and again I get it out, this is my one little pleasure in life. I know it is not politically correct at the moment, a bit like fur coats, but he once was the king of the jungle and I knew him. Often I sit here in my twilight years, when the whole world seems to be enjoying themselves. When everybody seems busy, except me. I sometimes feel a little left behind, but this skin, this beast, is a little reminder that I once also led a hectic and exciting life.

"With this jaguar comes a fascinating story that starts in the depths of Guyana jungle and ends here. So many years have passed that it all seems like a distant dream. This was once a magnificent and fearsome beast that kept an entire village in fear. I was there the day it died."

Sheila was one of my *old dears*. A sort of personal club made up from my favourite customers. I had looked after her machine for years and had often stared at the pictures and paintings of her on the walls of her bungalow.

There was one from 1948 at Butlins Holiday Camp just after World War Two. She looked fabulous, tall and slender with a face like Ava Gardner. She was wearing a revealing off-the-shoulder dress melting into a tiny waist. How she must have turned heads in her youth!

Now she stood before me with her grey hair bunched up behind her head in tight curls. Her fading eyes were pale pearls shining dimly in a sea of milk white skin. She was still tall but time had bent her frame and stolen her beauty to pass onto some other lucky young girl. She continued…

"When I was much younger, and the world was an exciting adventure, my husband was offered a job at a mine in Guyana. We both agreed it would be a wonderful adventure so we packed our bags, said our goodbyes and set sail for the other side of the world. We were on our way to a pristine rainforest where humans were just a tiny number in a huge wilderness.

"It was a long and arduous journey. Even when we arrived in Guyana it was another 60 miles up the Demerara River, you know where the sugar first came from. There were otters there the size of men, locals called them river wolfs. Piranha with sabre teeth like little monsters from Mars. Then dirt tracks for miles in 100% humidity, but eventually we arrived.

"We had running water and deliveries to a little village on the edge of the rainforest. The closest town was Mackenzie, now Georgetown and that was 45 miles of hard, bad roads and a long way to go for a drink.

"One day I drove there, it took hours and on the way back I ran over an ocelot! Not the sort of occurrence we have in Polegate!

"Our nights were not crammed with excitement but all that changed and how!

Jungle roads were hard work and dangerous

"Life was so very different. Washing our clothes and preparing food would take hours. I quickly settled into a daily routine as my husband went to work at the mine. We had a grand house on the edge of the village, on stilts to keep it dry.

"I learnt from the villagers a way of life that had remained unchanged for centuries. Many of their husbands now worked in construction, mining or forest clearance rather than scrape a living off the forest. However, although their way of life was altering beyond all recognition, they kept their traditions alive.

A typical village hut on stilts

"The days soon turned into weeks then years and I learned to love my new life in the forest. There were spiders big enough to eat birds. Possum crept into camp at night. It was a land of giants, everything was larger than life. I soon got used to my new world but all that was about to alter.

"It started simply and quietly when the guinea pigs, or cavies, started disappearing. They were used for food, but also they were surprisingly good at keeping the rats away from the chickens.

"Lovely little snack, a guinea pig, but you get them riled and they attack, they will simply not tolerate rats so they were great guards and dinner too!

"Then the chickens started to go, one by one. At first we all thought it was one of the village dogs as they were part-wild. Then two of the goats vanished. Goats were always running around the village feeding on scraps.

"Then, to our dismay, a dog disappeared!

"Now we all started to worry. Something was hunting on the edge of the village. It was silent and invisible. As the rains came our worst fears were realised. Huge jaguar paw prints were discovered, then deep claw marks on a tree where it had left its scent. From the large gap between the claws we could tell it was a monster.

"The fear was electric. This was a beast that was held in mystical esteem. Some almost revered it as a god, others the very opposite! Even the forest dwellers had not seen one of these elusive creatures for years. Only two of the elders had come across the silent hunter in their lifetimes in the jungle.

"They had seen markings from the beast everywhere but few had laid eyes on the elusive jaguar and now one of them was hunting around the village. The elders told how the jaguar was a hunter not only of animals but of souls! *To make eye contact with one was to look into the eyes of a Devil!*

"The jaguar had no remorse, no feeling, no emotion; it was simply a natural born killer. The savage rule of the jungle was in its blood, hunt or be hunted, eat or be eaten.

"We all knew that the beast was losing its normal fear of humans. It had happened occasionally in the area before. Although man-eaters were rare it was not a risk anyone wanted to take. The animal was becoming accustomed to our smell and our ways. Though we could not see it, somewhere in the forest mingled in with the leaves and trees it was watching our every move. In the shadows of the night walked our nemesis.

"It was only a matter of time before the jaguar would take its first child. We all knew that a fully-grown jaguar might take any living creature, especially as it grew old and could not chase its usual prey.

"It was the perfect scavenger, instinctively killing anything from a frog to a deer, though its favourite prey was the Capybara and monkeys. It had evolved into a faultless killer and, with its huge padded paws, it had superb swimming ability. The animal evolved from the primeval swamps and jungles and was superbly adapted to its surroundings.

Capybaras are a favourite meal of the jaguar

"Gauchos on the grazing plains feared the jaguar for its ability to destroy cattle. Before hunting was banned they used predator dogs to flush them out of the thick undergrowth, just like fox hounds were used here in England.

"Problem killers were still allowed to be hunted by professionals with permits. However, the jaguar's ability to disappear into the jungle, leaving no trace, to move through water and climb trees made it a formidable animal to hunt.

Only a few true professional hunters and poachers had the skill to outwit the ultimate killer.

"Over the decades as humans flourished in the area and as the jungle was felled the jaguar numbers diminished dramatically. It became a rare and elusive beast. It moved from real life into legend, to be talked about around camp fires on late evenings.

"The local name was perfect but the rough translation was *the creature that roars like thunder and kills in a single leap*!

"Just imagine that there was a stalker where you lived and you knew that he would follow you and perhaps kill you on your way home from work any day! That is how it felt in the village; it was a feeling close to terror.

**Beautiful but deadly, a young jaguar**

"The jaguar's method was to silently stalk its prey, watch and wait. The third largest feline, after the lion and leopard, it was a killing machine. Mainly nocturnal and at the very top of the food-chain, with superb hearing and even better eyesight.

"In the forest all living creatures feared the ancient hunter. Its ability to blend in made it seem even more super-natural. It would simply vanish. A person could walk right by the animal and not know it was there. All you would feel was that something was watching you!

"After killing animals, usually with a single crushing bite to the skull it would take some of its prey high into the trees, to feed on over several days.

"You could always tell a jaguar kill. All that would be found were a few bones and a skull with a single hole in it! The jaguar's tooth would have bitten through, clean as a bullet, straight into the brain. Fast and ruthlessly efficient.

"Respect for the perfect hunter had, with the killings around the village, turned to terror. The village panicked.

"Livestock was locked away every night also the children were protected, none left alone at anytime. The heavy vegetation, that made perfect camouflage, was cleared and extra fences built. All the men came back to the village and great fires were lit every night. Fear reigned.

"The elders retreated from the civilised world, back to the world of their ancestors. They made spirit dances to chase the beast away, and called upon their ancestors in sacred rituals to help and protect them.

"Some put on war-paint and sharpened their weapons. The bravest warriors painted their faces with soot from the fires to mimic the jaguar and feel the power of the hunter. They went out in packs to kill the beast, before it managed to kill one of their children.

"But as the dreaded nights came and went, the beast still stalked the village and no one came close to even seeing it. All that there was to see were its menacing prints.

"It would circle the village, coming in to the weak-dark spots and then out again looking for any fresh meat. It had become impossible to track or catch and seemed to vanish in daylight. It was at home in the dense forest, stalking the village animals and its inhabitants.

"Early morning and late evening people would sense the danger. Even the animals were worried. The village dogs became hyper-sensitive, barking at every movement and sound. This, in turn, made everyone nervous, expecting the beast to appear any moment and snatch an animal, or worse!

"One morning we found its prints leading up to our strongest fence. On the other side we could see where it had landed, perfectly, silently. The fences were no deterrent!

"Some of the villagers moved away, left. But many had nowhere to go. Some talked of evil spirits that had come to claim vengeance. So little was known about the animal that fear took its place. It became an all-seeing all-evil presence that sucked the life-blood from the once-happy village.

"My husband and the local police chief spent many nights waiting with rifles hoping to get a shot off. We tied a kid goat to a pole but the old hunter was too wise to fall for the trap. We dug spike-pits but once again the creature out-witted us.

"Weeks went by. No one even saw the creature. We were at our wits end and even the village chief was in trouble. His ability to lead the village was being challenged by an unknown assailant. His power was being sapped and his authority challenged.

"One night the Police Chief, a crack shot, was by the stilts, under of one of the taller buildings, waiting. He was quietly cleaning his gun when he felt hot breath on his back. He turned to see the jaguar not three feet away! He screamed, and in a panic actually threw his rifle at the beast before running for his life!

"By the time a group came back the beast had vanished into thin air as silently as he came! The Police Chief felt like an idiot but was alive to tell the tale!

"It all came to a sudden climax one evening.

"The Police Chief was returning to the village. Dusk was falling and he was travelling back along a dirt path in his truck. He had a sudden feeling that something was not right. He slowed his truck as a family of hogs ran across the clearing.

"He pulled over and got out of the truck. The light was fading in the forest, throwing deep shadows across the road. The sounds of the night were starting to penetrate the sticky heat. He opened up the back of his truck and quietly pulled out his rifle and started to walk slowly up the road.

"Every footstep was carefully taken, his heel touching first and slowly moulding the ground to his tip-toe. He moved about 20 paces, every hair on his neck was bristling, beads of sweat running down his face. He knew the killer was close; it was in the very air, the stillness was stifling.

"He pulled his rifle hard into his shoulder ready, waiting.

"He told me he could feel his heart pounding, his every breath made him shudder.

"Then it happened.

"Into the clearing came the beast. It was smelling the ground to pick up the scent of its prey. For one split-second it had not seen him. He aimed just as the jaguar's eyes focused on him. He stared the Devil in the eye, held his breath and squeezed the trigger. One shot, that was all it took. One perfect shot and the beast that had terrorised the entire community crumpled to the floor dead.

"He tried to load it onto the truck but it was so heavy that he could not. We later weighed it. It was a male of 280 pounds. One of the largest cats anyone had ever heard of.

"He rushed back to the village in great excitement and got men to pick up the carcass. As he drove back into the village great whooping and cheering broke out. Children poked the creature of the night with sticks and arrows. It was a sight to behold. The beast was an old male with a bad lower canine, which was probably why it had started to feed on easier prey.

"Even in death he was a majestic creature, beautiful, powerful and a true master of his environment. The village fell silent as they paid tribute to the mythic creature that stalked the dark hours of the forest. No one would purposely set out to kill such a beast but this was another matter. It could only end with bloodshed. It was either him or one of us!

"The chief, in great and solemn tribute, brought a knife and cut his warm heart out. It seems barbaric now but, my god, how happy we all were. He held it aloft and we all cheered. The women cried, men danced and children laughed.

"That night, a great party was had. The animal was skinned. The teeth pulled. The meat was cooked then eaten by some of the young men of the village, to gain the beast's magical hunting powers.

"We all danced and feasted until the first light came breaking through the trees. We were all drunk with happiness and a weird concoction that was quite potent. When we went to bed we were exhausted and exhilarated. At last the village was safe and free again.

"After the jaguar's demise the village animals all went back to normal. The families that had fled returned, all visiting the chief to see the jaguar for themselves. The guinea pigs bred like rabbits and were up to full strength in no time. The chief wore some of the jaguar's teeth round his neck and passed the claws on to his family, and also to members of his council as a sign of their authority.

"No part of the animal had been wasted. He had the skull boiled and cleaned. The skin was stretched, scraped, cured and treated on a large frame by the women of the village until it was soft and supple.

"The priest came on his stubborn mule to bless the village. To make the mule go he would sit on it and a boy would light newspaper and hold it under its bum. Now that was a sight!

"Some time later, when my husband's work was finished and we were leaving, the chief presented us with this skin that you see here.

"We knew that if the chief had sold the pelt he could have made a month's wages. It was a stunning gift.

"Now when you see this old skin you would never believe the story that comes from it, or the terror in which this creature once held an entire village.

"One day, long after I am dead, no one will ever know about the story of this animal. Its life and its dramatic death on the far side of the world.

"South America and Guyana when we were there was from another time. A time that had remained almost unchanged since the arrival of the Spanish conquistadors. It is all very different now, though I dare say that there are still some jaguars stalking the remote jungles.

"Well Alex, how about that for a story? I bet you did not expect that when you asked!"

"Wow! All I can say is **wow**! What a tale," I said in admiration.

I felt like a kid coming out of the Saturday-morning cinema filled with excitement and respect. I touched the animal, as if to feel its power its strength, to feel its very life. Before me was the mighty predator, the king of the jungle and collector of souls. Some of his distant relatives were still out there, still creeping silently though the undergrowth with their eyes glowing in the night.

I left feeling honoured to have been told such a fabulous story. It had sent a tingle down my spine

Once again I came to realise that our lives are made up of many weird and wonderful experiences and, however we might feel about ourselves, none of us are really ordinary.

If I had anything to do with it, Sheila's story would live on, even if it was just in one of my little books.

Can you imagine for one second the Police Chief feeling something behind him and turning to see the jaguar…

I bet he covered a hundred yards at Olympic speed!

## The End

## The Few
### September 1940

Angels were chasing devils through the burning sky,
Red heat tore the ether while God stood silent by,
Wings torn, in dying gasps both angel and devil fell,
One on their way to heaven, one, straight to Hell.
\*\*

In the warm autumn earth both warriors silent lay,
Our young hero returned forever to his sovereign clay.
Lacing the heavenly blue with streamers of white and grey
Weapons of death still danced above in an aerial ballet.
\*\*

Oh how they chased those devils, shattering the early glow,
Spitting fifteen seconds of fury at our mortal foe.
A cats-cradle is stitched by our planes in deadly flight,
Victory rolls the signal we'd blasted Hitler's might.

*All clear sirens*

Families from dark shelters climb, free from their strife,
In sweet silence they embrace the delicious taste of life.
But soon the wireless crackles to remind us of the day,
Trade over Hell's Corner boys, more bandits on their way!

*Alex I Askaroff*

*Many thanks to Dorothy Sullivan, (nee Freeman), Maureen Byrne, Jacqueline Johnson and Dick Huggins whose wonderful memories inspired me to write this story of a little chapter in our history based on true events.*

## Spies & Spitfires

"Doll, Doll, Dorothy! Wake up it's time to go," whispered her mum gently shaking her through the bed sheets. "We are going where the skylarks sing and the air smells of the sea, where dreams are made. Make sure you put on the old clothes I've patched for you!"

Before Big Ben had chimed four times, Dorothy, along with her mum, dad, brothers and sisters were walking into the great city of London. Dorothy had a small bundle wrapped tightly and placed in an old sailor's chest from her great grandfather, who had been at sea in the 1850's. The older members of her family carried the chest between them. It contained an assortment of worn out and well-patched clothes that had been saved throughout the year. Her mum had spent many hours patching with her old treadle machine.

She clutched her brother's hand tightly and the small group of figures made their way through the darkness into the city. Huge buildings loomed above her in the lightening sky and soft mist circled around the streetlamps like steaming cauldrons. It was September and the late summer air held a chill. The year was 1929. In America the Great Depression was about to start as the Wall Street Crash loomed closer. Ten years of post-war prosperity was about to crumble.

Factories in America had been producing far too many goods. Workers had their hours cut to avoid massive overproduction and so they could afford to buy less and less in the shops. The knock-on effect was a collapse in world trade. Effects were felt in Britain and by 1935 unemployment had reached as high as 68 percent in places like Jarrow. The Jarrow men, hard and proud shipbuilders, marched on London finishing at the Ritz and interrupting, much to her annoyance, Barbara Cartland's afternoon tea. Their efforts had little effect but became a landmark of the Great Depression.

Doll, totally oblivious to other worldly goings on, was jam-packed full of excitement. She stared upward at the imposing skyline and her eyes shone diamond bright as she toddled behind her parents.

At St Pauls Cathedral, they said goodbye to their dad with hugs and kisses. He was off to deliver the post for his part of Central London as he had done since the end of the Great War, it was a very different trade to his army postings in India but civilian life was an enjoyable one to him.

Dorothy looked back to see her dad waving on the corner. She would not see him again for many-a-week, she waved but he had disappeared into the mist. "Doll, catch up or we'll miss the train," shouted her mum who was beckoning to her. Now they were on their own, just mum and her band of kids skipping along the old London streets.

They had walked for nearly two hours, seen the sky turn pink then gold as dawn chased darkness up the streets of London. Shadows shortened as the great city slowly came to life all around them, much as it had done for over two thousand years. Street corner newspaper touts shouted the latest news into the cool air. Carthorses, buses, lorries, trams and taxis filled the streets.

Doll's family arrived at the steamy railway station, where whistles blew and trolleys rushed past with porters shouting. On the platform at London Bridge they boarded the Hastings train and Doll found a seat by the window. She peered over the wooden sill at the world rushing around outside. The train hooted, shunted and chased the shining steel rails out of the city. Mum handed out breakfast in brown paper wrappers. Doll munched on her sandwich, watching the endless rows of brick buildings slowly turn into rolling countryside as they clickety-clacked along. She laid her head on her mum's lap and drifted into sleep with a half eaten sandwich in her hand. Doll's mum gently prised the sandwich from her tiny hand and stroked her hair as she slept.

"Wakey wakey kids we've arrived," said mum, gathering their baggage from the overhead racks. Doll rubbed her eyes, brushed some crumbs from her front and smiled as the train blew its whistle.

At Hawkhurst Station, they all bundled onto the platform, walked outside and waited. Sometimes they would arrive closer at Bodiam but today it was Hawkhurst. The sun was up and the smell of fresh country air poured into her little lungs. She knew what she was waiting for. She had been here before, as had her brothers and sisters. Shortly before nine she heard the familiar clip-clop noise of the horse-drawn wagon. It drew up and they all clambered aboard, sitting on the hard wooden slats at the back.

"Walk on, walk on," came the strong deep voice of the wagon master in his thick local accent as he released the block-brake. The horse moved off at a slow plod. Doll sat smiling. She stared up at the trees as the wagon made its way along the country lanes toward Sandhurst, with the wagon master occasionally shouting commands and applying the blocks as they went up and down the twisty lanes.

They were on the Sussex-Kent border, heading towards Farmer Reeves' at Old Place Farm. Like many other families they were heading to the farms of southeast England.

As summer slowly turned toward autumn in the countryside it was a special time, it was hop-picking time.

Hop picking had gone on for centuries on the fertile soil of eastern England. A good pint of ale was enjoyed just as much a thousand years ago.

In its prime in ages past hops, a member of the cannabis and nettle family, spread the entire breadth of England from north to south. Their value made many men wealthy. A single acre of hops could bring more money than fifty times an acre of arable land.

First used in ancient Egypt as a medicinal herb for digestive problems, the humble hop, a fast growing weed, became known as *the wolf of the woods*. It was a valuable plant in any garden, its prickly tips eaten as a delicacy.

It is generally believed that hops found their way to England around the 1400's, after Germans or Flemish traders passed on their art of mixing the hops for fine ale to Winchelsea sea-traders.

Hops were first regarded with some suspicion for there sedative powers were well known. Folklore told that the hops would shorten life and cause melancholy. In part they were right. A few beers on a warm afternoon left you no good for work. However there was nothing sinister about this wild hedgerow creeper that could grow six meters in a season.

King Henry VI first banned hops for cultivation and use in beer as did Henry VIII but as they resigned themselves to the pages of history the hop flourished.

They say that the first cultivated hops arrived in the thriving port of Winchelsea before it was destroyed by great storms. By then the plant was being imported and cultivated across the land.

Doll's family had dressed in their patched clothes as they would be sleeping in old tin huts and working the fields throughout September. Doll would be doing little work as it was more of a holiday for her family. The old adage that a change was as good as a rest was true. For the next few weeks they would rise with the lark and pick hops for Farmer Reeve.

The cart passed the pretty village of Sandhurst, down one more lane and then into Church Lane. They passed a row of cottages on their left, then up the short hill toward St Nicholas Church, and there they were!

William Reeve came to the gate to greet them dressed in his usual farming breeches, held up with thick braces, his sleeves rolled up to the elbow and on his head his favourite pork-pie hat. To Doll he was a friendly old man. His craggy, weather-beaten face wore the years of sunshine and open air on it, like a well-used leather bag.

Locals said that he was made of iron pummelled together in an old Roman foundry near the village. He certainly had lungs like a blacksmith's bellows. As the decades went by, people came to believe in the old village tale. For, while the years changed, Farmer Reeve stayed the same. He appeared as eternal as the land he worked.

He greeted them and walked to the front of the horse grabbing its' chinstrap. He marched the wagon down the old track towards their accommodation.

Doll hung on as the cart rolled past the four large conical hop-drying kilns of the oast houses, that looked like plump Dutch maids with white bonnets. A gust of wind made the bonnets swing around to point out over the countryside toward the English Channel.

"They're just saying mornin' to you all," chirped up Farmer Reeve as his hobnail boots trod the path, tapping with the horses, down to the huts on the corner of the field.

"Look Mum, the sea, I can see the sea!" squealed Doll with excitement.

"Yes my dear and so you shall for many-a-week and smell that sweet air! Not like our London air is it? That is the smell of the countryside—the smell of heaven." Doll breathed in deep, her little face beaming.

They unloaded on the corner of a large field where a row of huts waited for them. Inside they unpacked all their belongings and made their single room a bit more homely. Outside they chatted to some of the other workers who had already arrived from Eastbourne and Hastings. Down at the barn all the Brighton families had made themselves at home, before long a pot was boiling and lunch was made.

"Enjoy yourselves kids," Doll's mum shouted to her children as they ran off to play in the fields, "for tomorrow you will be working for your supper!"

Sure enough, as the sun next rose, Farmer Reeve was calling all the hop-pickers and giving them their orders for the day. Which field and row to pick. Doll and the other kids followed behind their mums dragging old umbrellas, boxes and bowls. They got to the vines that stretched and twisted around the chestnut poles. The poles were lashed together at the top like totem poles and beneath their feet lay large coconut matting.

"Now all of you," sparked up their mum opening out the umbrellas and sticking the upturned points into the soil, "you remember what to do! Pick as many of the flowers as you can and drop them into the containers. When you have filled them I'll empty them into my sack," she said, pointing to her large sack. "If you fill five umbrellas I shall give you a whole penny! If you save your pennies you'll have enough to buy all sorts of little gems back home. Now off you go kids, get to it!"

Doll, with her brothers and sisters, attacked the hop poles with glee and stripped the hops' flowers from the vines. Doll being small would get the lower hops, while her taller brothers and sisters would reach up higher, leaving the rest for the adults. Doll had to be careful as the hops were protected by long prickly stems that would scratch if given half the chance.

Rows of pickers moved along in slow procession working the bines. Bines were the hairy-vines that grew up the strings supported by wires and chestnut poles. The bines were planted in small circles of four. They were twisted together at about waist height to run up the strings that then fanned out into the canopy above the ground. Once picked, all the hops were dropped into a bin or crib, which was a large sack, supported by a wooden-crossed frame with handles resembling a baby's crib. Four or more pickers could work around the crib dropping hops in as they picked. When they moved along they would tug the wiry bine down from its support and lay it across the crib, then pluck the hops carefully and drop them straight into the crib below. The farmer did not accept hops that were crushed or dropped into the dirt. No leaves, no crushed hops, no dirty hops! However, more often than not they would be chucked into the crib when he was out of sight, it all added to the flavour!

Once the long sinewy bine was picked clean it would be neatly wound up below the poles, and the pickers would move on to the next one.

Many farms had different methods for picking. Some would bring the poles of cut bines to the end of the rows to be picked, but at Old Place Farm they picked the way they had done for centuries.

The hop, once cut at ground level, would leave just the rootstock below ground. That would remain dormant until the following April when the plant sprouted. The best bines would be selected and in May *Twiddling* would begin. *Twiddling* trained five hop-bines, always clockwise, up four strings. One was always spare in case of damage.

In June earth would be heaped up over the mounds in hills, to stop all but the best shoots. Pests were kept at bay in case they ruined the crop.

Traditionally, in a good year, Midsummer's day was the day that the bines would reach the top of their strings. Growers monitored the next stage of flower, *pin, bullet* and lastly the *cone* stage. From that point the harvest date was clear and the cycle nearly complete.

After about 20 years of life the rootstock, always female, would be replaced with a fresh plant and the whole rotation, learnt over a thousand years, would start again. Occasionally a male plant was allowed to grow to fertilise the females and produce more stock.

Once the crucial date of the harvest was known, when the hops were at their biggest but not spoilt by moist mornings, letters were posted to the lucky families all over London and the South East, telling them to pack their bags and come to the farms as quickly as possible.

These letters were the talk of the street and often gossip would fly…why one family was chosen to pick and another not. But there was no time to lose, the hops were ready and money to be earnt!

Hop pickers in action, 1949

Families loved hop-picking with a passion that is hard to understand today. Can you imagine going on your annual holiday to work all day in the fields! Well, not long past the only holiday that many-an-East End London family could have was a paid one. An unpaid holiday was a luxury few could afford. A month in the countryside, picking, was as close as thousands of families would get. Also women seemed to be better at hop-picking than men, so there were traditionally many more women who went-a-picking.

Lorries were sent by many farms to pick up pickers but others, like Doll and her family, made their own way to their working holidays.

Back down on Old Place Farm pole men would work in front of the pickers, pulling down the larger bines of flowers, known as Burrs when they first bloom, from the top of the support wires.

Of course many farms had different ways to cultivate and pick hops and names often differed. The strings or coir that went some twenty feet up to the canopy to hold the bines were often cut for picking by stilt walkers.

Master stilt walkers would lumber along on their stilts, cutting the strings as they went. Funnily they were always a popular attraction at the summer fayres.

As this timeless yearly harvest went on, Doll would drag her umbrella up to mum for emptying, then run back to grab more hops. Playing, picking and generally messing around all at the same time.

The sun rose and shadows shortened. The cool morning air of late summer warmed and dozens of workers picked their way through the fields, stripping off clothing as the sun reminded them winter had not yet conquered.

In the hop fields Doll was in another world. The large hop plants towered over her like great pillars reaching skyward. Where the fully-grown hops touched in the middle of the rows the sunlight poured through them in a wonderland of green. Each way she turned, North, South, East and West, she was in a green world of rustling leaves and musical birds. She was in God's cathedral, far away from the noise, smoke and pollution of 1920's London. Oh how happy could one little girl be, how full of life and fun, running around in her own little wonderland.

Occasionally someone would start to sing. First one, then two, then the whole field of pickers would burst into song, filling the country air with Cockney songs that lifted and mixed with the skylarks and swallows.

At midday all the pickers would break for lunch. A *hop pot* would be swung over an open fire for hot tea, then sandwiches and cool beer would be passed around. There is no cup of tea on earth that tastes like a cuppa brewed from a *hop pot*.

The measurer, bin man, and a pretty bookie.

At *Bushlin time*, as the sacks were filled, the daughters of a local man, called *the measurer*, would measure the hops picked by each family. He would scoop out the hops from the bin with an oval shaped wicker basket called *a bushel* and fill a sack called *a poke*. It took many bushels to fill one of the pokes. As *the measurer* scooped his daughters would count, making a note of who had earned what in their books. Tickets of the amounts were then given to the pickers like a little receipt. The pokes were then loaded onto the cart and taken away for drying and storage.

Transporting the 'Pokes' to the oast house for drying.

This is where the oast houses came in. The hops would be layered over the warm, heated floors of the oast house for drying. A green haze would rise and hang in the warm air. Drying was an art and needed full-time attention. Coal, wood and sulphur mixed in exact quantities to dry, purify and colour the hops.

Later sulphur, also used as a pesticide for the crops, was discarded. On the side of the oast house, during the hop season, lived the men responsible for drying the hops. They worked, ate and slept next to their hops, never leaving until they had been successfully dried and poured into the long thin sacks or pockets ready to be taken to the brewers. Each pocket would be marked with the farm's name and parish.

Successful drying was imperative. Reducing the moisture in the hops to around twelve percent allowed the hops to be preserved but did not damage the flavour. In this way the hops could be used all year in their sacks until the next picking.

The brewers would then work their art using the resins and oils hidden in the hops to delicately flavour and preserve their beers. It was biological wizardry. Mixing solutions in big coppers with the sugars or *worts* from the malted barley. Each beer or ale was different and the skill needed to mix all the ingredients was carefully guarded by the brewers.

At the end of the Victorian era there were over six-and-a-half thousand brewers in the country. Today there is only a handful of specialist brewers left.

Hop-picking families would often save all their money until the last week of picking and use farm tokens to barter with. It was very useful to earn *'Christmas Money'* picking hops.

However if a family wanted, they could have a *sub* that would then be docked from their wages at the end of the month. Subs were common, for come the weekend many families were visited by their men-folk from the City. They would all toddle off down the local pubs, eat, drink and be merry. The pubs had to put a charge on the glasses as they had a habit of disappearing down to the farms. You only got your deposit back once you returned your beer-glass. You had to keep your eyes on your glasses as the local lads would pinch the empty glasses for the deposit!

Many pubs did not allow gypsies and there were often signs outside the doors barring gypsies.

The gypsies moved around the countryside with ease and on Sundays they would often make their way up to Horsmonden near Tunbridge Wells.

At Horsmonden, on the village green, there would be horse-trading every Sunday. Possibly where its name originated from!

Horses would be smartened up and some decorated with brasses and ribbons then trotted around the green, their masters running beside them. Local merchants and farmers would bid against each other for the animals. Gypsies were skilled horsemen and knew horseflesh like few other people.

It was a common fact that the gypsies' own horses were always piebald or spotted ponies. These dappled beasts were uniquely marked like a finger print, each one different, and each one impossible to steal without being instantly recognised by their owners. Plain coloured horses on the other hand were another matter altogether!

Gypsies were banned from most of the pubs as they were notorious drinkers and gamblers. Drinking often led to betting, and betting led to fighting. However there was usually a willing local lad who helped them get a tipple or two for a few pence.

As the sun fell at the end of the daily hop-picking the pickers would all return from the fields, their hands and clothes stained greeny-brown by the hops.

The farmer would always make sure there were bundles of firewood faggots by the huts. Over the open fire dinner would be cooked, stews made and potatoes boiled. There was a cook hut if it was raining but most families preferred to cook in the open air. Some used to take potatoes to be roasted in the oast houses earlier in the day and pick them up for supper.

As the evening wore on, the families would sit around the fire exchanging stories and singing songs. Kids would bake spuds and apples in the ashes. They would sit around the open fires prodding the food with sharp sticks to see when they were ready, watching the fire dance into the sky.

Under the stars, their faces warmed by the night fire and their bellies full of good country food, they were children in paradise. At the end of the evening still smelling of hops, families would retire to sleep the best sleeps of their lives. For hops were a great sedative, still used today in many herbal recipes.

Around the area there were several local village lads that were always playing around. One little urchin was nicknamed "half-a-penny" or "'ape-nee" by the cockneys. They say it was because he was so daft that if you gave him a penny for his thoughts you would get change! Although he was supposed to be a bit dippy he knew what was what! The scruffy little rascal was always up to mischief with holes in his shorts, mud on his face, scuffed knees and tangled hair. He had the smile of an angel. His giggle was so infectious he could make you turn to jelly and forget why you were telling him off!

No one knew if he could read or write but he could dance around the campfire and play the fool to perfection, stuffing hops in his hair, mimicking London Cockney slang.

His rendition of *maybe it's becoz' I'm a Londoner that I love London Town* was enhanced by his hopping around the fire like an old mother hen, with a branch protruding from the back of his shorts. This would reduce everyone to tears of laughter.

On Sunday, before people would arrive at St Nicholas Church, he would close the gate to the car park. It was open all week! He would then rest on the fence without a care in the world as if he was bird watching or something.

When the toffs turned up he would quickly run and open the gate, then dutifully nod his cap. Often they would tip him for his service. He earned a pretty penny on Sundays for opening a gate that was normally open!

He had wind worse than a camel. It was probably all the rough food he ate. More than once he was seen chomping on dandelion leaves and wild berries. He could almost burp in tune! When told off for his rude behaviour he would run away giggling and shout, "Better out of the attic than the basement!" He smelt worse than the oast houses when they belched out the hop-colouring and purifying sulphur.

During the war the village kids were always up to something, collecting scrap for the war effort, or keeping an eye out for potential spies.

If you left anything lying around it would not be there for long, a spoon or tin cup, the pram wheels, even the railing outside the houses were not safe, turn your back and they would be cut off and taken.

The kids then swapped all their booty for chocolate from eager government officials. Once a month it was collected and taken for recycling into military hardware. The kids collected for their Spitfire fund in the hope of putting one more plane in the sky against Fritz and his bandits.

During the hop season a daily routine soon fell into place at the farm. An old tin bath would be filled with water and dirty clothes cleaned when necessary, dishes washed, wood collected, tin huts swept clean. And so the month went by, picking, cooking, cleaning, in a cycle repeated every day come rain or shine. Doll loved every second. She dreaded the end of the month when Farmer Reeve would wave goodbye at the gate and they would head back up the old twisting lanes to the railway station.

Another year would pass in the city as they returned to the normal hubbub of urban life. But before long, time would come once more for Doll's favourite excursion to the country.

Doll would go to sleep the night before their annual hop-picking adventure bursting with excitement. She would fall asleep, as excited as she was on Christmas Eve, and wait for her mum to come for her in the early hours.

Years passed and Doll grew. At 15 she had already started work at a London printer's, but she always made sure she had the time off for the family's hop picking excursions.

The Second World War came but that never slowed the family down, they still made the yearly walk from their home in Islington, down to Alders Gate over Cheapside, past St Paul's to Blackfriars Railway Station, sometimes climbing over the bomb-damaged rubble as they went. Some nights in the city Doll would watch the German air raids as they dropped tons of bombs on the buildings. The *moaning minnies* or air raid sirens would wake children. As the sirens howled into the night, waking all, there was no time to dress. They would pull on their *siren suits*, a one-piece garment with a long zip up the front, and then run for the damp dark shelters.

Often Doll watched the great city burn. Searchlights would pierce the night sky looking for the planes, catching the barrage balloons in their beams that were laughingly known by all the children as *fat elephants* or *silver sausages*. Anti-aircraft guns or ack-ack spat out tracer missiles and fury into the darkness as the bombs dropped and debris fell. The pavements shuddered in a deadly dance of bouncing rubble.

Factories and houses fell and became no more than piles of smouldering ashes. In 1940 the government revived the Women's Auxiliary Force, the WAF, to help with the shortfall of manpower in the factories and fields.

By 1940 over a quarter of a million Londoners were homeless and thousands killed. A far cry from the new hit of the year, *a nightingale sang in Berkeley Square*. Months before the Blitz, on the 31$^{st}$ of August 1939, orders were sent out to evacuate the city. Over three million people were transported away.

Bevan's *silver sausages* had little effect on the relentless offensive of the Luftwaffe. Bombers, as many as 1,000 at a time, dropped as much as 500 tons of bombs a night on the capital.

On December 29th the Luftwaffe tried to burn London, dropping tens of thousands of incendiary bombs. The Capital turned black in the firestorm, but later in the night a sudden drop in wind saved the city.

The nightly raids on towns and cities from September 1940 to May 1941 became known as the Blitz, short for Blitzkrieg or lightning war. Casualties were appalling. For example on the 10$^{th}$ May 1941 one raid on Clydeside left less than ten of its 12,000 houses undamaged!

Evacuated children, labelled like baggage, gripping gas masks and bags were huddled onto trains and buses. In the lull before the Blitz as many as a million came home but were soon packed off again as the bombing started. On the 7$^{th}$ August 1,000 planes descended on London. Seventy six nights of continuous bombing followed.

Over one million homes and 44, 000 Londoners lost their lives in the hellfire. The 15$^{th}$ September 1940 was the fighting climax over our great capital. That day later became known as Battle of Britain day.

Churchill never left the capital because of the bombing, often walking with his bodyguard amongst the rubble during raids. Churchill had a supreme faith that he was put on earth to complete a mission and would never be harmed. It turned out to be true, every single attempt on his life failed.

The Germans had gambled on destroying British morale, it had just the opposite effect bringing strangers together in a common cause to defeat the enemy.

In the same year, the British forces known as the British Expeditionary Force (BEF) had withdrawn from Europe and Britain became an island stronghold. A last hope for freedom. The dramatic rescue of men from the beaches of Dunkirk made heroes of ordinary sailors and fishermen, who had used their boats to ferry many soldiers to safety across the English Channel, under fierce fire from Stukas and Messerschmitts.

Winston Churchill had only been in office a few days when he was faced with the daunting task of trying to rescue over 400,000 British and French troops. Churchill, by general consent of all the political parties, was chosen to lead Britain after all confidence had been lost in Neville Chamberlain. The bombshell was then dropped that the troops had been forced onto the beaches of Dunkirk and would shortly be destroyed by the advancing Germans.

Churchill had been unaware that the commander-in-chief of the British Expeditionary Force (the BEF) in France had given the order to retreat. To keep morale high news of the British retreat was kept from the public, who were informed that the war effort was going as planned.

May 1940 had indeed become Britain's darkest hour, it was the closest that Britain came to losing the war. Unless the BEF could be rescued, protecting our shores from invasion would be an impossible task.

At the Admiralty, operation *Dynamo* was rushed into effect overseen by Vice Admiral Bertram Ramsey. He had been rushed out of a comfortable retirement. His organizational genius was crucial. From his HQ at Dover Castle he started to organize the largest evacuation ever manned and one of the most extraordinary operations in British history. Dover and Folkestone were separated from the enemy by a thin blue strip of sea. Locals could watch the huge German guns fire from the French coast, count to 60, and see the one-and-a-quarter-ton shells hit British soil.

All available boats and ships were rounded up and sent to France. Fishing boats, yachts, Thames barges, cockle boats, anything that could float was commissioned to save the troops. Ramsey managed to procure around 900 vessels. On the 29$^{th}$ May at 22.00 hours the armada sailed. Boats that had no engines were strapped together and towed across the channel through miles of minefields.

All the Pleasure Boats from Eastbourne were taken. Founded in 1861 by the Allchorn Family, the Pleasure Boats had carried tourists out to sea from the Eastbourne beaches, plying their trade on the Sunshine Coast.

The toll was high. The Empress, Eastbourne's largest Pleasure Boat, went down as did the Commodore, owned by Henry Boniface. The Sayers Brothers boat, Britannia, was also lost. The Belle had so much shrapnel in it that it took a month to prise it all out!

One of the rescue craft, the Jane Holland, a lifeboat from Eastbourne. More than 500 bullet holes were found in her but she still floated!

On the shores of France, the lightly armed and retreating BEF was in disarray, hounded by Hitler's SS and the Wehrmacht's 3$^{rd}$ Panzer Division. When the orders were received to retreat, the BEF troops rendered the heavy artillery useless to the enemy and made for the coast.

Churchill hurriedly placed 10,000 men from the 51$^{st}$ Highland Infantry Division under French control. French and British forces engaged the Germans in a ferocious rearguard action, allowing most of the British troops and as many French as possible to get to the beaches in the hope of rescue.

The 29$^{th}$ Infantry Brigade and Royal Green Jackets amongst others were sent in to relieve pressure on the retreat, with instructions from Churchill that they were not to surrender! For many it was a heroic struggle to the end, fighting till their last bullet. Many of those that were not killed spent the war in work camps and salt mines.

As the BEF retreated to a small strip of beach at Dunkirk, the German Luftwaffe pounded the shores. Mercifully the constant hounding by the RAF and the soft sand reduced the effectiveness of their bombs, but they still killed thousands of soldiers and sank nearly 240 ships in the brave flotilla.

One of the ships saving our brave soldiers from certain death. No space was left unfilled.

The painstakingly slow evacuation was underway and Churchill was put to his greatest test as Britain's new leader. Peace talks and surrender were the most obvious option forwarded by Lord Halifax, but Churchill stuck to his guns and decided to go down fighting. If Britain capitulated it would have been the end of the war and Nazi domination in Europe would have followed.

It was not until the 31$^{st}$ May, days after the evacuation had begun, that the British public were finally made aware of the disaster happening across the Channel.

Ten German divisions closed in on Dunkirk. Hitler sensed that the end was near but did not realise how effective operation Dynamo had been, his hesitation was our salvation.

Numbers vary considerably but, in total, it was thought that nearly half a million troops, including over 300,000 British had been liberated and brought safely to British shores. The core of the army had been saved.

Tony Hibbert, a 2$^{nd}$ lieutenant, was commanding a half-battery of three-inch guns on a sand dune above Dunkirk. He was one of the last men off the beach. On the 1st June his post had run out of ammo, he was given orders to 'scupper' his mobile guns and to make for the water in the hope of rescue.

That evening Tony was up to his neck in the bloody, oil-coated water, praying for rescue. The scene he remembers was surreal. Oil tankers were aflame, the beach littered with bodies and vehicles, Junker 87 & 88's were attacking in force to try and eliminate as many troops as possible.

The dark water glowed with natural phosphorescence and, as the bullets and bombs ripped through the salt water it reacted and radiated with light, casting strange lights along the surface.

Tony later said it was one of the most dark-dreamlike but beautiful sights he had ever seen. Tony was one of the last lucky ones. Out of the darkness a rope was thrown and a friendly voice came, "Grab that son." Tony made it, exhausted, back to British soil. He, like every survivor, was issued with a card to fill in and send to relatives to let them know he was alive.

Finally, on the 3$^{rd}$ June the remaining troops on the French beaches surrendered. In a few days around 70,000 British and 30,000 French troops were captured, wounded or killed.

On the shores and fields of France lay not only the bodies of our brave soldiers, but the entire weaponry of the BEF 76,000 tons of ammunition and 2,500 guns. An army had been saved but their arms lost to the enemy.

Nine destroyers, over 200 boats and ships and 145 aircraft were lost. Britain was left with just her depleted Air Force to stave off the inevitable attack.

Britain became home to a rag-tag army of British and European troops, even some cavalry from India, including over 100,000 Polish who had fled from the pursuing might of Nazi Germany.

Churchill braced himself and announced the full extent of the disaster to the public. He then made one of his famous inspirational speeches that told of the disaster, but also lifted the fighting spirit of the British people. He described the evacuation as a miracle of deliverance and went on…

*"We shall not flag or fail. We shall go on to the end. We shall fight in France, we shall fight on the seas and oceans, we shall fight with growing confidence and growing strength in the air, we shall defend our island, whatever the cost may be, we shall fight on the beaches, we shall fight on the landing grounds, we shall fight in the fields and in the streets, we shall fight in the hills; we shall never surrender."*

Churchill was preparing Britain for the oncoming invasion that would happen once the Luftwaffe had cleared the skies of British planes. In Europe the largest forced migration of people in human history took place as German domination took hold.

By June, an ominous lull had fallen over the skies as both Germany and Britain prepared for the final battle for supremacy of the air. Churchill ordered all church bells to fall silent, only to be rung in advance of invasion.

Germany consolidated many of its captured airfields closer to our shores. They used slave labour from occupied factories to mass-produce arms. In Britain the Royal Air Force desperately trained pilots for the oncoming battle that all knew was inevitable.

*Operation Sealion* was the German codename for the invasion of Britain. The first part of their plan was to attack the radar stations and airfields, then the harbours and factories. This was to clear the skies and pave the way for the land-invasion.

Over the hop fields of southeast England the future of the country was to be decided. Young men hardly out of school would stand with volunteer pilots from all over the world, from New Zealand, Australia, Canada, South Africa, America, Poland, France, Czechoslovakia and Belgium. They stood against the mightiest fighting machine the world had ever seen. The Battle of Britain was about to begin and just over 550 fighters were to try and stop 2655 German planes from destroying Britain.

Surprisingly, hops were considered vital to the war effort, not only for their recuperative powers amongst serving men in the shape of a good old pint of beer, but also for their medicinal qualities and sedative powers. Because of that, hop growing continued throughout the war, as did, of course, hop picking.

**Girls from all walks of life joined the WLA**

Land Army girls worked the fields and planted the crops while their men prepared to fight the enemy. The girls of the Women's Land Army, WLA, formed in 1939, became fondly called *Soil Cinderellas* and worked for 18 to 24 shillings a week plus board. Over 80,000 women toiled the soil.

Allotments exploded, with over 1.5 million across the country after the Ministry of Agriculture started the Dig for Victory campaign to encourage more people to grow their own food.

Every spare piece of soil was used to grow food, playing fields were planted and economy recipes flourished.

At the outbreak of hostilities Doll had gone to work at a munitions factory and her family carried on as best they could. But as the hop-picking season arrived they would gather all their old clothes and head for the countryside for their special working holiday.

Guinness was sold as a tonic with seven benefits. One for each day of the week. How lucky was that!

Britain became a lone voice in a dark Europe. Anti-tank traps were dug all along the coast and thousands of small concrete bunkers called pillboxes peppered the landscape. Britain's coasts looked more like prison camps, where once children built sandcastles, the deckchairs and sunshades were replaced with endless miles of barbed wire, concrete and minefields.

Old soldiers, civilians and the Home Guard added to the numbers of the armed forces and manned the pillboxes with inadequate equipment, knowing it was their job to slow down any invasion as it marched on London. They all knew their pillboxes would have become their concrete coffins had the Germans arrived.

While working at the hop farm one year, Doll noticed that a foreign gentleman had rented a cottage just off the track to the farm. He had positioned a large telescope in the back window. The telescope could not be seen from the road but from the fields she could clearly see it pointing out of the cottage window. He would often be seen staring into his telescope and jotting down notes. He had a perfect view over a huge part of the East Sussex landscape down to the Channel and beyond.

"He's a spy," whispered one of the pickers. "I just know he is."

"Don't be so daft," came the reply. "Mind you it does make you wonder what he's doing all day looking through that telescope!"

"And he takes notes!" nodded another.

"And there is the flashing light at night from the back window down towards the coast!"

After much consideration, around the fire one evening, (which had to be covered in case of enemy aircraft) and with a few pints of beer to loosen up, it was generally decided to report the fact to the local constabulary. It may just be harmless bird spotting but it could be something more sinister! Anyway the police were sure to sort it out. If he was innocent then there was no harm done! *Loose lips sink ships* were the bywords of the day. Posters were everywhere warning of strangers and for the public to keep a watchful eye out for anything unusual.

No sooner had they reported the inquisitive stranger than all hell broke loose. It was as if they had given a missing piece of a puzzle to the police. First officials arrived and took all the women away, posting men on all the exits. Then the Ministry turned up and carted the man off. When he came out of the house he was in full uniform dress. That shocked everyone. After that a group of men came in and spent ages sifting through all the belongings in the house.

The hop-pickers gossiped for days and all patted themselves on the back for they had surely saved Britain from disaster! No one ever saw the stranger again!

In the summer of 1940 the ominous lull ended and dog-fights began above the southern skies as the enemy tested our defences. On the 12th August things really started sizzling and by the 30th Fighter Command launched over 1,000 sorties to intercept the enemy in one day! Young lads armed with 15 seconds of ammunition raced to the sky, many never to return.

In August the skies burned and by September it seemed like the world above was on fire. Doll later learned it was The Battle of Britain.

Germany had to control the skies for the prelude to their land invasion. Determined to wipe out our air power the Luftwaffe launched multiple attacks from all sides. German planes would come in low over the fields trying to get to their targets undetected. On the southern airfields, *squawk boxes* would wail and pilots would scramble to their planes to intercept the enemy. On Eagle Day the Germans launched 1485 sorties against our shores. On September 15$^{th}$ over 130 German planes were shot down.

Over the rolling fields of southeast England fierce fights ensued. Planes roared through the skies, bullets spat in anger, planes exploded and pilots died. When the planes crashed, the girls would rush over to the wreckage to help, but more often than not there were only bodies in the twisted burning metal.

One German pilot managed to crash-land his Messerschmitt BF 109E and was rushed to hospital. The unlucky British pilots were taken back for burial at their family churches but the Germans were buried in the nearest churchyard. At St Nicholas Church, near Sandhurst Cross, they buried several German pilots but after the war they were exhumed and taken home to their families.

One day as Doll and her friends were playing in the apple orchard they looked up to see a German bomber. Its tail was on fire. At first they all watched as several men bailed out, however they soon realised it was headed straight for them. They all screamed and ran up and down, left and right. No one knew which way to run, it always seemed to be headed right at them. In the last few seconds as Doll lay under an apple tree with her hands over her head, praying, the bomber screeched past, crashing into the woods in neighbouring Bourne Farm.

They all rushed over to the plane but the wreckage was so terrible no one could have lived through it. Later, when the fires had died down, they found and buried the pilots. To this day Doll was sure that the pilot had managed to pull the plane up just enough to avoid the children in the orchard. They later heard that one of the aircraft's crew who had bailed out, had landed on top of Hawkhurst church steeple!

There were several key figures instrumental in saving Britain in the dark days of 1940, such as Sir Keith Park. Sir Keith controlled the response to the German attacks hour by hour with superb skill. His brilliant use of the new radar defence, combined with observation posts, allowed him to organise the air defence minute by minute. Information was rushed to the air force allowing the pilots to scramble and intercept the German attacks.

On September 28$^{th}$ a fierce encounter took place over the southeast, known as Bomb Alley and Hell's Corner. Squadron 605, based near Croydon, was scrambled to intercept a large formation of ME 109 fighters. During the furious dogfights that ensued, Flying Officer Peter Guerin Crofts, who was 22, was killed in action.

Peter Guerin Crofts

He was one of the many that gave their lives for their country, a hero in every sense of the word. On Padgham Corner adjacent to South View Farm where his body was found, his mother kneeled and placed a simple wooden cross in the soil. Near Little Rabbits Farm there still stands a small cross, a reminder of our hero who shall never grow old, a young man who fought and died to preserve our freedoms and way of life.

In West Grinstead there is a memorial to Douglas Arnold, a spitfire pilot who was one of the lucky ones to survive the war. On his gravestone is one of the finest poems ever penned.

It was written by John Gillespie Magee Jr, a young fighter pilot flying Spitfires, for the Royal Canadian Air force.

John wrote this superb poem to his mother just a few weeks before he was killed on active service. He was 19!

### *High Flight*
Oh! I have slipped the surly bonds of Earth
And danced the skies on laughter-silvered wings:
Sunward I've climbed and joined the tumbling mirth
Of sun split clouds – and done a hundred things-
You have not dreamed of, wheeled and soared and swung
High in the sunlit silence. Hovering there,
I've chased the shouting wind along, and flung
My eager craft through footless halls of air...
Up, up the long, delirious burning blue
I've topped the wind-swept heights with easy grace,
Where never lark, or even eagle flew —
And while with silent, lifting mind I've trod
The high untrespassed sanctity of space,
Put out my hand and touched the face of God.

By the 6<sup>th</sup> September the huge German armada was prepared and Britain was put on Alert No 2, meaning that invasion was probable in the next three days. Hitler authorised his secret directive No 16. This ordered all landing preparations to begin immediately.

However all that was not to be. The Royal Air Force, against all the odds, beat the mighty Luftwaffe. The superb training that allowed planes to be airborne within 90 seconds of the first warning bell had paid off. *When you hear the bell run like hell!*

With the new-fangled radar to guide them the British planes intercepted wave after wave of Germans. Although vastly outnumbered by the enemy our young pilots went into the fury of battle and gave their lives in the blue skies above our precious land.

*A Messerschmitt Me/Bf 109 downed at Berwick on 12<sup>th</sup> August*. The pilot's boots were taken to hamper any escape attempt!*

By the end of September the German losses were so great that, on the 12<sup>th</sup> October a furious Hitler called off *Operation Sealion* and looked east for other conquests.

Goering, who had stared across the small stretch of water with his binoculars and promised his Fuhrer *'the greatest of all victories,'* was humiliated. Britain's shores had been saved by a small band of heroes.

We now know that 544 brave RAF pilots gave their lives in that awful but truly inspiring Spitfire Summer.

Later Churchill spoke the immortal words, *"Never in the field of human conflict was so much owed by so many to so few. And if the British Empire were to survive a thousand years men will say this was their finest hour!"*

The casualties had been devastating, one in five pilots had died but it was not the final toll. By the end of the war over a quarter of a million planes had fought and nearly 200,000 air crew had died in Western Europe alone.

However in the late summer of 1940 Britain had won its most important battle in the war, control of the skies! The country, with Churchill as their resilient and dogged leader, fought on in a desperate one-sided war. A war that only the foolhardy but wonderful British with their bulldog nature, born from centuries of war and invasion could ever dream of winning.

As hostilities progressed, Churchill gathered support among his allies across the globe and started to build a force that could free Europe from the tyrannical master race and their thousand year Reich.

Doll remembers the first time she saw American troops arriving in London in 1942. "We all ran out into the streets to see them march past. We were waving and shouting, clapping and cheering. They looked so big and strong and healthy. They oozed self-confidence, it was wonderful to see. Our boys had been through so much, thin, worn and rationed—but the Americans, Oh they looked magnificent! What a sight!

I was standing next to an old woman who was crying. I asked if she was all right! She told me that for the first time in the horrible war she had a glimmer of hope and there was suddenly light at the end of a long dark tunnel! 'I feel a heavy weight being lifted from the pit of my stomach and a knot untying from my heart' she sobbed. 'For the first time in two years I have laughter in my heart and a smile on my lips.' Suddenly I found tears welling up in me as well. We ended up both crying and waving together."

The Americans, as the Canadians had, brought with them more than just chocolate and hope, they brought with them laughter, enjoyment, silk stockings and the sound of Glenn Miller!

Where the Odeon Cinema stands in London today was the old Paramount Cinema and below it was a dance hall. The troops taught the girls all the new American moves. Doll would go to dances there and at the Hammersmith Palais (pronounced *Pally* by the locals, and cost a shilling to get in). It was a little bit of sugar on the bitter pill of war and thoroughly enjoyed. Where the English boys were polite and restrained the Americans lived in the spirit of the moment, no one knew what tomorrow would bring. As the big-band sound of *the jitterbug* shook the dance floor, the American lads would swagger over to the girls, waiting like the proverbial wall flowers, stare deep into their eyes and say, "Come on snake let's wiggle!"

Some nights the air raid sirens would screech out, but the band played louder and they just kept on dancing. Candles were lit when the electricity failed. As the bombs fell, dancers held close, skipped across the maple sprung floor in defiant bliss. If they were going to be killed, where better than enjoying themselves on the dance floor, instead of cooped up in a shelter wondering if the next bomb had your name on it. Live for today for tomorrow may never come! What great dance nights Doll had and what memories. *We'll Meet Again*, the new slow dance hit, would often finish the night.

After the battle of El Alamain, Churchill knew that invasion of British soil was almost impossible and announced to all to let the bells across the country ring, and joyously how they did!

In November 1942 at the Lord Mayor's Luncheon in London, Churchill, in response to our victory at the Second Battle of El Alamein said, *"This is not the end. It is not even the beginning of the end. But it is, — perhaps—, the end of the beginning."* And so it was.

As the all-important D-day approached, Britain amassed combined armies of over three million men to storm the Normandy shores. Day after day they waited, coiled like a gigantic spring, as the worst June storm for 20 years raged in the Channel. Finally on the 6$^{th}$ June 1944, with a short break in the weather, the order was given to attack. The largest armada ever assembled, four thousand ships, and over twice as many planes surged forward from Britain. Europe would be wrenched ditch by ditch, house by house from the clutches of a despised dictator. The black heart of Nazism that had held a knife at the world's throat would be crushed.

Before the attack by the AEF, now the Allied Expeditionary Force, large numbers of soldiers in over 11,000 camps were stationed all over the country, some not far from Doll's farm on the beach at Lydd, where hundreds of telegraph poles had been faked-up to look like gun barrels.

On the weekends they would send a truck to pick up Doll and the other young women, then proceed around some of the local villages. They would arrive back at the barracks with a truckload of girls. Passes were checked, and then they would dance the night away. At the end of the dancing the passes were checked again, everyone was loaded onto the trucks and dropped back all over the countryside to their various blacked-out villages.

What a way to spend time in 1940s England! Dancing the night away with soldiers in their barracks on the beach. For a few hours each week the thought of the impending strike on Europe was put far away into the back of their minds.

On the 7th May 1945 at 2.31am, at General Eisenhower's headquarters in Rheims, after frenzied retyping of documents, the remaining German generals surrendered, unconditionally. They marched silently into Eisenhower's office and without a word put pen-to-paper and left. Verve Clicko was drunk out of hastily gathered mess tins by the officers and staff. The war in Europe was finally over.

Hop-picking went on straight through hostilities and when Victory in Europe or VE day finally came, great celebrations were had by all.

May 8, 1945 was a beautiful day. The sun rose over a blue sky and the centre of the world on that fine day was London. Churchill made another immortal speech..."*This is your victory, victory of the cause of freedom. Advance Britannia!*"

Doll went up to St Paul's in London to hear a sermon, all the more meaningful as it was near the spot that she used to wave farewell to her dad.

At Buckingham Palace the gates shook as countless numbers cheered for the King. "We want the King, we want the King."

Slowly the large doors behind the balcony opened and the King, Queen and Churchill walked onto the balcony.

The crowd went wild, streamers flew, people cheered and sang with jubilation. There was pure joy in the air.

Doll then made her way slowly to Trafalgar Square, squeezing through the throngs of strangers that were suddenly friends along Pall Mall, dancing and singing as she went.

In Piccadilly tens of thousands gathered to celebrate and party until the early hours. Many then slept in the parks and gardens. A million people watched searchlights, that used to pierce the night sky for enemy planes, pick out the cross above St Paul's that had almost been lost in the firestorm during the Blitz, as it once was in 1666.

However the ancient oak, felled in the great forests of Sherwood for Sir Christopher Wren's masterpiece, had stood firm against foe, fire and flame.

The whole atmosphere was indescribable. Old ladies danced with young men, strangers kissed and tears of joy ran freely down faces.

For many VE Day was one of the happiest days of their lives. Some say it was one of the greatest days in the history of the world. That one day signified a free world, free from a dark engulfing terror that had been vanquished.

Although rationing had taken many luxuries away including high-heels (the maximum allowed was two inches) girls found different ways to look their best. Lines were drawn up bare legs with eyebrow pencils to mimic stockings; beetroot colouring was used as lipstick. A thousand new makeup tricks were learnt using everything from boot polish to gravy browning.

After the war the Americans, Canadians and forces from so many countries around the world packed up and shipped off home, many thousands taking their new British wives with them, who were glad to escape the drudgery of post-war Britain.

Our country lay in tatters and had lost a generation of young men and women. At first there was full employment and people celebrated. In 1946 over one and a half billion cinema tickets sold and millions were spent on gambling.

With a three-and-a-half billion war-debt to pay back Britain was working hard. But 1947 saw one of the worst winters for decades. Millions were freezing and over two million men could not work. Factories closed and men were laid off. Rationing bit hard. Britain slid into recession, borrowed even more, then spent 50 years paying back the debt!

America, unaffected by our terrible weather kept manufacturing and had zero unemployment. The States were on a boom. The lucky women who had followed their lovers to America forged a new life. Over fifty thousand British women had left the country and over 150 Eastbourne Girls went home with Canadian servicemen.

It was a hard time for Britain, but they say that the British walk proudly upon the earth and it is in the times of greatest hardship that their spirit shines brightest. It was a long hard road and rationing continued in some forms until 1954, though clothes-rationing ended in 1949. Men could wear turn-ups again and kids over 12—long trousers.

Surprisingly, Churchill was defeated in the post-war elections. Clement Atlee had stormed to power with the promise of a New Jerusalem and George VI handed him the Empire. His dream turned to ashes in the bitter winters that followed the war and the Empire collapsed. Although the new labour government had kept its promise of free health care for all it was not enough.

Churchill had retired for a short period to lick his wounded pride at Chartwell, in Kent, overlooking the same sweeping countryside that Doll and her family had worked. There he recuperated. He had been defeated at the polls before, but Churchill was a fighter and returned a few years later to taste a glorious victory at the 1951 elections.

Through his long life and endless deeds, his many failings were understandably overlooked and he became known as the greatest Briton that had ever lived.

From a shattered Britain the word had gone out to her Empire. Her heart had been damaged but not her soul.

Men came from all corners of her realm to fill the gaps left vacant by those who had sacrificed their blood for freedom. Indians and Jamaicans came to drive the trains and run the buses, Africans, Russians, Europeans and more all heard the call and answered with their sweat and toil. Polish officers were given automatic entry to Britain by Churchill for helping during the war.

On the 22nd June 1948 the Empire Windrush pulled into Tilbury Docks. On board were 494 West Indians, mainly from Jamaica. As they filed off the gang-plank few realised it was a turning point in British history. The Empire of old had crumbled but a new Britain was being born, a multicultural one. The Black History of Britain had entered a new chapter.

Most of the forces were de-mobilised—"*de-mobbed.*" Men rolled up their sleeves and went back to the factories and farms that had been kept going by women. Army barracks were changed and rebuilt. Billy Butlin bought up some of the old barracks and changed them into holiday camps. Just as before the conflict, he entertained young families, but now there was a newfound community spirit that had been forged in the furnace of war.

Slowly, our battered nation dusted off her clothes and stood back on parade. Eventually she would once more be counted amongst the great nations of the world.

And so the world turned and a new generation was born into a post-war era.

As for Doll!

Doll had finished up in the munitions factory where she had worked during the war years and returned to her job at the printers. There she fell for Patrick and in 1947 wedding bells rang out over a war-torn but re-energized London. The bells that year were not only for Doll and Patrick but for Princess Elizabeth and her dashing Lieutenant, Philip Mountbatten.

Two years later Doll decided to have one last trip hop-picking. The pound had been devalued by thirty per cent against the dollar and times were hard. The year was 1949 and it was a new world. Doll had a husband and family to look after — but just one last time Doll was going to find her green heaven.

Even all those years later Doll was too excited to sleep the night before she went hop-picking.

"Pauline, wake up my little darling wake up," whispered Doll in her daughter's ear. "I am going to take you somewhere very special. Somewhere dreams are made. We are going where the skylarks sing and the air smells of the sea. We are going hop-picking!"

Doll, with her daughter and the rest of her family walked the familiar path along the London streets, in their patched clothes carrying grandad's ancient chest.

Once more they saw the autumn sun rise over the old London streets. At the railway station they caught the southbound train and Doll stroked her daughter's hair as she slept. Doll smiled across at her mum and the train followed the gleaming steel rails to her little dreamland.

# Epilogue

The old hop names have long since faded into history. The Hop Pocket that would contain over 160 pounds of dried pressed hops. The Hop Pokes that held about ten bushels or 50 pounds of freshly picked hops. The Dead Men or concrete sleepers used to hold the posts erect.

The Hop Dogs and Cone Barrow, the Bines, the Ankle Binder, the Scu'bit or Scuppet Driver and the Monkey Feeder—all gone. So are the gangs of old experts such as the Brass Harness Boys.

The shouts roared out over the fields by the managers have folded into the rich soil to remain silent forever. **"All to work, no more bines, all to dinner, ge'ya 'ops ready!"**

The names of the many varieties of hops are now also scarce, The Amos Early, the Fuggle, the Mayfield and Canterbury Grape, Golden Tip's, Cooper's White. They are now just strange and unfamiliar names to all but a few.

Of course, old-man Reeve was not really made of iron. Although he had outlived just about everyone of his generation, eventually Father Time called.

There is a little corner of paradise down an old path on the Kent-Sussex border that leads to St Nicholas Church.

At the far end of the graveyard lies old man Reeve. He had lived until his $93^{rd}$ birthday. There he rests, eternally, above the land that he had worked for so many decades in his pork-pie hat, braces and breeches. He overlooks Old Place Farm with its hop drying oasts still standing like plump Dutch maids in the valley below.

The skies are peaceful now. No more dogfights or bombs, just birdsong and the wind whispering through the fields where the hops once grew and Land Girls once toiled.

The trenches dug for the field workers to run to when the German planes shot at them have all been filled. The songs that the Londoners would sing on their way home have disappeared like morning dew. *The monies all been spent, a'int none to pay the rent!*

Legend has it that in late summer, when the ripe grain is high and the hedgerows are full of honeysuckle and wild berries. When the breeze carries the scent of the sea and the skylark calls to the song thrush. If you stand very still and listen very carefully, you may just hear the sound of laughter and Cockney songs drifting over the countryside.

# The End

## Isaac Merritt Singer

# Touched by Fire
A brief history of a giant

What a man! When I first started, as a child, to hear stories about Isaac Singer, I was enthralled. He lived the American dream. This is the rags to riches story of a man who became a household name. A man who went from the gutter to untold wealth.

Over the next 40 years I gathered snippets of information which accumulated into the story of the greatest invention of the 19$^{th}$ century. I doubt if all of it is completely true.

They say that a few men are touched by fire in their lifetime. Isaac Singer was one of these men. He blazed a trail that the world followed, lived hard and died famous.

Let me tell you about one of the only men outside of religion who became a household name around the world, it really is worth the read.

Isaac Merritt Singer was the youngest of eight children. His father, Adam, was possibly of German-Jewish origin as there was a Jewish family in his hometown of Frankfurt, Germany, known as the Rei**singer**.

Isaac's father arrived in New York in 1769 at the age of 16. This German immigrant had arrived in America to chase a dream. Little did he know that his youngest son would fulfil that dream!

Who would believe that even today people sailing to America set eyes on one of Isaac's wives! Yes, one of the first sights they see when nearing Ellis Island is the Statue of Liberty. It is rumoured that she was modelled on the most beautiful woman in 19$^{th}$ century Europe, Singer's half-French wife and actress, Isabella.

Édouard René de Laboulaye had the idea of presenting a statue representing liberty as a gift to the United States. It was the sculptor Frederic-Auguste Bartholdi, one of Laboulaye's friends that turned the idea into reality. Gustav Eiffel of Eiffel Tower fame, built the structure in 1885 that enables Bartholdi's Statue of Liberty to stand proud, welcoming people from all over the world.

Bartholdi's Statue of Liberty modelled by Singer's wife Isabella

Bartholdi originally asked his mother to sit for the statue but she would, not stay still for long periods. Then he asked

Jeanne-Emile Baheux de Puysiex a woman he met he while holidaying in America. She later became his wife.

However it is still rumoured that Singer wife, Isabella, the French actress, said to be the most beautiful woman in Europe, was the model that finally sat for the statue.

Even as an old man, Isaac Singer's charm and wealth attracted beautiful women. As a young man, by all accounts, he had the devil in him. He was a renowned womaniser and father to at least 28 children by several wives and countless lovers.

However, I am jumping ahead. He has many miles to go and many hardships to face before he makes his millions.

Isaac's father, Adam Singer, set up business as a wheelwright and barrel maker, a cooper. He married and started a family. History tells us that he lived until 1855. He was 102, an amazing achievement for the hard frontier life of those days.

Isaac's mother, Ruth, left the family home when Isaac was a child to become a Quaker. It is said that in later years Adam Singer, at the age of 99, went to find Ruth, possibly to tell her of the fortune their youngest son was making. He tracked her down in Albany, NY, only to find that, at the age of 96, she had passed away shortly before his arrival!

I am not sure about the reliability of these dates as they do seem extreme and mean that Ruth must have had Isaac when she was in her 50s. I suppose it is possible, there was little birth control. Maybe Isaac's birth was the last straw for Ruth?

In the history books, Isaac Singer seems to have been born in several locations in the New York area. One humorous solution was that Ruth had a slow birth in a fast wagon! However for our story we will go for the most likely town.

Some say Isaac was born in the small frontier town of Schaghticoke, NY, in 1811, some say Pittstown. His dad Adam was already nearly 60! Although the family moved away, it would be back in New York City, many years later, that Isaac made an indelible mark on American history, building one of the first skyscrapers and one of the largest buildings in the world at that time.

Adam Singer remarried but Isaac never connected with his stepmother. Isaac, now in Oswego, NY, must have had a hard childhood for, by the age of 12 and still just a lad, he slipped on his running shoes and ran as far away from home as he could.

There is little detail of his early years. It must have been tough on the road at such a tender age. What would make a child run away from home is anybody's guess. He probably stayed with some of his older brothers who had left home earlier. There are tales that he worked part-time, and paid for rudimentary schooling between jobs as a mechanic and carpenter.

So how did the most famous name in the sewing world get into the sewing business? Isaac was smart, cunning and ruthless. He had to be to survive on the streets of 19th century America. The States was a bustling mass with immigrants flooding in, and prosperity booming. There were endless opportunities for those willing to grasp them.

After a few years in the wilderness Isaac reappears in history. He had learned the trades of mechanic and cabinetmaker. Two trades that later would combine to his benefit and make him one of the richest men in the world.

He was also a showman. He thought of himself as an accomplished actor, landing the role of Richard III with a group of travelling actors, when he was only 19.

As a handsome young man, with an inventive mind, we find Isaac at the age of 28 having invented a machine for drilling and excavating rock. He had no use for his invention and sold it for a year's wages.

With his new wealth he quickly put it to use and followed his first love—acting. He formed a group of actors called *the Merritt Players* and off they went around America *treading the boards*. Of course it was not long before his money ran out, and he was back to working for a living. His first attempt at the American dream had failed but he was not finished, not by a long way.

Isaac could charm the socks off anyone, as one hotel manager remembered. Isaac, his wife and children arrived at the hotel penniless. Isaac performed for the guests to pay for board. When Isaac packed to leave, the hotelier even gave him some money. He last saw the family heading out of town, into the wilderness on a buckboard.

In Fredericksburg, PA, his inventive mind was at work again, this time inventing a wooden printer's type. Don't ask me what that was, I haven't a clue! It was obviously not all that successful because, with all of Isaac's powers of persuasion, he never managed to sell it. However it did lead to his greatest invention.

Isaac was a practical man with vision, but he had a poor academic education. His writing, in later life, shows how much difficulty he had spelling even the simplest words. Hey I know how he felt! This did not slow the master showman down. His intellect was undeniable, even at a young age he was able to quote great chunks of Shakespeare at the drop of a hat. Always one for smooth-talking, the handsome young actor and inventor *wheeled and dealed* his way through life.

By 1850 Isaac had rented a basement at 19 Harvard Place, Boston, MA. He tried in vain to sell his printing invention, but once again failed to find a buyer. However, the light was at the end of the tunnel. He had rented his basement from a sewing-machine manufacturer called Phelps. Phelps, by all accounts, made poor sewing machines under licence for Lerow & Blodgett. None saw the huge potential in sewing machines that Isaac did.

Phelps asked Singer to repair many of the machines that kept coming back. In fact very few machines sewed well in those days. While working on the machines it became clear to Singer's inventive mind that improvements were necessary. Once again he went to work.

He raised $40 in capital from one of his business associates, a Mr Zieber. The story goes that the money came about from an accumulation of a bet between the two men that Isaac could make a reliable sewing machine. Zieber was onto a good thing. If Isaac did make a sewing machine that worked he would get his money back and much more. If Isaac failed- Zieber would win his bet!

The stage was set.

Isaac had just enough money to make a practical machine. Something that, in the entire history of the world, had yet to be done.

Men had tried through the ages to make a good sewing machine, but all had shortcomings. Ignorant of many of the patents of the time, Isaac went to work. At last the first practical sewing machine was being built in a basement by a 39-year-old who still had a passion to make a fortune and, of course, win his bet.

Isaac's version of events were naturally flamboyant. In later life, he often told of how he worked tirelessly for eleven days and eleven nights building the machine. How he went without food, and grabbed only a few snatches of sleep. That may be true. Whatever the story the result was the same, a sewing machine that actually sewed.

After a few minor hiccups, Isaac packed up his sewing machine and headed for the patent office in New York.

Against all the odds he had come up with the first reliable and practical sewing machine. His only problem was that he had infringed several patents doing it. His worst nightmare came true when he found himself in court against one of the most powerful men in America, Elias Howe.

After a shaky start in the sewing machine business Howe had successfully been charging all the other sewing machine manufacturers for the use of his patents, and Isaac Singer, the poor upstart, was going to be no exception. One day Howe spotted one of Isaac's machines being demonstrated in a shop window, and immediately went in to complain. Isaac was there and an argument ensued. Isaac nearly booted him out of the shop. Howe left flustered and angry. He was used to manipulating others, not being pushed around. He vowed Singer would pay!

Years later Howe tried to get his patent rights extended. Howe stated that the huge sums that he had made out of his patents were not enough. Needless to say popular opinion of him was not high. Later Howe hired writers to boost his colourful version of the sewing machine saga.

Singer used all his talent and cunning to try to avoid Howe's costs. Isaac's machines came onto the market at $125, a fantastic and impossible sum for most normal families.

Isaac no longer needed his old partners. He needed a legal brain. Firstly to fight his court case with Howe, and secondly to figure out how people could afford his machine. Into our story comes Edward Clark, who instantly sees a huge potential in the new venture.

Isaac bullied Phelps, one of his partners, out. Then, in a brilliant move, he conned the other.

Clark watched while Isaac did the dirty on both of his old partners. It appears that Clark was more than happy for them to be removed from what was to become such a huge financial boom. All Clark had to do was wait until Isaac needed him most, and then strike a deal. Clark had no money to invest but he had something more precious to Isaac, legal talent!

Zieber was in failing health, probably due to the pressure Isaac was putting him under. The story goes that Isaac went to his bedside and promised he would look after Zieber's family after his death. All he had to do was sign over his shares. Isaac would even give him $6000 to give to his offspring! It seemed too good to miss. If only he could have seen the future! He was about to make the biggest mistake of his life...

No sooner had Zieber signed the shares over than Isaac hires the best doctors of the period, to spare no expense in curing him. Zieber recovered!

In a stroke of devious genius Isaac had most of his business back, and for what would become a pittance. Zieber then had to work for Isaac as an employee, which he did, reluctantly, for many years.

It is extraordinary to think that Isaac could have been so cold blooded. Isaac and Zieber had been through so much together. When the pair had first met, according to Zieber, Isaac hardly had a shirt on his back, his jacket was torn at the elbows and he had not eaten. Zieber had clothed and fed Isaac, and spent many hours talking of living *the dream*.

Between them, they had been through great hardships. Zieber had also borrowed heavily to invest in Isaac, and had helped him in endless ways.

Isaac's deed showed his ruthless side where money was concerned.

However, he did not have it all his own way, for the brilliant legal mind of Edward Clark was a match for Isaac's more forceful tactics. Clark agreed to fight Howe in court, for a huge lump of Isaac's business. Isaac, now pretty much penniless and in desperate need for money, had little option but to agree.

After all of Isaac's cunning work, Clark got half his business without putting in a cent.

The partnership turned out to be one of the most successful in sewing history and, although they obviously did not trust each other, they both needed each other. They became uneasy bedfellows.

Incidentally, Isaac, with his persuasive manner also managed to get some of Elias Howe's sewing machine competitors to refuse to pay the huge licence fees that Howe was demanding. This enraged Howe who went around to see Singer. He told him the demand for his patent had changed from $2000 to $25,000. Once again a heated argument ensued and Howe was shown the door. The stage was set for years of legal wrangling and court cases.

This is where Clark earned his share of the business. Not only did he keep Howe's lawyers tied up in court, but he devised the first official **hire purchase scheme**. Everyday people who could not afford $125 for a Singer machine could pay $3 per month for their sewing machines, and so the *never-never* was born. Clark also devised multiple or group purchases where several people could get together to buy one machine.

This is one of a whole book of original hire purchase slips. I knew one person who paid for 15 years for her sewing machine from **1926**, making her final payment in **1941**. Could you imagine that today!

Of course, for hundreds of years before Clark there had been bartering and exchange, money lending and part-payment. But it was Clark who really did the paperwork and made it part of our everyday life. Who remembers the dreaded *Tallyman or knocker*? They would turn up once a week, or at the end of the month, to get their payments on borrowed money and check the numbers. They could lend money for Tommy's new shoes or a bicycle for the hubby, a little extra at Christmas. A million *knockers* kept their books of payments, and travelled around the poorer communities of the world before Clark's scheme.

Eventually Howe won his case and Singer reluctantly paid. Howe then gave up suing everyone and, on legal advice, joined the enemy. All the patent holders pooled their patents and joined *The Sewing Machine Cartel*. For the first time in history, in 1857, patent-pooling happened. This was really an illegal monopoly that ended up needing government legislation to bring it to a halt.

However, all that was years away and the all-powerful *Sewing Machine Cartel* sued all fledgling sewing machine companies and charged the rest royalties. This allowed **the few** to dominate sewing machine production for years, and become rich, stifling most American competition.

Once again we are jumping ahead, Isaac is not out of the woods yet, and he still cannot afford a new suit. In addition he makes mistakes. He failed to notice that the treadle cabinet, that he made to stow his machine in, and on which it is used, is unique. He was beaten to the patent office and missed out on patenting the treadle base of his machine.

Isaac was on the verge of untold wealth but it was not an easy ride.

Why buy a sewing machine? None of them had ever worked properly before! Why buy a Singer? Who was Singer? Certainly not the household name he is today.

This is where Isaac's superb salesmanship comes into action. Much like before, in his acting career, he packed up his machine and he and his entourage hit the road. He goes to shows, to theatres, to factories and displays—"Gather round ladies and gentlemen, come see the future!"

He tirelessly demonstrates his amazing invention that not only stitches but was also guaranteed to stitch for 12 months without failure! Something simply unheard of!

All of his acting skills, used to promote his machine, start to pay off. The master showman has a great publicity stunt up his sleeve. He goes to one of the largest sewing factories in America with the Press in tow. Here he has a race with not one—or two—but three of the fastest hand-sewing girls in a factory of over 3000 staff.

He unpacks his sewing machine and off they go. By the end of the race not only has he beaten all three girls, but the machine has worked flawlessly and with the much stronger *lockstitch*. The press were impressed, the factory was too—placing an immediate order for the machines.

Incidentally, rumour has it that some of the women in the early pictures, that Singer used to promote his sewing machine, were also his mistresses! One has to wonder, what with all his mistresses, wives and countless children how Singer managed to make anything at all! It seems like a miracle to me. He must have had the energy of an ox.

Was this one of Singer's mistresses?

Unlike Walter Hunt, an earlier inventor of a sewing machine, Isaac knew he was on to a winner and would not let *Hell or high water* get in his way. People say Hunt's daughter had actually put Hunt off his invention. She feared that thousands of women would find themselves out of work if he went ahead with making a sewing machine.

The facts turned out to be quite the opposite. Sewing machines created a whole new industry and cheaper clothes for the masses. Once, Isaac set up a demonstration just along the road from the famous P T Barnum. More people flocked to Singer's demonstration than Barnum's museum on Broadway!

Isaac, after struggling for most of his life, had finally come of age and so had the sewing machine. Almost single-handed, with bloody determination and against all the odds Isaac had ushered in the dawn of the sewing machine industry.

Machines started to sell at an amazing rate. For the first time in history, in America, proper mass production was going on.

The new age had arrived, which affected not only sewing machines but also more deadly inventions such as firearms! It is said that both Samuel Colt and Oliver Winchester gained knowledge for their mass production of arms from the sewing machine industry.

The money was rolling in. As word spread about the reliability of Singers, Isaac moved out of his workshops and looked for bigger premises as 10 machines turned into a 100 then a 1000.

Edward Clark's clever hire purchase plan also helped tremendously. It was copied by all the other sewing-machine makers of the day, and then by just about every company in the world. Clark also drew up a plan to trade-in old machines for new ones at a ridiculously high rate of $40 per trade. All old machines were quickly destroyed to stop them being resold. This policy continued right up to the 1960s and many Singer shops had presses in their storerooms to crush old machines. I know for sure that the Singer shop in Eastbourne, my hometown, had a seven-ton press in the basement for crushing competitors' machines.

At last, Isaac's machine, that he had *invented-copied-made* was to revolutionise the world and provide him untold wealth until his death. He had become the first Bill Gates.

His bank balance, along with his waistline, expanded rapidly. Isaac was a flamboyant and good-looking man at his peak—and now he had money rolling in beyond his wildest dreams. He let Clark run most of the daily grind of their business, while he set about enjoying the fruits of his labour.

By 1860, Singer's factory had produced over 13,000 machines at $125 a piece. At a time when the average wage was a few dollars a week it was already a fortune! He could not spend the money as fast as he was earning it. Within a few years the company was making over a million machines a year.

Isaac went on to embrace the good life. He had a string of mistresses and wives. He managed his affairs with little privacy and gave the papers of the day wonderful print material. As his wealth grew so did his excesses. His offspring rose in number, almost by the month. Many say that he had at least 28 children by a dozen or more wives and mistresses. He was allegedly even married to two women, and keeping a mistress, all at the same time… In the same city—New York!

How he managed to keep his intriguing life going is anybody's guess. He was burning the candle at both ends and loving it!

It is all too possible that he was over-compensating for his very hard start in life. Now, not only could he afford a new suit, he could buy the shop!

Isaac did everything in style. He had the grandest and most expensive parties, loved dancing and telling tales of his days of struggle and hardship. It is said that he even travelled to work in a specially commissioned coach. Bright yellow, 30 feet long and pulled by twelve black horses. He would ride up Central Park from his magnificent home to his office. Everyone would know who was coming, and children would often run along beside his carriage, shouting to him in the hope of a few coins.

The Singer building, finally completed in 1908, the world's first skyscraper over 600ft high.

Within a few short years he was the figurehead of a multi-national company that was expanding to every country. Singer machines were being carted across African deserts and shipped up the Amazon with new agents appearing in every town. In the larger towns there would be several agents and shops, all selling Singer machines.

Incidentally, Singer never made any sewing machines for anyone except Singer. This was unlike most of the other companies, who were only too happy to put any name you wanted on the front of a machine if you bought enough of them.

Eventually it all caught up with him. His constant womanising and a series of scandals turned many Americans against him. Their *favourite son* became ostracised from society and scandalised in the papers. Rude-mouthed, hot-tempered and arrogant. The women obviously loved it, though in reality he had a dark and dangerous side!

Clark, constantly embarrassed by Isaac, came to him with a deal that allowed Isaac to retire and spend his wealth on one condition—that he departed America. This time for good! Clark's wife was delighted. She was deeply religious and had always hated the man. She would not even let him step inside her house. Some stories vary here saying that he was being prosecuted for bigamy and fled while under bonded bail.

Leopards don't change there spots and before Isaac left he was once again courting (surprise, surprise). However, the woman had a daughter and the daughter was even prettier. Isaac turned all his charm and wealth on her. She was Isabella a half-French half-English beauty, described as the most desirable woman in Europe.

Singer wasted no time in enticing her, or maybe it was the other way around—who knows for sure! There is no doubt that the divorced beauty was a spectacular catch for him and, with his wealth, charm and looks how could she resist?

Before long Isabella was installed in Isaac's Fifth Avenue home and fell pregnant. Isaac had trouble with one of his divorces but, finally, married a very heavily-pregnant Isabella. Because they had to leave America the obvious place was Paris, France, where he had first met Isabella, and the city their son was named after.

Singers last residence in the United States was in a home nicknamed the "Castle" that Singer had built in Yonkers, New York. Not to be confused with the "Castle" that Singer

Company president Frederick Bourne built on Dark Island. Isaac Singer and family, Isabella and children, lived in Yonkers for about two years before leaving for Paris in 1867.

It must have been a sad day when Isaac and his new family set sail for Europe. He left behind his American dream and looked to the future in a foreign land. He had been to England a few years earlier but found the life in London boring.

At 53, Isaac and his entourage toured Europe before settling down in Paris. Their address in Paris was No.83 Boulevard Malherbes. Within a short time they moved from this address to several hotels where they stayed in royal apartments. However, things were not to be, and three years later, in 1870, the Franco-Prussian war erupted. Isaac packed up and headed for the safety of England.

After a stay in London, where he was the centre of society, the family settled in the West of England. Isaac laid plans for a grand house and gardens—palatial by all standards—with the most magnificent circular ballroom that he quaintly called the Wigwam.

Oldway Manor still survives in Paignton

The doors were large enough to allow a coach and horses straight in to unload, out of the rain, so as not to spoil the ladies' evening gowns. The Wigwam is still there, as is his house, now council offices. Well worth a visit if you are ever in the vicinity of Paignton down in the West Country.

While he may have been shunned by America, the wealth that he brought to England was most welcome. He employed hundreds of local workmen on his palace and became a popular sight around the town of Paignton. Isaac settled into his retirement with ease, enjoying his family and wealth.

**Isaac in his prime**

In July 1875 at the age of 64, Isaac died of heart failure. All the hardships of his early struggles had taken their toll, as had his over-indulgences in later life. He was deeply mourned, and his funeral was almost like a state funeral, with nearly 80 black carriages pulled by horses, some specially shipped in from France. Thousands of mourners and onlookers lined the streets from the early dawn, to catch a glimpse of the legend on his way to his final resting place.

Isaac never lived to see his precious Wigwam completed.

Isaac's final resting place

And so, the most famous of all entrepreneurs was dead. He had blazed a trail that would never be followed. He had lived life to the full and had grasped every moment.

I say *never to be followed*, let me tell you why. While Isaac's early life was spent in obscurity his final years were spent in a blaze of wealth and publicity. On most graves there are dates, birth and death. It is the little space between those dates that mean everything, the simple space that is the entire life of a person.

Isaac really did start from nothing with little more than the clothes on his back. He really was what the *American Dream* was all about. The son of an immigrant, he made the first good sewing machine in history—whatever other makers tell you. He helped kick-start mass production, pioneered proper hire-purchase, oversaw the first patent pooling and had one of the first truly multi-national companies employing nearly 100,000 people. Singer machines were the first mass-marketed domestic appliance in the world. Singer's machine may just go down in history as the most useful invention of the 19$^{th}$ century.

Singer was the first company to spend over one million dollars on advertising in one year. This, along with superb machines like the singer 12k, New Family machine of 1865 made Singer machines world leaders.

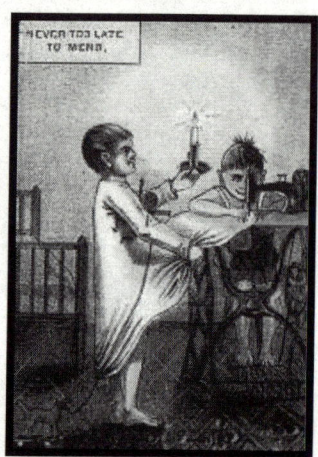

The Singer Company was the first to spend over $1,000,000 on advertising in one year.

The company went on to build one of the first skyscrapers that really did seem to touch the sky and, in his spare time, Singer fathered at least two-dozen children.

In his lifetime, and for the next century, his name was known by more people across the globe than any other person in history. What a simply amazing fact.

Moreover, when he died as a grey haired old man, he was married to the most beautiful woman in Europe.

Later, Clark sent his cousin and Ross Mc Kenzie over to Britain to build the largest sewing machine factory the world had ever seen at Kilbowie, Clydebank.

The factory had its own docks, shipyard, railways and even forests for wood. At its' peak the factory employed around 14,000 workmen.

One of the problems of getting men to work on time in the 19th century was solved when the Singer factory built the largest clock in the world, larger than Big Ben. Everyone in the valley could look out of their windows and see the time. There was no reason to be late again. Clark continued successfully to run the Singer Company for many years.

The massive Singer factory at Kilbowie, with a clock tower bigger than **Big Ben!**

In his will, Isaac generously split his enormous wealth among his many children, wives and mistresses. There were several claims by other children for money. They ended up in protracted court cases.

Had DNA testing been around we may have found out just to what extent Isaac was a ladies' man! What would the papers say today?

Isabella modelled for Bartholdi's Statue of Liberty before marrying a poor but handsome Italian Count. Several of Singers wealthy children went on to marry into high society, some into the European royal families. Some took up important positions around the world. A few even carried on in their father's ways. Paris Singer had an affair and fathered a child with the famous dancer, Isadora Duncan, before losing much of his wealth in the 1929 stock market crash.

All in all, the Singer name became synonymous with wealth and power. Not bad for a little runaway. Now you see why I started this story by saying *what a man*!

## The End

*Sussex Tongue*

The Sussex tongue is soft and sweet,

Laced with skylark and summer wheat.

It ripples like a babbling brook,

Thick and rich with a Cornish hook.

The Sussex tongue is almost gone,

To be lost amongst the meadow song.

In years to come you may search in vain,

For the Sussex tongue won't rise again.

*A I A*

# A Day of Stories

The trees were being shaken like rag dolls, and the leaves were being ripped off by a wind that was showing no mercy to man nor beast. The balmy Indian summer had been replaced with bitter Arctic winds. To top it all a flash flood had lifted the drain-covers in my garden, spraying sewage across the plants.

*I guess the fertiliser will do them good!* I had thought as I left for work deciding to worry about the mess later.

Bent against the storm, I struggled to my first call along the old redbrick alley towards the tradesmen's entrance of the Lansdowne Hotel on Eastbourne seafront. It was like walking in a wind tunnel. The rain slapped my face, the toolbox tugged annoyingly, like a misbehaving puppy on a lead.

I arrived at the entrance to the laundry just as the van driver dropped a box of fresh linen into a pool of water by the back door. He was cursing. I was wet. Another day's work had begun.

I soon had the linen-room's machine running perfectly. One of the hotel staff had crept in after work to repair her denim jeans. Somehow she had managed to shift the top shaft of the Singer 527 out of position. In her panic she undid the lower bobbin assembly, got in a right muddle, and scarpered. The next day she owned up and I was called.

It's funny how stories come. It was just one of my normal days. Mrs Lamb had called me out—once again. I sat in front of her machine wondering if it was her or the machine that was faulty. I re-threaded the machine, tested it, and pronounced it fit for duty. Thoughts of charging her disappeared when she smiled so sweetly at me. I left knowing that I would be back within the month.

My next customer went into a rendition of *Swing Low Sweet Chariot* as she made my coffee. She only stopped when the neighbour's dog howled louder than her!

By the time I arrived at my next customer's my head was pounding. I was soaked and my mood, like the weather, was getting darker. I was just thinking *what electric blue eyes the old man had* when his charming wife brought in a steaming cup of coffee.

"Wow! Now that's just what the doctor ordered," I piped up, with my first smile of the day.

"He's 91 this year," said the old dear, handing me the coffee, and a biscuit that was as welcoming as a fresh worm to a starving bird.

"I'm only 90! He does all the sewing—learnt it during the war in India where he was stationed."

*Story time*, I thought, as I sat down and sipped my drink. "Did you do much sewing out in India?" I enquired with my usual quizzical, tell-me-everything, expression.

"Hardly a stitch! I was busy maintaining Dakotas out of Assam. I had the training but we had a tiny gentleman who lived in a dirt hut near the base. He could turn a piece of scrap into a suit and a rag into a dress. We would go to the local market and buy Indian silk, then take it to him. He had a hand-operated Singer, old as Moses. He would sit cross-legged in front of the machine and sew, singing away to himself in Bengali. When he got to a tricky piece of sewing, where he needed both hands to sew, he would unfold his legs and turn the handle of the machine with his right foot! You had to see it to believe it. The best shirts in the area came from that little dirt hut. We arrived back from our tour of duty loaded with bags of clothes."

"I can see why you did not have to sew if you had such a person living so close." I smiled as I finished off my coffee, feeling, for the first time that morning, a bit more like a human being.

The old couple fussed around me as I left, almost dressing me, folding my collar up around my chin and pulling the zip of my coat up tight. With both hands loaded, I nodded goodbye and ran with my tools to the car.

My next customer was another delight. His family had a sewing pedigree that few could match. Court dressmakers to no less than King Louis XIV. Not bad eh! And more followed.

"Walpole's? That was it, Walpole's of Bond Street. Smack in the centre of London, on the corner of Oxford Street our shop was!" squealed Sylvia in delight as she sat down opposite me. "I spent several years there making skirts, blouses and dresses for the more refined members of the community.

"I remember it well. We were dressmakers to the gentry. An everyday dress, you know the sort of thing you would wear out to a meal with friends, would cost about eight pounds just after the war.

"Now let me think. Yes, I was earning 19 shillings a week, so a dress would have cost two months wages! Can you imagine going down to the shops today and spending two months wages on one dress? It doesn't bear thinking about.

"Not many people know but, before the war, some of the wealthy people stockpiled material. After the war they would turn up at our shop with the most fantastic material that was not available anymore. They would have ball gowns, dresses, skirts and blouses made from it. Garments from our store were pricey, but I remember that we were far from the most expensive in London. I suppose there are still people today that spend thousands on designer clothes.

Our quality was always perfect. A single stitch out of place could be enough for a garment to be rejected, and much was hand-made, not like today. In fact there was one seamstress in our shop who made the whole dress by hand. Not a machine-stitch in sight. It would always cost double, but there were people who paid. Toffs and their wives, the odd mistress of a lord or a cabinet minister and, of course, movie stars who dressed to kill.

Once I spent days making a fabulous dress in a beautiful soft fabric, a bit like velour. It was only when I had finished that I realised that I had made a terrible mistake. I had made the whole garment inside out! Reluctantly I took it to the owner. After a long examination outside in natural light he told me that it looked so good that no one would notice. He gave me the choice of unpicking it or putting it in the shop window for sale. I thought, what a nice man, but then he added a condition! The condition he made was that if someone noticed the mistake I would have it docked from my wages. I thought long and hard but decided to take the risk, and it was put on display.

The thought of unpicking the whole dress sent shudders down my spine. It would probably have been ruined. Anyway, it sold the first day and we never saw it again. I was lucky, but learnt from my mistake. From then on, if there was any doubt about the fabric, I would always get my manager to decide which side was the *right side*."

"Sylvia—you have made my day," I said as I turned the last screw in the top of the machine and ran a piece of cloth through. "I just love your story. I wish I could listen for hours, but I have to rush off to a school and fix a whole classroom of machines. I was supposed to be there by midday, so I am already late. Then I have to see Adrianne who's in a right pickle. You will have to tell me some more of your time in the sewing world on my next visit."

"If I am still here!" she laughed.

As I drove to the school the rain was still hammering down. The windscreen wipers squeaked away and the car rocked from the wind. I meandered through the puddles smiling to myself. All I could think about was the priceless image of a little man sitting on the floor of his little hut, turning his old hand machine with his foot and singing as he sewed.

In the afternoon I was at Adrianne's. She took me on a wonderful trip with her, down memory lane. I spent an hour or so listening to the most delightful story.

Adrianne's father had bought her a wonderful Singer 201k shortly after the death of her mother, when she was only 14. It was the best machine in the shop for his lovely daughter.

I had been called to repair that same machine and, while I brought it back to life, her childhood was revisited. I went along for the ride.

Adrianne moved to Sussex with her family from the East End of London in 1945, just after the war.

Her father had, with his two brothers, taken over their father's grocer and delicatessen business in Peckham, London, but her dad suffered from TB.

The London atmosphere of bombed-out buildings and smog only made it worse. His doctor advised him to escape to the country to improve his health.

Most of the family, including the grandparents, moved down to Heathfield, leaving the two brothers to carry on the London deli.

Adrianne's father bought the general store at the top of Heathfield's High Street, on the crossroads of Mutton Hall Hill and Tower Street. The family moved in and went to work.

The bustling store sold everything that a busy village might need. Adrianne described it as the small superstore of its day. They sold the whole kit and caboodle, from bread and milk to furniture.

The house and the shop were combined, and Adrianne said it was often hard to tell where one ended and the other started.

Adrianne's first day at the local school was a bit of a shock. At seven years of age she could not understand the thick Sussex accent of the local children, and they all teased her for being so posh!

Today, a Cockney accent would hardly be called *posh* but we are talking of a time when few children had travelled, let alone been to the great city. Remember this was the 1940's and Heathfield was just a rural town feeding the local farming community.

Because of her accent the teachers made her do all the announcing for the school plays and pantomimes. She would be pushed through the curtains to announce the forthcoming event in her best *London* voice.

After school, Adrianne would get back to the store and her jobs would start. Children were expected to pull their weight. Bagging sugar from big sacks, pouring rice into retail containers for the display and running shop errands.

One day a chicken escaped from the house next door and landed in Adrianne's yard. Rather than give the chicken back, to end up as someone's Sunday lunch, she hid it and fed it grain from the store. She kept it with her pet bulldogs in the yard and they lived happily together. The bulldog never ate the chicken's grain and the chicken left the dog's dinner alone. All was calm.

One of Adrianne's chores was to cycle round and pick up the grocery lists from the surrounding cottages and farms.

She would cycle for hours collecting lists for her father. Due to rationing, still in full swing, they would often do *swaps* for goods. The pig farmer would swap meat for cheese from the dairy, the woodsman would exchange firewood for eggs, and so bartering would get around the strict rationing of the time.

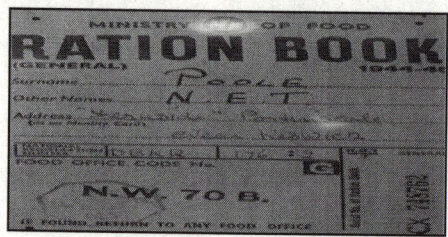

In fact rationing on farms was really a bit of a joke and almost impossible to police. When the odd official did turn up, there was always a nice slab of meat or some other goodies ready!

One of the only vegetables that was hardly ever rationed was the good old potato and many signs advertised the benefits of the trusty spud.

Only during the bitter winters of 1946 and 1947 did bread and potatoes become heavily rationed.

It is hard to imagine today with our central heating and supermarkets bursting at the seams with food, just how tough our relatives had it and how little there was to go around in post-war Britain.

Potatoes were always a great filler

A week's war ration was appalling. Four ounces of ham or bacon, two ounces of butter, half-a-pound of sugar, two ounces of tea, three ounces of sweets— if you could find any. Four ounces of lard, marg and jam, and one egg! Sausages were not rationed but they were almost impossible to get.

Every four weeks you were entitled to a packet of dried egg. Wow! To wash all this luxury down you were allowed a few pints of milk, depending on availability. When some old folk say to youngsters, "You don't know you're born!" You can understand why they say it.

One of Adrianne's favourite stops would be at Batemans, the old home of Rudyard Kipling. At Christmas the cook made the most wonderful Christmas pudding. They say that it was from a recipe that Rudyard loved, made with breadcrumbs rather than flour.

You can just imagine Adrianne cycling up to the big old manor on a cold winter's day to pick up their shopping list. Cook calls her into the kitchen and hands her a slab of warm Christmas pudding. Wonderful! It is still the best pudding that Adrianne has ever tasted.

Her father would often fish for the wild brown trout that swam silently in the little streams around Batemans.

On the weekend, with their old shooting brake van packed full, Adrianne and her dad would set off to deliver the weekly groceries around the East Sussex countryside. It was her favourite job.

As the store prospered her mum decided to expand the store's range of goods. Each month Adrianne and her mum would travel to the seaside resort of Brighton, to a wholesaler, and buy haberdashery and clothes. They would be brought back to the store. The living room was converted into an extension of the shop. Today it would seem strange to have a customer looking around your front room, buying a dress, while, just through the door, you cooked in the kitchen, but it worked like a charm. The whole family pulled as one and worked hard to make the business grow.

One day there was great excitement. It was announced on the crackling radio that rationing was officially ended.

A ceremony was organised and a huge party was held on the village green. The stern years of shortages had come to an end. Adrianne had only known those years, years of hardship and struggle from the end of 1939 to 1954.

Now they were over.

Great rejoicing and drinking carried on into the night. An enormous bonfire was lit and, with rounds of cheers and clapping, everyone threw their ration books onto the fire in a mass celebration of freedom. There would be no more rations of dried egg, no more trying to make one pot of tea last 10 cups, or slicing the bread as thin as cobwebs. Rationing, that was as popular as ants at a picnic, was finally over.

At last people could buy what they liked when they liked—when they liked.

Adrianne was growing up. The loss of her mother, when she was just 14, had a devastating effect but she carried on. The shop had to be tended, schooling, orders to be delivered, she chased her tail as the years flew by.

Adrianne blossomed into a beautiful young teenager and was made the village *May Queen*. She would be driven around in a classic De Dion car, opening fêtes and flower shows around the area.

Barn dances also had to be attended, more fun than hardship. An old minibus was acquired to take the youngsters from one village hall to the next. Adrianne even knocked up some curtains on her Singer for the local village hall.

Before long the beautiful 17-year-old had caught the eye of a young lad with a motorbike and, four years later, wedding bells rang out.

Forty years on John and Adrianne are still together. The busy grocery store is now just another house along the high street, indistinguishable from any other.

The land where the storerooms were, and the yard where the dog and chicken happily lived, is now a row of modern houses.

The old world that Adrianne knew has long gone.

The Sussex accents that were once so common in rural areas have all but disappeared. However, memories are harder to steal.

All of Adrianne's are all still with her. All the hard work and busy days mingled with the freedom and happiness of childhood. A childhood only few could dream of today.

Memories of cycling down country lanes collecting grocery lists from the local farms. Buzzing around in her father's van with the groceries in the back. Getting dressed-up for the summer fayres. Happy times—a time when the world turned at a slower pace and we all had time to laugh.

As I left Adrianne's I was in an up-beat mood. My day had flown by, and I was just so glad that her Singer had decided to grind to a halt, so that her story would come to life.

The leaves were dancing along the country lanes as I drove to my last call of the day, on the seafront at Seaford. Beams of light were breaking through a raging sky and the wild sea crashed down on the shingle, raking the pebbles into troughs. Gulls shrieked with joy as they played with the sea horses.

The autumn equinox had brought the all-conquering storms that make the trees dance and the grasses bow. England was preparing itself for the onset of another winter.

However, as the storm faded from my mind, all I could see in my imagination was a pretty girl bombing down a country lane on her bicycle, a bunch of grocery lists tucked under her belt and the wind in her hair. Oh, happy days!

# *The End*

# Nuria and the Clown

Nuria is one of my typical women—, if I have such a person with over 25,000 customers. She is a hobby seamstress, someone who sews purely for the pleasure of sewing. She has one spare bedroom in her lovely house dedicated to her needlecraft, the bed merely a table on which to lay all her fabrics. Rows of containers line the walls holding every shade of thread, buttons, zips and endless patches of cloth. In the middle of her sewing table, a Bernina Virtuosa sits proudly awaiting her work. Next to her Bernina sits a Frister & Rossmann overlocking machine also ready for work.

Her passion for sewing even survived a horrendous car crash on the Frant Road leaving her with multiple fractures and broken bones including arms, pelvis and knees. The main Tunbridge Wells Road was closed as she was airlifted to an emergency unit. I remember hearing about the accident on the news, never thinking it was one of my girls! Unfazed by her brush with death, and with a lust for life, every part of her sewing room oozes enthusiasm for the ancient craft of sewing.

Over the years I have often called on Nuria but seldom had the time to talk. However, as I was showing her how to sew stretchy fabric on her new overlocker we chatted about life.

You know my theory that everyone has a story, well Nuria's was a beauty.

Nuria's mother was part of the Spanish/Catalan aristocracy that fell from favour under the harsh regime of the dictator,

General Francisco Franco. Her father was an important doctor and they were often invited to attend parties and ceremonies. One evening Nuria, who was then only five years old, went along with her parents to a grand house up in the hills.

It was the home of none other than Salvador Dali, the outstanding and outspoken artist. Dali was in fine form, stroking his long, curling moustache and taking centre stage at his prestigious home. Now, all this pomp and circumstance was lost on little five-year-old Nuria and she soon became bored.

Holding her father's hand while he chatted to Dali, Nuria yawned, swinging idly on her father's arm. Dali's beautiful Russian wife, Gala, was entertaining the guests. Dali was quick to notice the, rather bored, child on her fathers arm. He tried in vain to excite her pulling faces and twirling his moustache.

As she tired of his efforts, she pointed at him and shouted over the crowd, **"When is the clown going to perform?"**

What a showstopper! You could have heard a pin drop amongst the gasping breaths of the guests.

The great Dali took it in good humour and they all had a laugh. He then suggested that rather than be bored by the grown-ups Nuria could take his little cat for a walk in the grounds. The idea sounded fine until they saw the cat. Dali returned with a fully-grown lynx-type cat, almost bigger than Nuria herself! The cats ran wild in the mountains and had wispy tuffs of hair on each ear. Dali had domesticated one and kept it at his mansion.

Unperturbed Nuria pulled the beast out into the garden and promptly disappeared.

Now you have to stop and wonder what sort of mother would let her child wander away with a large feline, even if it was domesticated, but that is not part of our story!

The party went on for hours with wine flowing, music and dancing. The noise drifted over the dark countryside and everyone forgot about the little child that had wandered off into the night.

That was all to change when Nuria's mother realised she was not around. They searched the grounds—to no avail. All the guests then spread out to search in earnest. The house party turned into a search party as they all scoured the area. What on earth had happened to the little girl who had gone off with a large cat?

Visions of a well-fed cat licking its lips sprang to mind as everyone frantically rushed around with torches, lamps and candles calling for Nuria.

Just as everyone started to get really worried one of the guests saw something under a bush. They carefully lifted the branches away and held a lamp underneath.

There, fast asleep, was Nuria with the lynx curled up beside her. A huge sigh of relief went around the guests and Dali told everyone to remain still and quiet. He rushed to get his sketch book, returned, then drew a rough copy of the pair of escapees, one fast asleep under the bush, the other perfectly happy to keep her company and stay by her side.

Somewhere in Dali's vast works there will be a scribbled drawing of a little girl cuddling a large cat with a diamond necklace.

Few will know that it is not one of his imaginative creations but a five-year-old called Nuria. A little girl who had mistaken one of the most important artists in the world for a performing clown!

Told you it was a beauty!

# The End

**The Liberian or Spanish Lynx**

# Faith

I met a woman who really made me wonder about life. This is a short story and amazingly true.

I was just fixing her sewing machine when she noticed that I had an unusual name and I told her it was originally Russian. Then out came this story.

One night she was fast asleep when she woke in an anxious state. She had seen a man in her dreams. A haggard thin man with hollow cheeks. He was in a terrible state. His teeth had been knocked out and he was starving in a dark cell.

She had an overwhelming urge to pray for this stranger. From that night on she prayed for him and his safety. One night she kneeled to pray and she knew she no longer needed to pray for her stranger.

Years went by and with her church she went to Albania. One day she was pouring soup into the bowls of the parishioners and she felt the strangest feeling. She looked up to see the smiling face of none other than the stranger in her dream. In the middle of the hall they hugged and tears fell.

They sat and talked for hours. He told her that he had been in prison in Russia and was on his last legs. There was no hope, no light only darkness, despair and death.

Then one night a sudden feeling came over him that someone was looking after him, someone cared about him. He never knew who or why, but the wonderful feeling gave him hope.

He survived his incarceration and was eventually released

from prison. He joined the Christian faith and never looked back. He never knew who his guardian angel had been until that chance meeting at an Albanian church.

As my father used to say; *With hope all things are possible.*

Well, is that the most amazing story of faith and love and unexplainable things!

# The End

## The Driscoll Incident
### With many thanks to Brenda Bremmer for inspiring this story.

In the 1950s, just off the High Street in Eastbourne, there was a special shop. So special that people travelled from miles around to visit it. Its fame spread far and wide and, in an austere post-war time, it was full of colour.

The shop was called Driscoll's. It had a beautiful front window displaying all the latest fashions for it was a dress shop. No ordinary dress shop, mind. Driscoll's was a cut above the rest.

As war rationing finally folded in the early 1950s, though coal rationing lumbered on until 1958, a breath of fresh air was sweeping the land and Driscoll's captured the exciting spirit of a new age.

Their display had all the latest high-fashion. Dresses, skirts, blouses, ball gowns and even a few pairs of women's trousers, although they were still frowned upon by many women. Haute couture in every detail.

They made dresses for the famous, for dignitaries and local officials as well as the upper crust. People like Lady Shawcross of Friston Manor and the Duchess of Devonshire. Dresses for debutantes' balls, dance halls and evenings at the Grand or tea at the Ritz. Outside of London, Driscoll's earned a premier reputation for beauty, class and style.

Some customers, that had been abroad or on Grand Tours, brought with them silks and other exotic fabrics that

Driscoll's would transform into startling costumes and gowns.

Beside their outstanding seamstresses, one of the secrets of Driscoll's success was their superb artist. She scoured the daily papers and magazines. She even went regularly to the flicks. Her job was to sketch all the latest outfits. Anything that Ava Gardner or Elizabeth Taylor was wearing was quickly copied.

Before the main features at the Cinema, newsreels of the latest stars and what they were up to were shown. Marilyn Monroe, Judy Garland, Joan Crawford, Bette Davis, or Ginger Rogers. They were all there and many more, all 30 feet high in the hottest new frocks.

Back at the shop the pattern cutters cut, seamstresses sewed and window dressers dressed. Eager eyes peered in at the new styles and the latest fashions. All keen to get a peek at Driscoll's latest masterpieces.

There were several other dressmakers in town and furriers in Grove Road selling beaver and mink or whole fox stoles, complete with feet, head and tail, to wrap around a lady's neck! Those were the days, eh?

When I was a lad, out near Arlington was a mink farm where thousands of mink led short lives in cages, bred for a collar or coat. I used to cycle past the long-low huts on my way to my favourite fishing spot.

When fur became unpopular, the mink were mysteriously released as there was no use for them. Some say it was an animal rights group that released them, others that it was the owners not wanting to kill them needlessly.

The outcome is that, even today, wild mink hunt the Sussex wildlife. Eventually, after the furriers in Grove Road had had their windows smashed time and time again, they closed. The anti-fur adverts used to say,

*It takes forty dumb animals to make a fur coat but only one to wear it!*

Driscoll's main competition was Bobby's in Terminus Road. But no shop matched their style, quality and elegance and, as their machinists used to say, "... or their stripes and checks!"

They even had one girl that just did bead-work, sewing countless beads and pearls onto beautiful gowns all by hand. Driscoll's ruled Eastbourne supreme, la crème de la crème.

Next to Driscoll's was a milliner with a superb range of hats of every description. You could lean over the shop front, toward their recessed window, and look left or right into side-mirrors. You would see a hundred images of yourself disappearing into infinity. As a kid it would always be my first stop in town.

When I was older I would look on with quiet jealousy at other kids leaning over the shop front doing something I was *too old* to do. If the shop were still there today I would be leaning over that front again! I'm at that age!

Driscoll's was a family concern run by Mr and Mrs Driscoll, who would greet their customers and find a suitable girl to look after them. Polite conversation was conducted with customers, to pass the time in their elegant premises, while measurements were taken.

Rolls of fabric would be laid out and pattern books examined. Orders were taken and doors opened for departing clientele. Farewells were exchanged with polite nods at the door.

"Good day to you, Madam." Mr Driscoll was charm personified in his smart three-piece suit, a sparkling gold watch-chain curving across his waistcoat.

"And good day to you, too."

All in all it was a most pleasurable shopping experience.

Eastbourne was a conservative well-respected watering hole on the edge of the English Channel. The sort of place that well-set Londoners might have travelled to when taking the soothing air or the healing waters.

Certainly not the place for loose gossip!

Brenda, the lovely lady who shared her story with me, was well into her apprenticeship at Driscoll's when a very embarrassing incident occurred. An incident that, over fifty years later, was still sharp in her mind.

As an apprentice Brenda was responsible for all the menial jobs like unpicking, clearing up and matching sewing threads to the fabric. A thing of utmost importance. Around the corner in the High Street, near where C&H Fabrics is today, Dale & Curlies the haberdashers offered their wares. Brenda would take a snippet of material and match it with silk or cotton thread from the shop. It had to be an exact colour, a 'dead match', or there would be hell to pay back at the shop from Mrs Driscoll.

An apprenticeship was five years of hard work, early starts and long hours for little pay. But you learnt a trade that would gain employment all around the world. For a fifty-four-hour week Brenda was rewarded with two pounds!

Still, in the 1950s, for a young girl, it was enough to pay some rent to mum and still have money for lipstick, a magazine and a trip to the flicks. And, of course, she knew where to get some beautiful clothes. Even at trade prices, however, they were often more expensive than everywhere else.

One day Brenda arrived for work as usual and the shop was full of great excitement.

Mr and Mrs Driscoll had been called to The Palace, in London, for a fitting! They were to make some dresses for the beautiful young Queen Elizabeth. No higher honour could be bestowed on a shop than to become a Court Dressmaker.

"We could become 'By Royal Appointment'," said Mr Driscoll excitedly, fiddling with his gold chain and prancing around the shop like a fresh cockerel on a sunny morning.

"Yes, and think of the business! We will have all the stars in here. Oh, one can just imagine! It is so exciting!" retorted a buzzing Mrs Driscoll.

On the appointed day Mr and Mrs Driscoll, dressed to perfection, with pattern books and measuring tapes, took the train to London. Their great day at the Palace had quickly arrived. Surprisingly quickly as it turned out and for a very good reason!

The shop staff waited with bated breath for their return. Why the urgency? Well, it transpired that Queen Elizabeth was pregnant and in the way that The Palace works they like to let out details at specific times to suit them. For the time being, while Elizabeth carried on her engagements, her pregnancy was to be a closely guarded secret.

The normal London fashion houses were ignored and Driscoll's was carefully selected, not only for its quality, but because it was far enough away from London and reserved enough to keep the 'Palace Secret'. Eastbourne still had that conservative reputation where discretion could be kept.... Well... almost!

No sooner had Mrs Driscoll returned and told the shop staff of the great news than tongues started wagging in that most feminine of ways. It was not long before Mrs Driscoll had told just about everyone she knew that they were making clothes for none other than the Royal Family. She tried her hardest to keep her mouth shut but it just kept bursting open and out poured the exciting news, "**Elizabeth is pregnant!**"

Well! It was not long before another summons from The Palace appeared!

Mr and Mrs Driscoll were called back to London to explain how news of Elizabeth's pregnancy had escaped from a most curious source on the South Coast!

Mr Driscoll, fearing a beheading, was faking all sorts of near-death illnesses but Mrs Driscoll was not going up there alone.

They both appeared before The Palace once again and apologised profusely for the leak. Mrs Driscoll could not understand who could have done such a thing! The Palace forgave them with a telling-off and one little extra detail. They returned from London, still with royal consent to make their clothes, but with a little extra paperwork!

From that point on, all employees of Driscoll's had to sign the Official Secrets Act. Even Brenda the apprentice!

And so Driscoll's became famous. Not only for their clothes but also for their discretion. They made beautiful dresses for The Queen and a stunning honeymoon dress in pale lemon for the gorgeous newly-wed, Princess Margaret.

Mrs Driscoll managed, with great difficulty, to curb her wagging tongue. Mr Driscoll made an astonishing recovery from his illnesses and they all lived happily ever after.

## The End

## Winter's End

As the sun rose I was sipping tea in the kitchen and wondering about the day ahead. I glanced towards the outside thermometer. It read sixteen degrees! Could that be possible, was winter, with her endless cold days departing?

I took my tea and went to explore. I opened the front door and a warm wind greeted me like an old friend. I spent the next half an hour in my jim-jams slowly walking around the garden taking in the first, real, spring day.

Everything was on the move. The birds were noisily gathering twigs for new nests. The plants were all ready, as if they were at the starting line of a race for the new season, about to charge off with a furious spurt of growth.

I was totally entranced by Mother Nature and was examining the outstretched petals of a yellow celandine when a voice flew over the gate, "See you haven't lost your Christmas belly yet Alex!"

Instinctively I pulled my stomach in, but that loosened my pyjama bottoms. I stopped, realising it would be far better to show my postman a fat belly than the family jewels!

The jim-jams stayed put as I grabbed the post from his hand and grunted, "Well look at you in your shorts this time of year—you're like a schoolboy!" I replied, spilling a bit of my tea in frustration. He walked off with a smile and a wave whistling *Oh what a beautiful morning*.

With the wind singing through the trees and the lark on the wing, I hit the road to my first customer and her troublesome Singer Centenary 221.

"Ah, come in Mr Askentoff," Mary said as she opened the door. *That's about as close as anyone gets to my name* I thought as I went in.

"Call me Alex and I'll call you Mary, if that's okay?"

"Fine Alex. Come and see Brutus! I call my machine Brutus because it's a brute. I hate this machine. Don't hate many things but I have hated this machine for 50 years."

"Surely not Mary! It can't be that bad."

I was wrong. She went on to give me graphic details of all the times the machine had failed, all the garments ruined … all the tears … and, in the end … Hate!

"My dad taught me one thing when I was young, before he went off to war and didn't come back, he used to say *buy cheap buy twice*! Remembering that, I have always bought the best and this machine was the best the shop had to offer. It cost me 50 pounds! Almost a pound for every year I have cried over it. I've taken it to four Singer shops but eventually gave up as it never worked any better when I got it back. Once I was so angry I put it on the floor and was about to stamp on it when my husband caught me. He gave me a right telling off. I felt like a little kid. I was sixty at the time. At school they nicknamed me Mad Mary. Now I'm older I can see why!"

After hearing Mary's troubles I decided that I needed to change tack as Mary seemed to be working up a sweat. The last thing I wanted on this perfect spring day was a trip to the hospital! "Mary you get the kettle on and I'll take Brutus apart and see what's wrong."

It didn't take long. The problem was obvious. A manufacturing fault had left a bit of the casting rubbing against the automatic tension release, randomly jamming it. This would mean it would work, or not, depending whether or not the thread was in the tension unit properly. By the time Mary was back with the drink I was well into repairing it. Being so erratic it had been banished to the back of the cupboard for years at a time. The result was a near-perfect machine that looked as if it was purchased yesterday.

"How did you get into sewing Mary?"

"Arthritis!"

"Well that's a first!" I laughed.

"Everyone told me I just had growing pains. I was still a teenager when they had diagnosed arthritis. My old quack prescribed two aspirin a day, three spoonfuls of cod-liver oil and gentle exercise. Before cycle machines were available a sewing treadle was a perfect substitute. My mum knew from school, that I didn't like sewing because I made such a mess of my school efforts, but she never said anything, just let me use her treadle. When part of the school burnt down, including the sewing wing, I laughed and sung all the way to school for a good month after.

"For the first few days I sat at home and treadled away, watching the machine turn round and round, bored senseless. It was not long before I thought I could be making something as well as sitting at the machine treadling. It was then that my mum, who had already cut out a skirt for me, taught me how to sew.

"She was not so silly, my mum. Patience was her virtue. Something I have never had. It took me a week to get the damn thing to start in the right direction. Did I curse! Mind you, only when mum was not in earshot. She would have washed my mouth out with soap, and she only used the cheapest carbolic for that! Treadling was like trying to pat your head and rub your stomach at the same time. Still, I got the hang of it eventually and never stopped.

"And so things turned completely around and I learnt to love the sound of a treadle machine rocking and stitching. The sound can still bring a tear to my eye as quickly as a cold breeze in winter. There are so many memories all wrapped around old treadle machines. You could say that the sewing machine sings in tune with the music of my youth.

"About ten years ago doctors found out that I had an overactive thyroid, causing me to be really moody and a terrible fidget. That explained my moods as a child. I can't sit still for a moment. Still that's how I got into sewing."

"Well Mary, when I've finished you'll have to treat this machine like a new one and find it a new name, because it'll sew like it has never sewn before."

"Believe that when I see it," she snarled at the machine.

An hour later Mary was a convert. She had sewn everything from pure silk to five layers of denim without a hitch. "It's beautiful Alex, really beautiful. I am so happy I could kiss you."

Before I knew it Mary gripped me around the neck and planted a huge kiss, smack on my lips! "Mary you naughty girl," I stuttered. "What's my wife going to say?"

"I won't tell if you don't!" She laughed.

I escaped from Mary's with a flushed face and a feeling of satisfaction that you only get from a good job well done.

Before long I was rolling down Dog Kennel Lane towards an old farm along Criers Lane. The farmer shook my hand warmly and ushered me to his ailing machine. "Do all me own sewing," he announced as we got to the Frister Star on his table. "Have done for 60 years."

As I worked away I listened to how he had sold the family farm after his first heart attack at the age of 68. His only condition of sale was that he be allowed to live in the farmhouse at a fixed rent until his death. It seemed a pretty safe bet that he would not last much longer, so the deal was struck.

"The new owner was in such a rush to grab the cheap deal, but it came back to bite him," he said with a defiant smirk. "You know what they say? *Act in haste, repent at leisure*. Twenty years later I'm still on the same rent. I bet you the owner gets down on his knees every night and begs for me to die."

"Don't help him much as every day I wake up and find myself still here. First thing I do every morning, when I open my eyes and realise I've been given another day, is smile. I reckon another day vertical and above ground is worth smiling about."

"I reckon you can measure life by many things, money, assets—even wives—but none is better than a smile. I have always had more smiles in my life than tears boy."

I could not help but like the old farmer who had found himself in such an enviable position. He reminded me of my dad—and you know what it is like when you see someone who looks like a person you like—you can't help but like them as well.

I was just thinking how right he was when he returned with a cup of tea. It was so strong that it was almost black. When it arrived I looked down at the cup and then up at his smiling face.

"That do you boy?" He asked handing me the cup.

"Lovely job—yes, thanks. That's just what the doctor ordered."

I stopped work and took a sip. I nearly spat it out. It was like licking the tar off a telegraph pole! God only knows what he had made it with.

I left the cup on the side until he popped out of the room. Quick as a flash I opened the window and threw the contents of the cup out. I sat down just as he returned. "Another cup boy?" He asked seeing that I had finished the first.

"Oh no! Not for me—really. But thanks anyway."

"It was a real experience," I added quietly under my breath.

His machine, which had been disabled—well sabotaged really—by inserting an old Willcox Victorian needle into the shaft and knocking the timing out, was soon fixed.

Farmers have the amazing habit of trying to make something out of anything they have to hand.

"It's all about what you know boy, that's the secret of success in business. There's an old joke I used to tell. It went like this.... A man pushes his broken car into a garage. He asked the garage owner if he could take a look at the car to see if he could get it going. The garage owner looks around the car then under the bonnet, and then strokes his chin. He then goes and gets a big hammer. He returns and gives the starter motor a good whack. The owner turns the key and bingo! The car starts. The garage owner then says… that'll be twenty pounds."

"Twenty pounds!" The owner shouts. "All you did was whack the starter motor. I'm not paying you twenty pounds for that!"

"You're not paying me twenty pounds for hitting the motor. You're paying me nineteen pounds for knowing where to hit it and one pound for hitting it!"

"You see," he finished, "it's all in the knowing lad. All in the knowing." He was grinning at me across the table like a wide-mouthed frog.

After I had fixed his machine, he sneakily talked me into altering his trousers for him. They needed to fit an expanding waistline. Something that I had considerable sympathy with!

As I left the house I noticed a terrible brown stain on the grass under the window. I just hoped that the grass would survive his tea until rain rescued it!

I waved from the car and drove back up the track towards Uckfield and my next customer. In the back were a dozen fresh eggs and a bag of spring onions that had been dug that morning. I couldn't help but wonder how many more years the landowner would be on his knees, begging for the old farmer to pop his clogs!

In Uckfield I called at a retirement home, Grants Hill. Before the home was built an old house had stood there. It became notorious as one of the last places our most villainous British lord was seen alive.

On 7 November 1974 the legend of the infamous missing lord began. The story alleges that Richard Bingham, 7th Earl of Lucan, overwhelmed with gambling debts and alienated from his children, wrapped some surgical tape around a piece of lead pipe and entered his Belgravia home. He battered the nanny to death and left his wife seriously injured. He escaped and sped from his London home to friends at Grants Hill in Uckfield.

There he told a story that he had seen another man attack the nanny but had failed to stop him! Covered in blood, with his wife running down the street screaming murder, he panicked and bolted. Some story!

Lord & Lady Lucan in happier times

A nationwide search started. The police scoured the country. Three days later the Ford Corsair he had been driving was found abandoned in the seaside port of Newhaven. Inside was another piece of lead pipe wrapped with tape! It became obvious that he had made good his escape from Britain and, to this day, has never been found. He had disappeared into thin air.

I knocked on Esther's door expecting her usual greeting. The door opened slowly and I looked down at the diminutive Esther, all four-foot-ten inches of her. She used to be five-foot-one in her prime, but time had taken its toll and three precious inches had departed. She always saw the bright side and often laughed that her lower centre of gravity kept her safely on her feet. She walked with the help of a zimmer frame, which she had nicknamed her Ferrari!

All her sewing nowadays was to adjust her clothes. Being so small she had always made her own and had become an accomplished seamstress. Although she had used several machines, she never managed to master her latest troublesome machine.

Esther went off to finish her breakfast, a bowl of prunes, "I won't be long. I think, today, I will be marrying a beggar man!

I have already found six pips, and you know how the saying goes? *'Tinker, tailor, soldier, sailor, rich man, poor man, beggar man, thief.'* Last week I was married to a rich man and a tailor so I mustn't complain too much."

I heard Esther laugh and the light *clink* of her metal spoon on her bowl. "Gives me a chuckle and keeps me regular too!" She shouted.

I simply couldn't resist the urge to pop my head around the corner and take a peek at what she was doing. "Have you ever heard all the rhyme Alex?"

"No Esther, I can't say as I have."

"Well I can remember most of it. *Tinker, tailor, soldier, sailor, rich man, poor man, beggarman, thief. 'When do I get married?'* the rhyme goes. *'This year, next year, sometime, never! What do I wear? Silk, satin, cotton or rags! And how do I get there? A coach, carriage, wheelbarrow or cart!'*"

"So there you have it, the whole kit and caboodle. My," Esther laughed. "I haven't told anyone that since my school days when all the world was still in black and white!"

With a beam on my face and the sure knowledge that I would probably forget the whole verse before I left. I went back to work on her machine.

When Esther returned I happened to mention about Lord Lucan. "They'll never find him. In my opinion Lord Lucan never went nowhere," said Esther. "I remember that night as if it were yesterday. What the papers don't tell you is that same night that he disappeared there were shots heard coming from the house. Lots of people heard them and reported them to the police. No one ever investigated—so close to bonfire night, see!

The police must have assumed it was kids with bangers, or hoax calls. Mary, the housekeeper saw a man with a suitcase leaving at four in the morning but was it Lucan or someone laying a false trail!

I wouldn't be surprised if they find his bones under the foundations of this place. Probably shot himself after it dawned on him what a dreadful thing he had done. I bet someone moved the car to distract the police and press from the house."

"Well that's a theory and a half Esther! We shall just have to see if he ever turns up."

I left wondering about the old tale and the new slant Esther had given the story. I glanced around the property as I drove off, looking for a good spot where the body of our most infamous lord might be hidden.

My next call had me sewing an insert into the left cup of a bra! That was after I had removed the marble that her grandson had pushed into her machine. I was calling on a woman who had had a mastectomy. I sewed away and tried not to sew over the wire insert in the bra. After a few tense moments I passed her the bra. She held it up and announced that I had done a fine job. I was most impressed with my work. Few people realise that I do not sew well. There is a lot of difference between fixing a machine and using one! Rather like a racing mechanic and a racing driver, two very different skills.

I watched as she slipped a prosthetic into the new pocket. I did not wait to see what it looked like when she was wearing it, but she was delighted with her machine and my sewing!

"My next job is new knicker elastic," she giggled as I left. "I was walking by the church last Friday and I felt them slip. I had to say good morning to the vicar with one hand on my knickers. Most embarrassing!"

By now it was late morning and I turned my beast from its furthest call and headed toward home. I had a call in the pretty hamlet of Berwick then another near Cuckmere Haven on the coast.

The spring day was just inspiring. It was truly a gift after winter and coming so close to the Spring Equinox it was just too perfect to waste. I parked and walked up the soft grassy slopes of the South Downs to a viewpoint overlooking the English Channel. I sat on one of the famous chalk hills of the Seven Sisters, called Haven Brow, and stared out to sea.

The coastal cliffs stood proud, welcoming the warm breeze that still held a touch of winter's dying breath. She was on her way out, pushed by an ever-eager spring and it would be many months before winter would bring her biting frosts back to these hills.

The breeze shook the early spring flowers. Patches of primrose leapt out from the grassy tufts and cowslips elbowed their way through to get a peek at the beautiful sunny day. A small clump of snowdrops or *Fair Maids of February* danced a little jig to the delicate rhythm of the wind.

I heard my first cuckoo or *Gowk* as Sussex folk call them. I subconsciously shook my loose change, something I had done ever since I was a kid and first heard the old tale. Folklore tells that if you shake your money when you hear the cuckoo you will never run out of cash. It has always worked for me!

The shaggy Sussex sheep were still in their thick winter coats and nursing tiny lambs that could have been only a few hours old.

I sat breathing-in the delicious scent that is unique to these parts as it rolls off the open sea and combines with the wild flowers, herbs and grasses from the thousands of acres of downland.

I have always thought that there are a few people in history that shape the time in which they pass, leaving their mark for others. One such person was William Wordsworth. In the last year of his life he came here to sit and contemplate. He wrote... *There is no more precious gift than this*. That was in 1850 and it is as true today as ever.

The beauty that lay before me was priceless. The white cliffs stretching out along the coast in a curve towards Brighton were being lapped by an emerald sea that, in turn, was being stroked by a warm westerly wind full of the scents of far-away lands.

Birling Gap, with its untamed sea and ancient cliffs, is where heaven and earth meet in an intoxicating mix of wild abandon. On such a day it was clear to me that Mother Nature had crafted some of her finest work in this special place. Strangely enough, it was here at Birling Gap that the

Council for Rural England was founded to stop greedy land developers ruining this patch of heaven.

Developers had planned to build a whole town here with a main London railway link. Luckily they were defeated and Birling Gap, the old smugglers cove, was saved for all.

It is funny to think that smuggling was so rife here at one time and that Crowlink, just over the brow of the hill became renowned for quality booze. *Crowlink Gin* was a sought-after tipple.

People often think smuggling is an old forgotten trade. Far from it. Government figures show that smuggling still costs the Revenue over four billion pounds a year in lost revenue.

They say it was smugglers who first started to use nicknames to confuse the customs men. *Bones, Gruff, Crutch, Joker, Knuckle, Old Screw, Slippery*, all local Eastbourne fishermen's nicknames. The Allchorn's from Eastbourne's last Pleasure Boats had names such as *Old Bogey, Merry Legs, Billy Bags* and *Early Doors*. Jack Allchorn, who lived next to my mother-in-law, at eight Eshton Road, earned his nickname, *Early Doors*, as he was on the matinee doors and cheap seats at the Hippodrome.

I lay back on the warm grass and crossed my legs. My left hand ruffled the grass. It felt like I was running my hand through a giant's rough hair. I gazed up at the priceless sky. It was a pirate sky straight from the Caribbean. Great bellowing clouds in shades of whites and greys, blues and yellows played hide'n'seek with the sun. Gulls called as they soared high on the fresh winds.

Old seafaring folk say that the seagulls carry the souls of the mariners lost at sea, set free to roam the wild waves for eternity. On a dark day when the sea becomes brooding graphite grey, they cry for their old bones turning in the surf, picked clean by the squabbling crabs. The gulls skip over the white peaks, pitifully calling for the loved ones they will never see again. But today was not that kind of day; it was a blue-heaven day.

In a moment I was whisked back to my childhood. We've all had those precious moments, lying in the sun with the warmth on our face, the sound of the world turning all around. Life doesn't get any better than these simple moments.

I thought that if the last thing I saw on earth was the glimmering jewelled sea under a blue sky, I would die a happy man. I feel for those vain few that think our blue planet, this amazing creation, is all just an explosion of coincidental chemicals.

I had long ago learnt that there is more to life than life itself and if you ever lost your soul, your purpose, seek out the countryside and the wild sky, then it will find you.

I leant on one arm. About half a mile out at sea, rocking on a bed of sparkling diamonds, I could see the small fishing craft, the Sharlisa, that Brian and Jeff used. This time of year they would be after flat fish. Patiently biding their time. Waiting for the lobsters and bass to return with the warmer waters that would soon follow. I knew they would be sitting silently in their boat. They spoke little and never wasted a precious word. So typical of old-Sussex folk. *Fair winds and following sea to them*, I thought.

I could have remained on Haven Brow forever but time was passing and I had a niggling thought that I had to be somewhere. I strolled back to the car, brushing the grass off my clothes as I went I drove the twisting road along Beachy Head, towards home, passing the council workers who were once more removing the snowdrift fencing from the downland. A yearly job and a pleasant one.

"Alex, where have you been?" Squealed a flustered Yana. "We have to be at the theatre in 20 minutes and there is a man waiting for you. He is a dry-stone waller! Whatever that is! He has driven all the way down from North Yorkshire and has a huge machine in his old truck for you to fix. Apparently you are the only person who can do it!"

"Bung the kettle on while I talk to him," I said walking in to meet the customer.

"All she needs is a little fettlin' lad," he pronounced, plonking a huge Singer model 45 onto my workbench as if it weighed nothing.

*Fettlin', fettlin'?* I had no idea what that meant but I could see he was serious! I examined the rusty old machine that had not worked for years. I sighed knowing that my next few evenings would be taken up cleaning, oiling and setting the huge brute to get it to stitch.

It turned out he needed a machine to sew through several strips of thick leather. By the look of it he must have found the machine under one of his stone walls. Now all he needed was someone who could get it to work! That someone was me.

He left after shaking my hand so powerfully that my whole body shook. The shuddering went up my arm along my shoulder. Then I felt my neck click! Dry-stone walling must have given him muscles no normal people have. I had never shaken a hand so firm or held a grip so hard. It was like clutching the end of an iron drainpipe that had come loose in a hurricane. I waved him off from the gate and stretched my neck, rubbing it as I ran indoors.

My working day was nearly over. I relaxed and slowly unwound at the theatre, watching *Arsenic and Old Lace* being performed beautifully, while listening to the hearing aids of the Eastbourne old-brigade crackle and whistle.

Eastbourne might be getting a younger demographic, with lots of families moving here, but they were not at the Devonshire Park Theatre on that Wednesday afternoon!

In the evening, armed with a cup of tea, I headed for my garage. I saw the celandine that had been fully open in the morning sunshine had folded up its tiny petals and gone to sleep, bathed in a soft light from the full-spring moon.

A few clouds scurried across the night sky as I closed the garage door and turned on the lights and radio. Eva Cassidy warmed the workshop with her perfect supple tones. While I tinkered away I thought about the customers I had seen on our first spring day. Once again during my travels I had met so many characters, all wonderful, all individual and all so unique. The diversity of the human race never ceases to amaze me.

We are all here for such a short period, tiny grains in the endless shifting sands of time, and will soon be forgotten. But today, this glorious spring day, I had touched some lives, seen snippets of different worlds and lived new experiences. I had captured a moment where all of these people exist. They live, they breathe—as do I.

I worked on the big old brute of a machine that my Yorkshire friend had dropped off earlier. Its owner was probably bombing up the motorway heading for the moors and home, the steering-wheel of his old Morris pick-up gripped with his hands of iron.

I could see the old farmer, whose landlord was probably on his knees about now praying for his demise. He would be trying on his enlarged trousers and checking my stitching. The sweet dear with her prosthetic breast and knicker elastic would be in front of her mirror—or perhaps asking her grandson about the marble I had pulled from her machine!

Then, of course, there was Mad Mary! I did not mention to my wife that I had been snogged by Mary in a sudden fit of passion—! Albeit against my will. Mary would be busy catching up on 50 years of sewing. She'd left a message on my phone saying that she had renamed her machine Merlin, because her machine was pure magic now!

Tiny old Esther at Grants Hill would probably have her tin of prunes ready for the morning so that she could count all her pips and decide who she would be marrying and how she was getting to the church! Or, then again, she may have been peeking out of her curtains into the moonlight, wondering. Wondering just where Lord Lucan's body could be hidden!

Finally, Jeff and Brian, the Birling Gap fisherman. They would probably be sitting by their fires, smoking their pipes, watching the crackling wood burn in the hearth. No words spoken. Sussex lads born and bred.

Tomorrow, come what may, they would be down on the beach, peering out to the horizon, wondering if the sea would be calm enough for another trip out in their little boat.

And me? As always I would be packed up with my tools, on the road to more customers and more adventures.

And so the world turns.

## The End

*The finest jewels in all the land*
*Could never compare to the happy*
*Sun-spilt petals of the celandine*
*Heralding spring.*

*A.I.A*

# Messerschmitt's and Blackboys

Sometimes I feel I must have been blessed by an angel. I was standing in Babs' sitting room with a cup of tea in one hand, crippled up with laughter pains, trying to steady myself with my other hand on a table.

I was watching the old dear run around her garden with a stick. She was screaming at the neighbour's tabby cat while trying to smack it with the stick. One of her hands was swirling around her head like some possessed medieval knight trying to slay a fleeing dragon, while the other was firmly pressing down upon her wig that was lifting off her head like a bird escaping the nest! The noise coming out of her mouth was not repeatable and should never fall on children's ears least they be scarred for life.

It had all started when she brought me the tea. I had stopped for a break and was staring out of the window at her beautiful garden in full summer bloom. Babs handed me the cup at exactly the same time that we both saw what was taking place in her flowerbed.

Babs' cat, a pedigree five-year-old prized English Blue called Princess was being, how can I say it, romantically engaged with next-doors flea-ridden mongrel tabby. Babs had spent the last year protecting her princess since the mongrel, along with new neighbours, had arrived on the scene. In a single moment of horror Babs had screamed, "She's being raped!"

I had swung round wondering who she was talking about until it dawned on me she was referring to her cat!

It seemed obvious to me that Princess appeared to be a willing partner in the affair but Babs had other ideas. The 93-year old was out of her back door like an Olympic sprinter.

Oh how I wished I could have filmed the scene, I would have won first prize in any contest. I made a mental note to scrutinise her diet when she got back. She must be eating something that gave her an abundance of energy and I needed some of it!

Most people would have been dead and buried 20 years by Babs' age but there she was, mad as a hatter at 93, chasing next door's amorous cat. It all came to a crescendo when she cornered the hissing tabby against the corner fence. For a split moment there was a stand-off, the cat hunch-backed and hackled, feet splayed fangs out. Babs menacing. It was like a sketch straight out of a cartoon comic... Then she swung.

The tabby went one way, her wig went the other, and I spat tea all over the table.

Babs seemed to hate all living creatures except for her beloved cat. She had an arsenal of weapons ready for any occasion. There were mats soaked in creosote to scare the foxes, netting for badgers, sonic repellents for the cats and moles.

She greased the trees to stop squirrels descending and had a powerful water-pistol to shoot seagulls from her roof tiles. Almost all living creatures were held in disdain and persecuted in her little garden.

I never had the heart to tell her that most of her problems came from her old neighbour, who was her complete opposite. She loved all living things.

Every week without fail her neighbour would buy a large chicken from Sainsbury's. Cook it for Sunday lunch, eat just the breast meat and then feed the rest to her animals.

At four-o-clock Sunday afternoon a troop of foxes would appear for their chicken legs, wings, bones and other delicacies.

They would promptly go and bury some of it in Babs' garden, which drove her insane with rage. After dark the badgers would turn up for their feed. Every morning at six-thirty the seagulls would appear tapping on the conservatory roof. She would open the kitchen door and they would enter for their breakfast!

I had serviced Ellie and Norman's machine (the old neighbours not the newcomers on the other side) many times over the years and often got the run-down of her daily feeding regime.

She had a name for every animal that visited, right down to the current loving Lance Corporal Coal, the blackbird that had white wing feathers with little stripes on each wing.

Since her husband's death she had become a recluse with an iron fist. No one messed with her in the street. They would feel the wrath of her steely tongue if they brought up a topic not to her liking. Her wild animals were her joy.

High fences and overgrown trees had kept her little paradise a secret from prying eyes. All the neighbours ever saw were the animals making their way to her isolated home. Her little house on the prairie.

The last time I had called it was shortly after Norman passed away. He had the perfect demise. Ellie was beautifully philosophical about Norman's passing. At 95 Norman was not on any medication at all. Not a single prescribed pill, which was astonishing. He was sitting watching the cricket on television with a large glass of whisky and ginger ale in his hand when he closed his eyes forever. As Ellie put it, he had finished one journey and started another.

The couple had been married for nearly 70 years. Once Norman had leant over to me and quietly whispered in my ear, "The secret to a long marriage is to argue everyday but remember that you are both wrong!"

I had often come across opposites in life, like these neighbours. This world seems to be balanced like that, rain and sun, good and bad, balance in most things. Not often however so close to each other as a garden fence! In my life I had seen both sides of the human soul, dark and light. It is what makes this life, this world, so exciting.

By the time Babs returned to the house, embracing her cat like the proverbial long lost relative, I had almost cleared up the mess that I had made. It was awkward as the tea was ejected at such high pressure and so quickly out of my mouth that some of it dribbled out of my nose as well! It was awful but hilarious.

In all the fuss Babs had not put her wig on straight. What a sight the bright-red old dear looked with a crooked wig telling off her pedigree cat, as if it were a delinquent teenager.

The cat looked down her smirking nose at Babs with complete and utter disdain. Of course we humans still don't understand we are here simply to feed and comfort cats. Sort of domestic servants if you like.

After the cat went to eat, Babs slumped into her chair. "Oh dear me," she gasped through sharp intakes of air, "I have a touch of the palpitating vapours. Next door's tabby has to go!"

I noticed she did not put one ounce of blame on the willing partner in the scenario, her precious Princess!

"It's not surprising you're out of breath Babs," I replied. I timed you at a four-minute mile as you went down the garden. I don't think I could run faster with a tiger chasing me! I see the neighbour's cat got away scot free?"

"I'll get the bar steward one day…, mark my words."

*She probably would*, I thought. There were few people that I had met in my life with such determination.

I left with Babs sipping iced water to calm her 'palpitating vapours' while stroking her beloved Princess. I could not wait for my next visit to see if there were mongrel kittens running amok.

It was the first day of July. Summer was here at last and winter was just a memory.

Soon all the schools would break up leaving the rush-hour traffic cut in half. The early morning roads would be devoid of screaming kids and stressed out mums late for school.

The kids would be busy all summer making memories for when they were old. Paddling in the sea, camping in the woods, picnicking in the sun. Plus a thousand other missions that would eat up their summer holidays in a blur. Mums would be queuing at the shoe shops to get the kids shoes at the last possible moment to get a summers growth out of the way first! Then the kids would all be meeting up again at the school gates to swap stories. Aah to be young again.

I was looking forward to six weeks of easy driving and summer sun. I had encountered my share of angels and demons during the last few months, some wonderful customers with great stories and some monsters who I wished I could forget.

A few months earlier I had spent the morning at a little unit down Finmere Road fixing two industrial machines smashed to pieces by immigrant machinists and heavy work. When I went to leave, the office staff made some excuse about not having a cheque handy but promised to drop it off later in the day.

Three months went by and several phone calls chasing the payment, and loads of excuses. Then the phone rings, "It's Upholstery Logistics here. We are so sorry we mislaid your bill but we have your cash if you would like to pop in."

*Great*, I think, at last the bill will be settled for my parts supplied and work done.

Later the same day I 'popped in' to collect my overdue payment. The cheeky little devils then made up some ridiculous story about mislaying the cash, but while I was at the unit could I fix one of the machines, then they could pop all the money in later! Yeah right. Could you believe the cheek! They were trying to cheat me twice and it almost worked. They had managed to get me back to the unit.

I politely explained that I needed to 'pop out for an emergency job' but would be delighted to fix the machine once I'd changed the light bulbs along the seafront!

I made a mental note never to return. Another demon to be avoided if I wanted to live a healthy life without a stress-related heart attack. I would wipe of their debt and never set foot in the premises again.

Today however, I was in such a positive mood that my very veins were bursting with energy. Bright clouds scurried across the beautiful blue sky sending shadows rushing over the Downs towards me. It was as if the downs were welcoming me with open arms. The warm westerly was full of sea-scents and wild flowers, its honeyed breath caressing the countryside. It was simply a beautiful smell.

I know I am always going on about the beautiful smell of the downland but anyone who has not smelled one of these priceless days on the downs has missed out on one of the immense simple pleasures in life. You breathe in and just go wow! Then you breathe again and the nostrils just explode with joy. It is akin to smelling a great wine or great cooking. No place on earth smells as sweet as the South Downs on an early summer day after the rain has gone.

Some town-folk or 'townies' as locals often refer to them, have no idea what country-folk see in the boring countryside. The very idea of moving away from their hectic city-lifestyle and going green is just weird. I am quite happy for them not to understand the magic of our beautiful quiet places. Could you imagine for one second if all the millions of townsfolk moved out! The countryside would be no longer the countryside and we would lose our beautiful areas.

When a townie does suddenly understand what the countryside is all about it can be like an epiphany, a revelation, an awakening of the soul and spirit. That is the moment when they know they can never live in a city again.

As I drove along the South Downs from East Dean to Meads, a farmer was rounding up sheep on the wide open grasslands. I stopped to watch the art of a master and his animals working flawlessly together. Two border collies, working in perfect unison, raced from the farmer in wide arcs behind the alert sheep. They were watching the dogs intently. As the dogs reached their apex and moved in, outlining a perfect heart shape, the sheep huddled and moved toward the farmer. No words needed— just superb communication between animal and man.

I noticed a man with a walking stick ambling along the Beachy Head path. I suddenly remembered bumping into another old man many years before when I was riding my motorcycle across the Downs (something that was very pleasurable and quite illegal). More than once I was chased by the policeman on his large horse that used to patrol the green hills. He never caught me and I never did any harm. I certainly left less marks than his horse-hoofs. Back then, in the early morning, you hardly saw a soul up there, so there was no danger on the clear long runs. I used to ride along the slopes finding places to watch the sun come up over the ocean.

On the day that I was waiting for one such sunrise, with my camera poised, the old man appeared from nowhere. We exchanged pleasantries and he was very interested in my Yamaha DT250, having ridden a motorcycle during the war. It was during this discussion that he told me something simply fascinating.

He was on the hills for a trip down memory lane. During the Second World War he was part of a military team that was assigned the task of manning the guns that were hurriedly placed all along Beachy Head. He pointed to a place where the guns once were. Today there is nothing. He told me that underneath the chalk there are huge hidden observation and communication bunkers. They are still there to this day. If you could only find the entrance what a tourist attraction that would be!

During the first part of the war German planes used Beachy Head for navigation. It was one of the first points that they saw coming over the featureless Channel. By lining up on Beachy Head they could get their course for London or to attack places like the dummy airfield, RAF Friston, near Gayle's Farm. Fake mock-up spitfires were lined up there to lure the Luftwaffe into traps.

The British military quickly saw the German planes using Beachy Head and placed guns on the high points to shoot at them. At first they were successful in bringing down a few planes.

One pilot, apparently named Horst, was rescued from his crashed plane that landed near East Dean.

The local bobby, Harry Hyde, commandeered a grocer's van and rushed to the scene. He arrested Horst and took him to his police house. While they waited for the armed forces to pick him up Harry's wife made him a cup of tea. Of course escape was impossible, Mrs Hyde had taken his boots!

The German pilots, now finding they were being shot at as soon as they neared the coast, took sneaky evasive action.

As soon as they spotted Beachy Head they dropped to sea-level and came in fast and low over the waves then roaring up through the troughs in the Downs, especially around Birling Gap and the Seven Sisters. The planes were actually coming in lower than the guns.

The guns that had been designed to shoot upward would not go down low enough to attack the planes. The pilots were safe.

The old man and his colleagues regularly manned the guns in a valiant but vain effort. In fact some of the planes came so low and so close that the men had a clear view of the pilots. Often the German pilots would wave to the gunners. You can guess the sort of two-fingered wave they got back!

It was hard to imagine all the noise and fury that once happened at this stunning place. Now it is a quiet, serene, and beautiful place. We sat on the grass and talked as we waited for the sun to come up. We then watched in silence as it rose from the horizon majestic, supreme, immortal.

He then went on to describe how Belle Tout was used for target practice by bored forces, some in tanks at Cornish Farm. The rolling Downs were the perfect practice areas for tank training. The lighthouse was blown to pieces and was just a ruin by 1945. You would hardly believe it now looking at Jack Fuller's fully restored masterpiece.

He told me about being on duty one day gazing out to sea early in the war around 1940. He was idly watching a ship making its way along the Channel when all of a sudden it exploded. The ship was so close that he could see the name, the Ocean Sunrise. It blew up just off Seaford. Because there were no planes around, he surmised that it must have been a mine that the ship hit.

Once a damaged munitions barge broke anchor and drifted into Newhaven harbour and exploded. The earth shook for miles around and every pane of glass in the town was shattered! It was the largest explosion on British soil in the war and was heard all the way to Portsmouth!

Strange thing war, we are all fascinated by it and dread it at the same time. The old man talked about his youth with pride and excitement.

After our chat I helped him up. He put his hand into one of his pockets and pulled out a small piece of metal polished and worn. "Shrapnel from bombs dropped just over the hill. See that crater?" He continued pointing to a large dip in the hillside. "When I picked this up it was still warm," he said rolling it between his old fingers. "It has been with me ever since. The difference between life and death was a split second. I was standing less than a hundred yards from where the bomb fell. Over 30 years I have kept that piece of shrapnel to remind me how lucky I am."

We stood in silence staring at the small piece of metal in his hand. He suddenly held it out and said, "Yours now boy I won't be needin' it, brought me luck all these years."

I thanked him profusely. We then said our farewells and he wobbled off with his walking stick. I started my bike and shot home. He went one way and I went the other. I never saw him again, but he left me with a priceless memory that I still have.

I often wonder where the openings to the secret bunkers are at Beachy Head. Somebody knows!

I sometimes try to imagine Beachy Head, how it was for those few tempestuous years, planes roaring overhead, tanks rolling over the Downs, ack-ack or pom-pom guns spitting venom at the sky, such a complete contrast to the quiet beauty it holds today. How unique and strange we civilised British are. We rescue and capture a German pilot who was out to cause death and destruction then make him a cup of tea!

*****

"Vivien Leigh is scattered over the mill-pond!" I repeated in disbelief. "I thought she died in London when I was just a kid?" I had remembered as she was one of the most famous actresses in the world, and her untimely death caused quite a sensation. Vivien Leigh had played the immortal part of Scarlett O'Hara in Gone with the Wind, opposite one of my favourite actors, Clarke Gable.

I was sitting in a little cottage down a tiny lane near Blackboys, called Tickerage Lane, and my customer was telling me just another astounding piece of hidden information about my area.

"Yes dear, as sure as I am standing here Vivien Leigh's ashes were scattered over the pond. She supposedly died of tuberculosis while rehearsing for a play in London, though rumours persist that she drowned herself in the mill pond and it was all quickly covered up. Very strange the whole affair, but that is where her ashes ended up. The coroner's report noted that she had water in her lungs but that was put down to her illness. A sad end nonetheless. I loved her as Blanche Du Bois with Marlon Brando in a Streetcar named Desire. I don't care for the pond myself," she finished, with a strange note in her voice, almost like a warning!

After I had fixed her machine I decided to explore down the lane and find the Mill Pond to see where Scarlett, or rather Vivien, was scattered.

It was a steep descent along a small road that was also part of The Vanguard Way. The road was bordered by large woods that became deep and menacing. The woods were dark with none of the usual twittering birdsong. An eerie wind rustled branches behind me, it wailed as if in pain, as if it was searching for something and could not find it. I kept looking backward and had the feeling that I was being watched. There was no life in the woods, it was unsettling and I quickened my step.

I made it to the old mill where the road split the pond from a stream. There was coolness in the air, quite the opposite of the summer day. I looked across the water and felt a shiver run through me. *I don't want to be here* I thought. It was as if her tortured soul, never peaceful in life, was still haunting the place. I turned and made a quick-march up back through the woods and was glad to get back to the familiarity of my car.

If it was like that on such a perfect day what would the place be like in winter? I decided that I would never visit the spot again. Some places seem to be out of balance with nature and that was one of them. I am not sure how to explain it but you just don't want to be there.

I sparked up the Land Rover and made a hasty retreat to the more familiar territory of the Uckfield Road. No wonder there were rumours of Vivien's death around the place. It just seemed to be itching to be haunted.

Blackboys, where I had just been, gets its name from the old lord of the manor Sir Phillip Blakeboyes. Early records show the village of Blackboys around the $14^{th}$ century, however there is another popular belief.

The whole area was the centre of the first iron industry right back to Roman times. When Queen Elizabeth was building her armada, to stave of the Spanish attack in 1588, huge amounts of the forest were destroyed for her ships and more importantly, to forge her cannon.

Young men flocked to the area to work at the local furnaces deep in the woods. At the end of a hard day's work they would come out of the woods with their charcoal blackened faces and quench their thirst at the local inn.

A traveller entering the inn for the first time would be confronted with the black-faced men supping ale. The inn became known to travellers as the Blackboys Inn. Eventually the whole village became known as Blackboys. Now that's much more fun.

I had a stop near Worth Farm just below Uckfield, then one more at Chiddingly and a last call at Rattle Road in Westham. After that my work-day would be over.

Farmer Corner who had named his new home Renroc, his name backward, had worked Worth Farm most of his life. From the time his hands were large enough to milk a cow he was up with the lark. From the age of six he worked the farm with his parents. Worth Farm is so old that it is mentioned in the Domesday Book. A beautiful place set in wide open pastureland with panoramic views over the countryside towards Lewes. Next to the farm two oast houses stand like impatient twins waiting to play in the fields.

Seventy-six years later the old farmer still gazes over the land he worked all his life, and still drinks a pint of milk for breakfast!

By the afternoon the temperature was soaring. After months of cool weather the sudden summer was as engulfing as a sand storm. At 28 degrees I was sweltering with the windows open as I drove.

I rolled down the back roads to Horam, onto Gun Hill and Chiddingly. I parked up near the Six Bells public house. The pub is a great venue for live music, good food and happy chatter. It was once a bikers' pub full of sweaty leathers and macho men, bandanas and beer guts. Although it is still popular with biker's it now welcomes all. There is one story I know about the pub which is simply amazing.

Many years ago an old man wandered into the pub. He ordered some food and drink and sat quietly doodling away on a beer mat. The locals did not take much notice until he came to leave. He walked over to the bar and placed the beer mat on the counter. "I will leave this in payment for my bill," he said in a broken foreign accent. "**What**," replies the burly barman.

"I will leave this as payment."

"The Hell you will. You pay up like everyone else silly old fool."

"Do you not realise who I am? I am the great Pablo Picasso."

"Yeah and I am the king of Siam," Replies the irate barman. "Now pay up or I'll throw you out."

"No, no, no! I am the famous artist Picasso and this is worth much money." Retorts the old man pushing the bar mat forward.

The barman, now realising the trouble and attention the old man is causing comes round the bar and physically gets hold of the man and escorts him, sharply, out of the pub. "Silly old bugger."He shouts throwing the bar mat out with him. The old man picks up his scribbling and hobbles away towards Chiddingly.

Back into the pub everyone has a laugh and carried on drinking. A few try to pay with bar mats!

Later in the week one of the regulars comes in. "You'll never guess who is staying with Lee Miller our local celebrity photographer, none other than Pablo Picasso!"

The whole pub was shocked into astonished silence. His scribbling would now be worth a fortune! Needles to say they are more careful who they throw out of the pub now!

After my call at Chiddingly I headed up to Vines Cross taking Laundry Lane to Grove Hill, slowly making my way towards the last customer of the day. Cinderford Lane to Cowbeech and then Ginger's Green. Through the ancient flatlands of Horse Eye Level which used to be under the sea to the depth of a horses eye. Then to Rickney and Hankham, by the Dog House where Ian Gow, our superb MP, met his grisly death at the hands of terrorists in the summer of 1990.

From Hankham down the back road to Gallows Lane ending in Rattle Road just a few yards from my last call of the day. I had bypassed every major road and hardly passed a dozen cars all the way.

One of the glorious benefits of growing up and travelling in the same small area all my life, is a map etched in my brain of every back lane and hidden road.

I parked and walked up the garden path to my customer. The narrow brick path, laid in a herringbone pattern, had rows of lavender growing up each side. My toolbox rubbed over the lavender throwing up a beautiful scent and chasing the bees from their work.

I knocked on the front door and turned to see the Rattle Road sign along the road.

Rattle Road has its name in local folklore for a morbid reason. Rattle Road is met by Gallows Lane, that leads to a crossroads a few hundred yards away cut by Peelings Lane. This is where the old gallows stood.

Unfortunate wretches, who ended up at the old crossroads for their crimes, were hung on the gallows and left to rot as a warning to all.

As the bodies rotted birds would peck and rip at the flesh. Woodpeckers living in the woods nearby loved the bugs and maggots that ate the rotting corpse. Because of this habit they became known as the Gallows Birds, a nickname long forgotten to most. The flesh would peel and drop from the victims, blowing up the road at the crossroads. The road in turn became known morbidly as Peelings Lane. As all the flesh decayed and was eaten, the bones were held together by sinew and tendons.

When the wind blew the skeletons rattled in the wind and could be heard all the way down to the main road. No one ventured up to the gallows except for the morbid few and children on a dare. The main road then became known as Rattle Road as people hurried by on dark nights.

So there you have it, one more piece of old local history I had been told over the years, even though it is rather grisly! I wonder how many newcomers to the area know of the legend.

"Hello duckie," a large woman said as she ushered me in. In her left hand was a leaflet that she was using as a fan. "It's so hot I can hardly breathe! The machine is on the table. If you need me I will be in the kitchen keeping cool."

"No problem," I replied. "I'll get on with it and give you a shout presently."

Before long I was well into the machine, sorting out all the usual problems and within the hour the machine was stitching along a treat. I had not seen hide-nor-hair of the old dear from the time she opened the door, just the occasional huffing and puffing coming from the kitchen.

I packed my tools and called to her but there was no answer. I then decided to go and find my old dear and was confronted with a sight that will stay with me till my dying day! I was always impressed by the versatility of some of my customers but this one was a beauty. She had found a unique way to stay cool...

Before me sat the old dear oblivious of my entering the room. Luckily I entered from behind her otherwise I may have been scarred for life!

She sat on a chair, one elbow on the table and her head resting on her hand. Her body was slumped like she had melted onto the chair. In the other hand was her leaflet still being waved lazily over her face.

The table, covered with a plastic tablecloth, had a jug of iced water on it and a half-empty glass. She was wearing one of those typical old-fashioned floral dresses hiked up to just above her knees and unbuttoned to her midriff. Pop socks strangled her chubby thread-veined legs which were stuck straight out in front of her, about 30 degrees apart.

Her feet were pointed directly at her fridge like fallen bollards. The fridge door was propped open with another chair. On the chair was a fan pointed directly into the fridge. Her table and chair had been pulled as close as she could get to the open fridge. The sight was unspeakable. The humming fan blew air into the fridge. Then it came out and went straight up her dress ruffling it like a flapping flag between her legs.

Frozen, I stared boggle-eyed at the sight. I was astounded at her ingenuity and the scene set before me. What to do next…? I coughed loudly behind her.

"Oh hello duckie," she said not moving an inch. "Who needs air conditioning eh?"

"Not you for sure." I replied.

"Your money is on the shelf duckie. Is the machine saved?"

"It sure is. The machine is stitching like a dream," I said as I folded the cash into my shirt pocket, trying to keep my back to her as I shuffled by.

"See yourself out duckie. Pull the latch will you, I'm concentrating on keeping cool."

I hurried out and pulled the door shut. As I left I burst out laughing.

*Can you believe it*, I thought to myself as I pushed my toolbox into the back of the car. There is never a dull moment in this job.

# *The End*

# Evacuation for Flo

"We thought there was something up when school was called back early from summer holidays. Milly just said that they had the dates wrong and we would be sent home to play, but I knew something was fishy. I just did not know what!

Milly was my best friend, my closest neighbour and she lived next door. We had grown up together, went to our first school together. We were inseparable.

At the time I was 13 and Milly was a little older. We dressed like twins wherever we went. Our mums must not have minded as they made all our clothes to match. When we went to the Saturday morning flicks, we would fold our arms through each other's and skip all the way to the cinema.

I think it was 1940—but I can't be sure anymore. But what I do know is that our beautiful summer holiday was abruptly over. We had to immediately return to school.

Well, Mum had told us that war had been declared with the Germans, whoever they were!

We went to school arm in arm carrying our sandwiches and a funny little cardboard box, tied with string, with a gas mask. The gas mask was awful. It stank of rubber and made me feel quite sick. It was only when Milly put hers on and looked like a pig that I laughed so much I forgot about the smell.

In our lockers at school we all had a labelled suitcase, or a bag, full of spare clothes.

The days were normal, except for one thing. We had been taught that each time the bell rang we should follow teacher. What a game! The bell would go and we would follow 'Old Snotty'.

No need to explain why he had that nickname. He always had two hankies and needed both of them!

We would march around the playground. Sometimes up the street and through the churchyard. In fact we went with him whenever and wherever.

This went on every day for the first week. Then one day the bell rang, we grabbed our masks and suitcases as usual and followed 'Snotty'. He took us to reception where we all had labels attached to us and marched us straight out of the school and down the street. We walked and walked. We ended up in the railway station. It was really exciting in a scary way!

I stuck to Milly like glue and we sat in the same carriage. It was not like you see on telly today. On our platform there were no parents crying or anything like that. Most of us were having a ball.

The train went for miles and miles. When I saw my first real cows I squealed with delight! Having grown up in a big city the countryside was a mystery to me, and in 13 years my dad had never taken us on holiday. We had had the odd day out, but they were mainly to relatives at Christmas—that sort of thing.

I should have known something was up when my mum had asked me what I would like in my sandwich—she never normally asked. It could be anything from a bit of cheese to some lard and sugar—or dripping with salt. That day I had butter and honey, my all-time favourite. I remember Milly had salt beef, which I also loved so we swapped— half each.

Eventually, as it was getting dark, we arrived at a small place, which seemed to be in the middle of nowhere. Of course, looking back now, we were being evacuated to the country. But at that time I had no idea. Not one of us did—it was all a magical mystery.

From the station we marched to the village hall. Gathered there were loads of strangers who were eyeing us up like meat. For the first time Milly and me were scared! We all huddled together as the strangers walked around us, picking out one at a time. They would walk over to a man with a book, who seemed to write down information, and then they disappeared with one of our classmates. On the book was written Operation Pied Piper. It was the name for the evacuation of the children all over the country.

One by one all of our friends went. Suddenly I was aware of an old man standing next to me, eyeing me up.

"How old are you girl? Speak up! I don't bite."

"Thirteen," I replied sheepishly.

He felt my arms and huffed and puffed. "You'll do, follow me." I froze.

He came back and pulled me. I did not move. Milly was gripping me so tight that, as hard as he tried, we would not budge. "Let her go, you!" He said to Milly.

"**We're together**," she screamed at him. He almost leapt back with shock.

"You've got some lungs on you girl, what's your name?"

"None of your business. **Go away**."

Far from this upsetting the old man he laughed. "Got some spirit too I see! Well I'll take the pair," he shouted over to the man with the book.

All this time I never spoke a word. Milly said I was as white as a sheet! After a long time and a lot of chatting by the people in the hall, we were told to follow the old man and we would be fine. I looked back at 'Snotty' as we left with a terrible feeling of dread.

I need not have worried. The old man was harmless and walked us to his cart, chatting. We rolled out of the town into the dark. Excitement took hold of us again. Soon we were giggling and pointing at the stars and all the strange shapes in the dark. We travelled for what seemed like an age, and eventually pulled onto an old dirt track.

At the top of the track was a lovely crooked house, with a warm light falling out of the windows, and smoke trailing up—disappearing into the deep-blue night sky.

In the doorway was a fat old lady, very short, with an apron tied around her. "What's kept you Da? I was getting worried."

"Had a spot of bother at the hall Ma."

"I see! The bother looks like it comes in twos. Now that you have a pair where are they going to sleep?"

"They'll share the bed, just like me brothers and me when we were kids."

Inside, the room was full of warmth and wonderful smells. I realised that I had only eaten a sandwich all day. "You must be starving you young 'uns. Come on, I have supper on the table."

Ma was so friendly and comforting that we were soon tucking into a feast. Pudding was something special. It was sponge fingers floating in a plum sauce. Blood 'n' bones Ma called it and it was just the most wonderful thing I had even eaten.

Warm and fat, we went up the narrow stairs to a small bedroom where we fell asleep in seconds.

In the morning I opened my eyes and saw the oil lamp on the table that Ma had used to show us to our room. I got up and looked out of the window.

Down in the yard the chickens were running around—being chased by a boy with a bucket. Two dogs, full of life, followed him closely. The sun was just coming over the hill, and there was a mist in the valley where we had driven in the cart the night before. I thought I must have died and gone to heaven.

I opened up the creaky window and smelt a smell that will stay with me 'till the day I die. It was the fresh smell of the countryside. A magical smell of all the grasses and flowers, of animals and wild things. "Milly. Milly, come and look, I think we are dead—we must be. I think we are in heaven. Look—look there is so much to see."

Milly was at the window in an instant. She thought it must be those Germans that everyone was talking about! All our commotion at the window had caught the attention of the boy who was feeding the chickens.

"Morning girls," he shouted, touching his cap and smiling a smile as bright as the sun that was lighting up the valley. We giggled and ran back to the bed. "Where do you think we are Milly?"

"No idea Flo, but it sure looks like we have ended up somewhere nice. Did I dream it or did I eat the best meal I have ever eaten last night?"

"That was no dream Milly that was roast chicken! I had one once before. When we go down we will ask the old man what is happening. I am sure he'll explain everything."

Over breakfast the old farmer and his wife told us how we had been taken from our homes in the city to be safe in the country where the nasty Germans could not hurt us. Soon we would be back with our parents, and we should just treat our time at the farm as a working holiday. It all seemed strange to us as we had never upset anyone called German! But we did as we were told, and looked forward every day to Ma's wonderful cooking.

We posted official cards with our new address and soon letters arrived from home. We fitted in at a local school. It was a bit cramped in the classroom but we managed until Portsmouth was bombed.

Then there were loads of other kids and a sorry state they were in too! Some of the poor blighters did not even have shoes. They were the poorest children I had ever seen, and growing up in London I had seen a few.

In classes the teacher would ask for a spare pair of size fives' for Jimmy or a jumper for Billy and before long they were clothed and settled.

Because of all the extra children we only went to school in the mornings, there was not enough room for everyone. In the afternoon the other evacuees used the school. We did nature studies or worked on the farm. It all worked a treat.

We settled down to farm life. Jed, the son, was a little marvel. He made us laugh and taught us how the farm worked. Everything that Jed did not know, Ma and Da taught us.

Days turned into weeks, seasons came and went. Milly and me just gazed in wonder at country life, and the changing cycles that did not exist in a city.

We learnt how to get a milking stool close enough to the cow's back leg to let milk in the bucket but not enough to let the cow step on or into the bucket. There was the knack of milking the four teats, the closer you could get to the natural suckling of a calf the easier it was and the more milk we got. Mind you, more than once, I had a glass of warm milk straight from the udder. The creamy ambrosia rolled around my mouth and slipped down my throat. I still think no better drink has ever been made.

We always kept our cows happy and well fed; Ma and Da knew happy cows gave good milk.

Milly and Jed became more than friends. Jed was exempt from war duties because of the farm but felt he had to do his bit and signed up. The day that Jed went off to war was a sad day. Tears flowed from us all, but none more than Milly—who was inconsolable for weeks.

Our parents came to visit and stuck a deal with Ma and Da to keep us as long as possible. We were in a safe place far away from the troubles.

I know a lot of children from Yeovil went back home after the Germans kept trying to bomb an aircraft factory near there. It was more dangerous there than in the middle of a city. I remember, on market day, passing the huge 'fake factory' they had built to fool the bombers. It did not stop them strafing anyone they could though!

We were not old enough to join the forces, I think you had to be 18 or 20 if you were a girl, but there was only one place for us. The Women's Land Army. We knew that Land Army Girls were in demand and by hook and by crook we ended up working at the farm.

We even dressed as Land Army Girls and dyed our jumpers green, wore long woolly-ribbed socks and stitched up trousers. Da made us wide leather belts that looked just like the real ones. When we were *'in kit'* we looked better than the real thing. The WLA would have been proud.

One a trip to Yeovil we even bought Forces knickers. There were two types, thick winter ones which were called *black-outs* and light summer ones—*twilights*!

We played our part from feeding the animals to planting the spuds.

Loads of leaflets were available telling us how to make ends meet with our rations. We learnt a few tricks along the way as well like digging up dandelions and roasting the roots. We then ground them and made a passable cup of substitute coffee. Of course there was Camp Coffee if you had the money and the vouchers!

There were several, 'surprise,' visits from the Ministry to make sure everything was in order, but when they called any sneaky 'goings on' were well hidden. You see we always got *the nod* from our postman, who cycled past us to his home down the road a smidgen, so we knew they were coming!

We had a hidden store dug below an old oak tree that had fallen years before. If the Ministry was calling, all surplus goods for the local community were hidden there. It wasn't really black market stuff, just food for everyone when the coupons ran out.

Not once did they ever check the field. Mind you, Hercules, our bull, would put the frighteners on anyone, and it was his field! He was a softy, really. But a fiercer-looking animal never set foot on this earth. We used to feed him dandelions—they were his favourite. He would grunt at the gate until we fed him and made a fuss of him.

The Ministry men were always well treated. They went on their way with a pack of sausages or the odd chicken in their boot.

Leaflets were always handy when rationing took hold.

Towards the end of the war we were told that Jed was to go abroad. There was no other information, but we later learnt he was in the second wave of D-Day.

Unknown to us, Milly and Jed had made a secret pact to marry as soon as war finished. It was a happy day. Jed had returned with a parachute or *brolly* as he called it, that he had found in a field. He had smuggled it all through Europe. He said it became his lucky charm and his pillow. When he slept on it he would dream of Milly wearing it on their wedding day.

There was only one problem—all over the parachute it was stamped *Property of the MOD*. This was overcome with loads of small bunches of flowers sewn over each stamp. It looked a picture.

We were always using up odd pieces of fabric. Nothing was ever wasted. It seems amazing now but we would unpick something and even try to keep the thread!

Jed bought the wedding licence, seven shillings and sixpence, plus a penny stamp and the day was set. It's a bit more expensive to get married today!

For Millie's going away dress—they went to stay with her aunt for a week in Torquay—a neighbour kindly pulled down her kitchen curtains. These were unpicked and made into a lovely two-piece floral outfit. When they returned to the farm the dress was unpicked, then carefully made back into curtains and re-hung in the neighbour's kitchen. You could hardly see all the seams. What fun!

I remember Ma renting the most beautiful fake—wedding cake! We did not have a real wedding cake, no icing, no marzipan. When it came to cut the cake the outer pretty fake-cake was lifted up to a great round of applause and underneath was a simple sponge. How we laughed. It was just a hollow cardboard cake for show. Can you picture that? The sponge was lovely.

When the war ended Milly and Jed lived at the farm and I went back to work in the city. Most years, when my aching bones allow, I still travel to the farm and spend a few days with Jed, Milly and their children. They had nine and they are all grown up and have flown the coop, save for two of the sons who work the farm. Ma and Da are long gone but never forgotten.

They were days of heaven, days when the heart soared and the soul was full. We were so lucky, our evacuation had been the happiest days of our lives. Looking back now it all made sense. I had come home from Sunday school just after lunch in September of 1939. Mum was crying next to the radio and dad was comforting her. Although she quickly dried her tears and would not tell me anything. They had just heard Neville Chamberlain announce that we were at war. For many evacuees times were harsh, but luckily my world changed for the better. I had the journey of a lifetime.

The best day of the week at the farm was Sunday morning before church. Every Sunday Da would slip out of the back door before sunrise, a rifle under his arm. He would return with a young rabbit or two. Ma would coat the tender rabbit in seasoned flour and gently fry it in beef lard. To this day no food has ever tasted finer.

When Ma served up the breakfast, Da, sitting at the head of the old wooden table, with his hanky tucked in his shirt, would start to sing **Run, rabbit, run, rabbit, run, run, run**.

We would all join in and sing the whole chorus around the table finishing with... **Bang, bang, bang! goes the farmer's gun, so run rabbit, run rabbit, run, run, run.**

We would finish with a sombre moment of silence as we looked down at the poor fried rabbit. Then, with roars of laughter, we would tuck into the best breakfast ever made.

Oh happy, happy days."

## *The End*

# Misty Mornings

I was sitting in the kitchen of a modern semi-detached house in Eastbourne, scratching my head, staring at a Singer Magic Number Nine. Something was very wrong and, in a lifetime of fixing the little sewing machine monsters, this one was different. The whole top shaft seemed to be out of line.

In my usual suspicious manner I donned my imaginary Sherlock Holmes hat. I turned to her and asked my customer, in my most pleasant voice, if anyone had touched the machine?

"Oh no, no one has been near it," came her reply.

Humm! I was stuck.

I could guess for an hour or two—or leave. I need not have worried—rescue was at hand and from a most delightful source. In the doorway appeared a beautiful bubbly girl of about six years old. She had strawberry blonde hair dancing in curls around her happy freckled face. From her lips fell priceless words.

"Oh mummy," she says, "don't you remember? You went and got daddy the big hammer from his tool box so he could hit it!"

*Out of the mouth of babes* I thought as a big grin spread across my face. I looked up to see the mother with eyes the size of saucepans and her jaw dropping open big enough to park a car—sideways.

She had been caught red handed and grassed on by her own sweet child!

Of course, once I knew what 'helpful hubby' had done, it was no trouble setting the top shaft back to where it would have been before he had hit it. I had to wonder what was going through his mind.

I often fancy having a sign saying, **I fix the machine your husband has tried to!**

I left my customer—with the biggest smile on my face.

As I walked down the path I heard a tapping on the window behind me and looked around to see a strawberry-haired angel waving goodbye.

Some days my job is just priceless.

My next call, a stone's throw from Honey's Green, was a sheer delight. I spent more time picking ripe tomatoes and French Beans than I did fixing my customer's machine. The next was in a beautiful Georgian farmhouse not far from Earwig Corner, near Lewes. I was on a roll. Some days are like that, many are not.

As I entered the old farmhouse, I walloped my head on one of the low beams and disturbed the husband. He was leaning out of the back window with his air rifle. He held a finger to his lips and whispered to me, "Just trying to pop off one of the wild rabbits for supper. They're always eating my veg and now it's payback time."

The sewing machine I had come to repair was a Singer 15. It had unusual markings, and when I asked about them, it turned out to be an early Scottish Singer exported to France just before the out-break of World War II.

Mrs Fletcher had been given the machine on her $16^{th}$ birthday but, before she could use it, war broke out. She lived in a region of France that bordered on Germany, and they moved their precious belongings into a large bunker for safekeeping, just for the few weeks while the war was on!

When the French soldiers came across the machine they asked if they could use it for their uniform repairs, she agreed.

That did not last long—the Germans overran the fortifications. They found the machine and carried on using it for exactly the same purpose. She dare not ask for her present back.

Toward the end of the war American soldiers captured the bunker. She asked for the machine back but they would not let her have it. It was too useful. The 'few weeks' had turned into several years.

It then passed to the British, and it was not until after the war ended that she finally got to use her birthday present. She was 21.

She ended up marrying one of the British soldiers she had met, and he was now shooting rabbits out of the back window!

Autumn was coming. You could just feel it in the cool morning air. I was a bit early for my next customer, and decided I had time to stop just above Alfriston for a quick break.

I stopped at Frog Firle just above the sleepy village of Alfriston on the Seaford Road. At that viewpoint I watched Mother Nature preparing herself for the oncoming of winter.

The season of soft fruits and mellow-misty-mornings had arrived. The sun had lifted majestically out of her nightly ocean bath and risen refreshed for another day.

Farmers were busy ploughing, into the soil, the remaining stubble from the newly-harvested crops. The tractors were being followed by flocks of noisy gulls that wheeled and dived into the fresh furrows, as the steel ploughshares turned the chalky downland soil over as easily as fresh cake mix.

Down in the Cuckmere Vale hundreds of geese were gathering for their annual migration. Their epic winter journey across our planet was soon to start.

There was an air of expectancy. Autumn was here and winter was on its way. Mother Nature was creating another work of art, a masterpiece.

The first September dew was underfoot and the chill in the air was as refreshing as a cold shower on a hot day. The air was full of the scents of autumn, of rosehip and blackberry, of sloe and damson. It was the season of fresh earth and ripe fruit.

All the wild fruits were being gathered—no longer by humans but by the animals and birds. Finches squabbled over the elderberries that shone black and bright like magpies' eyes. Sparrows pulled and pecked at other bountiful hedgerow fruits. A blackbird was busy demolishing a damson while chubby rabbits foraged on the hillside grass, showing their little white tails as they hopped from one clump to another.

When I was a child there was a well known company called Delrosa. They sold the best syrup in the world, made from wild rosehips. It was a tonic, or cure-all, full of vitamin C. It tasted divine.

The syrup was produced from the berries of the wild roses that ramble through the endless hedgerows of good old Blighty. In Scotland they are known as itchycoo! I'll explain in a mo.

As autumn arrived so did the little rugby-ball-shaped orange-red berries or hips. The syrup made from these little marvels would be poured over hot rice pudding, or made into a warming drink when we were ill. It was always expensive, so kept as a treat for when we were not well.

Actually, it was really useful during the war when vitamin C was in short supply and was supposed to be for the babies, but the adults loved it as well.

The company, Delrosa, paid schools to pick rosehips from the hedgerows during the autumn. The schools welcomed the extra revenue, and would allow the children to take the afternoon off from lessons so they could pick the hips. The best pickers were rewarded with certificates and badges.

In this way Delrosa managed to acquire tons of wild rosehips to make their wonderful elixir.

Kids, especially me, loved Delrosa

Today there are a few paltry dried tea bags available with rosehips in health food stores but the splendid Delrosa has long gone and how I miss it.

Rose Hip Syrup disappeared when our prim and proper education system could not possibly approve children taking the afternoon off from school, even if it did help raise funds. *What would they think of next?*

However, I have absolute confidence that such a brilliant product will not disappear forever. Mark my words… It will be back!

Oh, and *itchycoo*! One other thing that the little devils cherished about rose hips. If you prised open the rosehip bud you had the most awful itching powder ever discovered—and hell for the kids who had it stuck down their necks in class.

Mind you, if you were not the subject of the attack, it was funny to watch! I always think there is a little devil in all of us.

The lazy morning air was alive with sounds. The countryside chorus that was so familiar reminded me of an orchestra tuning up, before the annual performance at the village pantomime. Sheep bleated aimlessly, cattle called in deep long steamy moans. Geese trumpeted like annoying aunties at a garden party. The swallows were chirping, busily feeding on the wing. The crows were cawing. Pheasant cackled as they ran for their lives, scampering across the open fields like poultry at a farmers market.

Down at the farm, deep in the valley, a cockerel stretched its neck to the sky and announced another new day. All was well in our little world.

In the bright cold morning some hot-air balloons drifted across the Sussex countryside. Up on my high place they floated by in silence, great ships in the sky.

Out at sea, far out to the emerald horizon, huge container ships ploughed their trade, full of merchandise bound for distant continents. I knew that in the shallows the sea bass would be playing, rolling in the surf and feeding on the last of the crabs and prawns before heading for deeper, warmer, waters for winter. They would not return until next June.

All the tents and tarpaulins for the summer fayres had been rolled away for another season. The summer fêtes and flower shows all gone. The farmers' bales of hay stacked and counted.

The countryside was a lazy brown colour, and the pigeons were fat. The meadow flowers had turned to seed—soon to be carried away and scattered on the winter winds. Insignificant little tufts and pods—mini-miracles—that held next year's summer splendour.

Things to be done. Places to go, I had to get a move on but did not want to leave. One of the farmer's tractors lumbered over the far side of the hill and disappeared from view, followed by flocks of eager seagulls like children following a schoolteacher after playtime.

Funnily enough, I realised as I was standing transfixed as summer turned to autumn, it was Michaelmas Day. A special day, rooted in the history of the old calendar. It was taken as the last day of the harvest and the beginning of autumn.

It was the time of year that farmers would decide which of their beasts would be kept and fed over winter—and which would be preserved, salted and dried to feed the family.

Traditionally this day was the start of many livestock fairs and a time of plenty for all. A busy time of preparation and celebration. Michaelmas Day used to be celebrated with a nice fat goose, something of a rarity on most tables now.

Michaelmas Day is the feast of St Michael the Archangel, who sat on the right hand-side of God. St Michael led the army of angels in the great battle of the heavens against Satan. The battle ended with Satan being cast out forever.

Fables say that when the Devil fell to earth he landed in a patch of brambles. Old folklore warns not to pick blackberries after September 29th as Satan, in his disgust, trampled and spat on them! The damp mornings, this time of year, cause the blackberries to spoil quickly, adding weight to the old tale.

That old Lucifer has such a lot to answer for!

I snapped out of my trance, got up and walked back to the car. I took one backward look at heaven, then joined with the traffic and drove down the winding road toward my next customer in Seaford. I had two more stops. One at a convent, which I always enjoyed, and one at a miserable old bat's whose objective in life was to make every one suffer.

The convent in Seaford has a mission in Africa where they take old hand machines. They teach a person how to sew and to look after the machine. The effect is dramatic; one of the nuns told me that a man could go from poverty to middle standing in the village, just from the sewing machine. More often than not, within the year, he has also found a wife and was living a good life. What a difference! The machines that we treat almost as junk are priceless to them.

A sister lives at the convent. A wonderful nun who is a regular visitor in Seaford town centre where she gets her shopping. Nothing is unusual about that except how she gets there.

Sister gets her lift into town in the most extraordinary way. She just goes out of the convent and walks into the middle of the road, and stops the first car coming down the road. She asks for a lift and away she goes. Who would deny a nun?

Well you can guess what happened. After all the years, and endless warnings, she came across a short-sighted driver. She stepped out in front of him and was promptly run over.

After a hip operation she is fine and is getting back to normal. Just think what the poor driver must have thought. He is going to have a bit of trouble when St Peter pulls out his list at the Pearly Gates. Running over a nun is not a *get into Heaven quick card* for sure.

Did it stop Sister from stepping out into the road for her lifts? Of course not, now she just waves her stick.

My visit to the convent flew by and all I had left was 'my last pain' back in Eastbourne.

I drove the winding road that skirts the hills and forests between Seaford and Eastbourne, passing New Barn Farm. The farm is tucked away in the valley just over the ridge from the Cuckmere, on the edge of the forest where the crows make their messy nests. Few people know that one of Britain's most famous writers spent some time at the farm.

Sir Arthur Conan Doyle found it a wonderful spot to slip away to and hide from prying eyes. Even now, once a year, members of the Conan Doyle Society come down from London and take pictures of his secret haunt.

My last customer only ever phoned after she had taken her machine apart. Then she would moan incessantly about the cost of the repair while I worked on it. However I was refreshed from my wonderful morning and was ready for battle.

Arriving behind the coalman, delivering coal for the winter, I stopped at her house. The world may have turned thousands of times but not every old trade had vanished.

I have always fancied writing a story called Last Man Standing. It would be about all of the trades—including mine—that have been slowly declining for years.

My job was going the way of the tinker, tailor and candlestick maker and I was fast becoming the last of my kind. A skilled and trained professional who plied a trade that had taken years to learn. I knew that I was repairing machinery that, one day, will simply be classed as disposable.

I remember bumping into an old man who back in 1951 bought his wife a sewing machine. He paid £53 for it and worked out that his first house cost him just over £500. He had paid just ten times more for his house than his wife's sewing machine!

It is inconceivable today to think how expensive these machines were, ten machines bought a house! No wonder some of the old dears treasure their machines so. Who would have ever thought that sewing machines, like so many new domestic appliances, would eventually become so cheap and throw-away!

Still there was work for now, and my last customer of the morning loomed closer.

I braced myself, toolbox in hand, took a deep breath and rang the bell. I was now ready for anything the old bat could throw at me.

"You're eight minutes late! I was just about to ring!"

*The End*

# The Witching Hour

A slow dawn rose over a drab grey day. This was no day for a poet. Shakespeare would not have been inspired to write any of his glorious words today, *"But soft, what light through yonder window breaks? It is the east, and Juliet is the sun. Arise, fair sun, and kill the envious moon who is already sick and pale with grief that her maid art far more fair than she."* No, today was no lazy lover's day, it was a dull day and no sun would rise to kill the envious moon. Drizzle smeared the windscreen of my trusty Land Rover as I ploughed the country lanes to my first call.

I glanced down at the speedo just as the odometer clicked over another mile. It now read over one hundred and forty thousand miles. This car was just one of the many that I had used on my endless travels as a sewing-machine repairman. Over the years I had travelled the equivalent of several times around the globe in my endless pursuit of faulty machines.

No wonder I called her my trusty Land Rover. She had never let me down, from the freezing ice-filled days of mid-winter to the hot dusty paths of summer. The old girl just rattled along uncomplaining. Tools in the back—and addresses to visit on the passenger seat.

I rumbled by the old village pubs, The Peacock Inn, The Black Horse and The Griffin at the small medieval village of Fletching, where they had just held their bonfire night. As usual they had burnt effigies of Guy Fawkes, one of the conspirators attempting to blow up The Houses of Parliament back in 1605. The old poem sprung to mind:

*Remember, remember, the fifth of November*
*The gunpowder treason and plot.*
*I see no reason why Gunpowder and Treason*
*Should ever be forgot.*

Nor has it! Four hundred years later we are still celebrating his failed attempt, with bonfires and fireworks. Poor old Guy, A catholic freedom fighter, was caught red-handed in the cellars of Parliament with 36 barrels of gunpowder made at Powder Mills near Battle. Guy had planned, along with his fellow conspirators, to blow up not only James I, but his whole parliament on the state opening.

His attempt to bring the religious war, that had been raging in Europe to England, and change a nation's faith through force, failed.

Parliament reconvened and one of their first acts was to institute *'a public thanksgiving to almighty God every year on the fifth day of November.'* And so bonfire night was born.

Guy Fawkes met his death in front of a jeering crowd. One consolation was that before he was hung, drawn and quartered he actually fell off the scaffold and broke his neck. They hung his corpse anyway!

Of all the bonfire celebrations in England, the town of Lewes holds the most spectacular. They celebrate not only Guy Fawkes but the poor martyrs who were burnt at Lewes under the reign of Bloody Mary.

Her short and bloody reign saw the burning of hundreds of Protestants who would not renounce their faith. Henry's little pearl had turned into a dragon, torturing, hanging and burning all who opposed her religious fervour.

Her attempts to destroy everything her father had done and bring England back under the Roman Catholic faith died with her. Three years of failed harvests, storms and tempests preceded her demise. She died in agony in November 1558 at the age of 42.

No more would bags of gunpowder be tied around burning martyrs necks to hasten their horrific deaths. Parliament later passed the Act of Settlement, forever banning Catholics from succeeding to the throne.

After her demise a sweet little rhyme came to life. It is still sung by children today but few know of its dark beginnings. *Mary, Mary quite contrary how does your garden grow? With silver bells and cockle shells and pretty little maidens all in a row.* Mary was Queen Mary, the silver bells and cockle shells were euphemisms for the instruments of torture they used trying to convert the Protestants and the pretty little maidens all in a row were the condemned women on their way to execution! Not such a sweet rhyme now eh!

Centuries later up to 80,000 visitors still cram the narrow streets of Lewes to see burning barrels roll down the old cobbled highways. Thankfully festivities have replaced religious intolerance. Costumed revellers dress as anything from Red Indians to Zulu warriors and, as fireworks fly high into the sky, they run around whooping and shouting far into the night.

How I used to love bonfire night, even the run up to it when dad would appear with a box or two of Brock's or Standard fireworks. We would sneak the lid open and peer at the little bundles of exploding delight inside. There were all their weird and wonderful names, *Green Goblin, Jumping Jack Flash, Traffic*

Lights, Red *volcano*, Golden Fountain, Snow Storm or Mount Vesuvius.

Every lad yearned for fireworks

Then came the night, cold and star-bright in my memory, even if it rained. Parents gathered and gossiped around the bonfire with hot chestnuts that burnt the fingers and stained the hands. Spuds pushed into the embers to roast. Warming cups of hot chocolate clasped in both hands with lips blowing steam from them.

The weird multi-coloured glow on everyone's well-wrapped face as the fireworks erupted. However small the explosion or pathetic the firework, it was always greeted with enthusiasm and eager anticipation of the next. The drifting pungent smell of sulphur, which stayed in the nostrils for hours, erupted from the crackling demons.

Brock's long gone now.

I loved the strange shapes we could make waving sparklers around before they fizzed out their short but spectacular lives and the final hiss as they were tossed into the bucket of water. The disappointment as the boxes of joy emptied and however hard we looked into the boxes there were no more fireworks to light.

And then the next mornings search, amongst the spent fireworks, in the hope of finding an unexploded bundle of fun.

Pains, another old favourite.

Of course there were also the bangers that we wasted all our hard-earned Penny-for-the-guy or paper-round money on to terrorise the neighbourhood with, but that's a whole different story.

I arrived at my customer's to find an eager neighbour's dog trying to snuffle into my groin as it was walked up the road. I sort of patted and pushed the mutt away in a friendly attempt to stop further embarrassment. I managed to coerce the mutt away with the help of its owner, and rang Wendy's doorbell

Wendy is part of the Heathfield Heffle Quilters. A small and enthusiastic group named after their patron, Dame Heffle, whose most important task of the village annual calendar was to release the cuckoo out of its wicker basket at the yearly Spring Cuckoo Fayre.

The Cuckoo Fayre was established centuries ago in the reign of Edward II. The name Heffle was just gypsy talk, or pigeon English, for Heathfield.

Legend tells that gypsies, traders, and pedlars from all over the area would descend to a clearing in the forest at Cade Street, near Heathfield, every spring. The fayre was always April 14$^{th}$ each year.

Dame Heffle was not, as one may think, the lady of the manor but in fact was one of the local gypsy girls who was granted the most important task of releasing the birds.

How the gypsies used to catch the elusive cuckoo to set it free was always a mystery.

The cuckoo would be released by Dame Heffle and as soon as its distinctive call was heard trading could begin. No trade was binding if made before the cuckoo's call!

Of course just in case the cuckoo flew off never to be heard again a gypsy would be waiting in the nearby woods to make the call.

**The Heathfield Village sign still depicts the cuckoo being released.**

Even Rudyard Kipling would make a pilgrimage in his Rolls Royce to the fayre from his home at Batemans.

In its prime a huge procession would march up Heathfield High Street to the fayre. At the head would be the honoured gypsy girl dressed as the important Dame Heffle and her basket of birds.

Once the cuckoo's distinctive haunting call was heard amongst the countryside all knew spring was here. The beautiful and tricky female cuckoo can lay up to 25 eggs in various nests before heading back to Africa.

Nowadays pigeons are used instead of cuckoos but the Heathfield village sign still depicts the old tradition. A cuckoo Fayre is still held at Halland each spring and tradition has it that no true cider brewer will tap or taste his barrels till he hears the first call of the elusive visitor to our shores.

Wendy's Heffle Quilters were attempting, with great success, Bargello Quilting, piecing tiny pieces of material together in an arrow-shaped pattern across a quilt.

Very time consuming—but the perfect job for her little Featherweight.

The 221 loves the small pieces where some of the larger modern machines with wide, zigzag, needleplate slots just cannot handle them. Over the years I have supplied many of her friends with the fabulous 221's that were born for quilting.

A stunning 1950 model 221 sewing machine. Perfection in engineering.

Along the lanes to my next call I spotted a witches hat in the gutter, probably lifted from some child's head in the high winds of late.

It reminded me of All Hallows Eve that had just passed, and the traditional **trick or treat-ing**. The witching hour had come and gone, where all the witches gather to make pacts with the Devil to keep the winter deep and dark, so they may play havoc. They must have got it right because the weather had been dreadful since Halloween.

People often think that Halloween is an American import but nothing can be further from the truth. Halloween is set into ancient Celtic roots long before Christianity or America was even discovered.

The Celts used to celebrate a time called Samhain (pronounced *sow-en*). It was the beginning of their new year and was celebrated at the first full moon, closest to what we now call the month of November. The dates changed a little after the Gregorian calendar was adopted in 1752 when we lost a few days. Today the Celtic New Year is accepted as being October 31$^{st}$.

The Celts believed that on that last night of the old year the dead could contact the living. It was the time when the two worlds of living and dead were closest. Now, that is okay if you have a nice dead relative, but what about someone who hated you or that you had killed in battle!

The Celts lit huge bonfires throughout the night to keep evil spirits away. They also made scary masks to chase away the demons. Part of that tradition survives in Halloween.

The Romans, always eager to assimilate a good thing, copied this religious belief and introduced their own harvest festival and, in typical Roman tradition, named a goddess after it. Pomona was the goddess of fruit and trees, she is often symbolised by an apple.

With the arrival of Christianity the whole affair was originally frowned upon as black magic. But, rather than upset everyone, it was sneakily accepted into its traditions.

November $1^{st}$ became a day to commemorate all the saints and became known as All Saints Day—or All Hallows. The preceding night became All Hallows Eve. So, all the saints who did not have their own special day could be celebrated on All Saints Day. In one simple stroke no one was forgotten

In ages past, the poor people and beggars would take the opportunity, for a small sum of money or for food, to pray for the living of the wealthy—for their continued good health and prosperity.

One of the foods that they were paid with, on All Souls Day, was a specially baked Soul Cake. It was a treat rather like a Bath bun or currant bun.

This treat was the origin of Trick-or-treating.

One unlucky 'learner' witch! Kings Drive, Eastbourne.

So how did Halloween get to America? Well, during the terrible hardships and potato famine of the mid-nineteenth century, countless numbers of Irish and Scots emigrants headed for a better life in the Promised Land.

With these emigrants went their traditions and Halloween found a new home. It was across the seas that children sang out the words from their homelands, *the sky is blue the grass is green now may we have our Halloween?*

America took the celebration to heart and, with their usual flare, made it into a fun-filled yearly event. Halloween, witches-and-all, returned to Britain many years later and was rediscovered, so-to-speak. What I am trying to explain, in my usual silly way, is that the tradition is much older and much more European than many people realise.

Witches on the other hand were very different. Sussex has a long history of witches and many met a grisly end. King James I, even wrote a book on them.

In olden days a witch would be tried and sentenced, as was Joan Usbarne in 1572. A Sussex Witch of some repute, she was sentenced to one year in prison for killing a neighbour's bull, poor girl. Many a witch had to suffer a dunking in the village pond—and many more nasty punishments. Another witch, Susannah Stacey, was well known and lived near Lewes. She was an accomplished faith healer and very popular in her time. Of course, most witches or cunning folk were simple herbalists who knew the ways of the wild.

My mum could always tell you ten ways to kill someone, with simple seeds and plants like hemlock, witchbane, yew, foxglove and laburnum. In old days she would have had to run—or end up on the dunking stool! I remember well her days at the Ripe Summer Fayre dressed as a gypsy, reading palms in her tent.

Suspicion ran rife in medieval times. Holly was grown along hedgerows to prick the witches' feet and stop them running along the top. Chimneys were built with twists and turns to stop them climbing down to steal the children. In Chester, in the North of England, one builder became rich building barley-twist shaped anti-witch chimneys.

Fires were lit on All Hallows Eves to scare away witches, before the Witching Hour in the dead of night. Witches were persecuted for several centuries, and countless poor souls went to their death because of the stupidity, intolerance and hatred of the period.

The most famous witch to be burnt at the stake was the poor village maid who rescued a kingdom and died for her beliefs, Joan of Arc, the Maid of Orleans. She was a pawn, in a much larger and dirty political power struggle. The young woman, who had inspired a nation, went to her death on the 30$^{th}$ of May 1431 and became immortal. Fables say that, as hard as they tried, her pure heart would not burn.

Besides the strange event in World War II when Helen Duncan was incarcerated as a witch for predicting the sinking of the HMS Hood and the HMS Barham, the last real witch trials in England were in 1682. Temperance Lloyd, Susannah Edwards, Alice Molland and Mary Trembles were all tried at Rougemont Castle in Exeter, Devon. The judge said that he thought that they were just senile old ladies, but the jury convicted them anyway. In 1684 they were hanged in Bideford, Devon. Only Alice Molland, though sentenced to death, escaped with her life. They were the last people to die for the crime of witchcraft during those awful times.

My favourite local fable of a witch from olden days was Nan Tuck. She lived just north of Buxted right in the middle of my area.

Nan Tuck is almost forgotten now to all but a few. She used to make potions to heal lame animals or sick children. A wise woman or witch, she knew the ancient ways of the woods. She was invaluable to the local community until one day she went too far. The story goes that she made a deadly potion to knock someone's husband on the head! When the local villagers found out it was her who was responsible for the death, they were out for blood.

A hoard of angry villagers with burning staffs headed for her hut in the woods. Nan Tuck ran for her life. She was chased through the thickly wooded area down to Buxted.

The villagers caught her and at midnight hung her from a tree in the woods. Her body was left to rot but the local vicar felt sorry for her, and buried her in unsanctified ground, under a stone slab, just outside the church wall by Buxted Village Church.

Today all that is left of her memory is Nan Tuck Road in Buxted. Few know of her passing but let me tell you, local legend has it there is still a place, under an old gnarled tree in the forest where she was hung, that no vegetation or flowers ever grow!

They say that her apparition still haunts the area, and she has been known to rise up from the ground behind the church wall, surprising young lovers on dark nights.

Centuries have passed since those dark days and all that remain are clues like Nan Tuck Lane or Witches Lane in Fletching.

Nowadays we can all look on the brighter side and enjoy the ancient ritual of Halloween in the spirit that it was originally meant to be, and great fun it is.

Just look how fashionable herbal remedies are now. Why, you can even buy them in the high street. Whatever next!

Katie & Laura have to be bribed with sweet things or else!

At Cherry Cottage I fixed a very over-worked Frister & Rossmann Cub while the owner told me of her great grandfather, the village tailor, who had passed some of his skills down through the family. He had earned such a good living from his trade that he lived in one of the largest houses in the village. I left, full of warm coffee and old stories and headed toward Lewes, passing her granddad's imposing house in Fletching as I went.

It might have been a drab grey day but at this time of the year there is still much to see in Sussex. Around the little villages and country lanes the wildlife prepares for winter, and farmers tidy up their land after the autumn storms.

The Land Rover rumbled down to The Bluebell Railway Line, then to Lewes and my next customer.

From Lewes I headed up-country. I could not help but wonder, as I drove, if I would make another hundred thousand miles fixing sewing machines, with my trusty old steed by my side. I smiled to myself, dropped the old girl into fourth gear and chugged up another twisty Sussex lane.

In Burwash Common I fixed my last machine for the day and headed toward home.

Passing Heathfield, I came to Cade Street. It is easily missed but a place of real interest to any historian. It is on a small back road, the B2096 out of Heathfield towards Battle. In Cade Street there is a small memorial to one Jack Cade. It marks the spot where, legend has it, that Jack Cade was captured.

Who was Jack Cade I hear you ask? Well hang on a mo' and I will tell you what I know about the man. I have mentioned Jack before in one of my books but have since learnt more about the man who shaped our past and left his mark on my area.

The whole area around Cade Street is ripe with history and, although Cade Street actually existed before Jack Cade came into this world, there is no doubt that it is because of him that it will be remembered.

Many areas were named after the families that lived in them, so it is more than probable that Cade, being a family name, could have been used for generations before the most famous of all the Cades left his footprint on history.

Jack Cade was a man of importance and, going by the place names, his family had probably farmed the area for centuries. Although some historians dispute that.

In the middle 1500's there had been unrest in the country for some time, and temperatures were running high. In 1450 Henry VI was up to his old tricks, raising taxes once again. It was the final straw. Cade and the countryside exploded with fury.

I feel for him, we seem to be suffering the same problem today. It seems that if the government could tax fresh air they would, all they needed was to find a way.

Henry had surrounded himself with sycophants and yes-men, he handed out land and favours to the select few. He knew little of what was happening to his subjects and cared even less.

Jack Cade and a few others managed to stir up a huge rebellion, of some 30,000 working men, and marched on London. Henry sent his royal troops out to meet the uprising. They clashed at Sevenoaks, so named for the seven oaks that grew on the common.

Henry's troops were defeated with pitchforks and scythes. They had completely underestimated the strength of the men that worked the land for their livelihood. Then the exuberant rabble of Sussex and Kentish yeomen marched on to the capital.

When they arrived, although their blood was up, the horde had lost sight of their objectives. They did not receive the welcome from Londoners that they had expected. The Londoners were not happy to see them. Propaganda was put about that they would kill them all! What was happening in the countryside ale houses of England was of little concern to Londoners as long as their food and goods arrived.

After a few minor skirmishes in the capital, around Blackheath and London Bridge, Henry, who had fled to Kenilworth Castle in Warwickshire, was ready to bargain. He sent the Archbishop of Canterbury and the Bishop of Winchester to bargain on his behalf and calm the rabble.

Cade presented his manifesto listing all the poor men of Sussex and Kent's grievances, Henry simply promised the leaders whatever they wanted.

Cade was sceptical because he had heard the King was on the verge of madness. He wanted to continue his quest for fairer taxes and changes to the law, but his colleagues, of who some were just out for plunder and gain, thought it better to grab what was offered and run.

The rabble faltered, the rebellion foundered, Rochester was plundered and Cade's men deserted. Frustrated, many of his faithful men dispersed and drifted back to their smallholdings and farms in Kent and Sussex.

Henry wasted no time and placed a large bounty on Cade and his henchmen. Jack Cade changed his name to John Mortimer, one he had possibly used before, and fled. However with such a bounty on him it was only a matter of time before he was caught.

While making for the coast in disguise, with the sheriff of Kent, Alexander Iden, hard on his heels, he was cornered in a garden near Heathfield. Cade put up a ferocious fight right to the end.

Legend tells that he died from his wounds before he could be officially put to death in London. However that was not going to deter the King out for retribution.

A ceremonial beheading of his corpse took place at Newgate. His head was preserved and placed on a spike on London Bridge for all entering the city to see. His body was quartered, wrapped in oil and tar cloths to stop it from rotting. Parts were then taken to each of the centres of unrest around the country and displayed as a warning to other troublemakers.

Jack Cade was a hero of the people, who met a gruesome death for his beliefs. He was a man out of his time, centuries before the first unions.

Shakespeare later wrote Cade into his play *Henry VI part II*. Cade was a believer in a state that no king could ever imagine, one that put the people first. Cade was the sort of man who often rises from a crisis, a man with beliefs so strong they can change empires.

It took another 500 years for his dreams to be realised.

All that is left to mark this great historical event is a small monument near Heathfield, at the spot where Jack Cade met his untimely and violent death many centuries ago.

He has crept into Sussex legend, and just one more of the local characters that makes this area so rich and fascinating.

# *The End*

*1066*

# W.O.M.B.A.T
*Wretched men starved, the land laid waste while Christ slept.*
England 1087

The Land Rover trundled down the back road from Battle on its way to Rye.

On my way to work I was cutting through the exact spot where William, Duke of Normandy, had risked all for the bounty of England. The prize of Europe was there for the taking and William had been the man to try. A blood-relation of the just-dead king, he was going to fight for his birthright and, on one furious Saturday in 1066, every inch of this place was soaked in blood.

In 1966 my dad took me to Battle to see a re-enactment of the great Battle of Hastings. I was nine years old and totally enthralled by this amazing centenary spectacle.

The sights of knights in armour clashing, spears and arrows flying, men shouting, attacking, retreating and dying was simply awesome to a bright-eyed child. All day I pushed through the crowds to see the action and get my first real taste of history.

Battle High Street is still full of ancient buildings

I have been captured by this special place ever since. William and Harold's world had been brought to life for me. As an excited child I lived the day as if I was there to see Harold falling, clutching the arrow in his eye. I saw William struggle over bodies to stand on the blood soaked ridge. To raise the Holy Flag and give thanks to God. I saw the corpses of the fallen and a country lost to an invader. A forgotten world had been reborn.

This tiny place, where England fell, is as special as any in the world, as special as the Little Big Horn or Pearl Harbour, Dunkirk or Stirling Bridge. It is where history was made.

Harold's final moment depicted on the 230ft Bayeux Tapestry.

My ardour was not diminished even, when later in the afternoon, I bumped into a rather drunk King Harold stumbling out of a pub, miraculously raised from the dead, still with his arrow attached to his helmet. He grunted, laughed and raised his beer glass to salute me. I ran off to try and tell my dad, who was buying commemorative stamps, that Harold lived!

From that moment on I studied every piece of information, every documentary, film, book and piece of gossip from the battle. I lived it and loved it. Even now as one of Battle Abbey's most frequent visitors I absorb more information. Being in the middle of my area and with a superb new coffee shop my stops are now more frequent than ever. I'll have my own seat soon!

I often stand where Harold fell, on a slight rise, probably one of the highest spots and last stands of the battle. His men would have fallen like Custer's, surrounded and doomed. On windy overcast days when visitors stay at home or linger in tea-rooms I feel the spirit of the battle rage around me.

This plaque marks the spot near where Harold fell.

William, the consummate politician, had a strong claim for the crown and had offered to settle his case in the courts but Harold knew that that was too risky. There were also rumours that the previous king, Edward the confessor, had promised William the throne in 1065 to stem Harold's power. If William produced evidence of this—his case was won.

It is a little known fact that William was on French soil even after he landed in England. William was no fool; the ground work had been prepared by his father years before. The whole area, known as Rameslie, was, although in England, owned by the Norman Abbey of Fécamp. It stretched from Hastings right through to Rye.

This gateway to England was the perfect place for William to set up camp and prepare his advance.

Fécamp monks acted as guides showing William the best way to advance through the land. For their service they were to become a huge influence in England for decades after the invasion.

It was not until 1247 that Henry III bought back the lands from the monks, however they kept one little piece just in case!

Just north of Rye on the Peasmarsh Road the Abbey of Fécamp still own land. To this day it is known as Rye Foreign!

Back to my story. Whatever his reasons, Harold, the popular new king, refused mediation. He would gamble with his life to keep the throne of England. It was to turn out to be a bad gamble.

Where my wheels now rolled two great armies had fought and thousands had died in bloody hand-to-hand combat. It was to become the most famous battle in British history.

It was the age of the axe, the sword and the spear. The age of muscle, bone and sinew. The age when the mighty took from the weak and great knights on chargers ruled. Where fortune favoured the bold and life hung on the blade of a sword. The very soil oozed their blood. For real history is far more than a tale of nobility, it is also the story of the common man.

With the land here so thick in history and the past so close, it's a wonder that the dead were not leaping out in front of me, ready to do battle once more.

A depiction of the High Altar built where Harold's blood soaked the ground.

William's more modern military machine won the day. They were a new breed of warrior, set to dominate Europe.

Their archers darkened the skies with piercing death moving ever closer to Harold's inner circle on the high mound. Huge armoured battle horses made constant massed attacks on Harold's troops. The Normans stood in their stirrups, legs straight and braced against their steeds. Lances tucked firmly under their arms. The Anglo Saxon warriors stood shoulder to shoulder, shields held tight, spears protruding. The ground shook. Horses, eyes-wide smashed head-long into the ranks.

Men were trodden into the boggy earth by flaying legs, horses were cut down. Norman knights would fall and be hacked to pieces. Many would be rescued, surrounded by following footmen. On foot, blades would be drawn, sword would clash with axe. A quick retreat, a new horse mounted, and another charge.

William and his paid mercenaries from across Europe had been fighting on foreign soil. However William took the precaution of destroying many of the ships that had carried his army to our shores. There would be no surrender and no return. This was a fight to the death. His men knew if they lost there would be no escape.

As the Bayeux Tapestry shows—it was all too much for Harold's men. By the end of the battle the new king and his men lay in pools of blood, their shields peppered with arrows.

William had brought with him the latest weapon of death, the first European crossbows! No armour was safe. The crossbow felled peasant and nobleman alike in a shuddering violent instant.

Although supposedly outnumbered, the hard-fighting better equipped Normans won the day. England was their prize.

The age of the Anglo Saxon, who had ruled England since the Dark Ages was brought to a brutal end, the time of the Normans had begun.

William was a true warrior and led from the front, having two horses cut from under him in the battle.

He was used to fighting out-numbered. Several of his previous battles in Normandy had been won against the odds. In fact he was alive against the odds. There had been a number of attempts on his life even as a child.

One assassin had managed to infiltrate his home and murder William's guardian right in the young duke's bedchamber, before being stopped seconds before he would have killed him. The result was a hard fighting, god-fearing man, the supreme ruler of the Normandy Dukes.

They say William only cried three times in his life. Once when he was crowned King of all England, when his wife Matilda died and once more on his deathbed when he repented his many sins!

At the battle for England he knew God was on his side. On his finger was a ring from the Pope with a lock of St Peter's hair, and in his camp was a consecrated banner waiting to be placed on his new throne.

William was a superstitious man, even promising an abbey if he was successful in his bid for the richest land in Europe. Having powerful priests on his side was healthy insurance.

How fewer than ten thousand men managed to conquer and then dominate the two million inhabitants of England still amazes me—if it is true!

Pevensey Court House holds details of nearly 900 ships landing at the old Roman fort which adds up to many more men than some records state.

Also I once came across a copy of an ancient Sussex Map and in the corner was some brilliant information. It goes roughly as follows—

*William the bastard Duke of Normandy* (obviously not a supporter, the bloke who wrote this, though technically correct, he was the son of a tanner's daughter.) *making his claim to the crown of England by affinity, adoption and promise arrived at the port of Pemsey with 896 ships furnished for war on the 28$^{th}$ of*

*September in the year of our Christ's incarnation 1066. And on the 14th of October, the following being a Saturday joined battle with Harold, King of England who in the field valiantly fighting was slain by the shot of an arrow into his brains. With him died Gerth and Leofwine his brethren and 67974 men besides. The place where they fought ever since does in memory thereof bear the name of Battayll.*

The story goes on to say how the Saxon rule of England was crushed and replaced by the Norman conquerors.

In truth there is no way that so many vessels held so few men, even with supplies and horses. For example, Viking long-boats held 80-90 men on a long voyage, not a quick cross-channel hop.

When Emperor Claudius attacked Britannia, centuries before, he brought with him 40,000 troops to subdue the country.

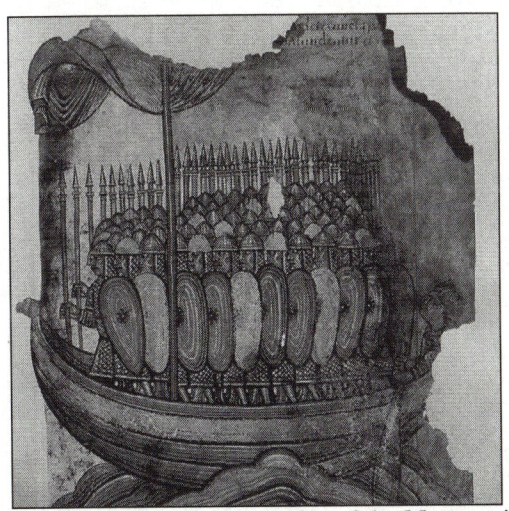

This rare, early medieval, manuscript of the Norman invasion shows one of Williams ships crammed with soldiers of fortune. Many of them went on to found the new aristocracy of our country.

William had spent years planning. Even if William's ships only held 50 men each, leaving room for equipment and horses that would make at least 44,000 troops.

This number is much more likely to suppress the most powerful country in Europe at the time. It would also give some credence to the Norman Chronicler, who stated that thousands of Harold's men were slaughtered in each of the fake retreats that William feigned during the battle.

At least twelve thousand men tried to come across in 1588 with only 122 ships during the Spanish Armada and Nasty Napoleon amassed 500,000 troops for his conquest. So the historian's numbers may be subject to question.

Whatever the real number, what we do know is that his victorious rule was truly murderous. Any who opposed him were slaughtered, their lands forfeit, their wives and children forced to work as serfs.

Where the actual battle took place the skies darkened with the black-winged carrion that fed upon the slain in bloodied fields. For a decade there bleached bones lay as a reminder of that terrible day.

Harold's mother fled to the Isle of Flat Holm to spend her days in mourning and solitude. It was from there, many years later, that Marconi broadcast the first radio waves.

You know what they say! To the victor belongs the spoils. Nothing was truer than this in William's case. He had won a battle and a nation. More land and wealth than he could have dreamed of.

One man now owned England! He could dispose of it, or anyone in it, as he wished. He quickly distanced himself from Rome so that the church did not have too much power and control.

The battlefield where King Harold and thousands of his men fought to the death is now quiet and tranquil. It is hard to imagine that for one day in 1066 this spot was filled with blood and screams as Norman and Saxon battled for England.

Modern historians are now trying to paint a different picture of William's reign, one of give and take, of compassion and tolerance to his subjects, but this is far from reality. The Normans ruled with power and fear.

Some 20 years after the Battle of Hastings, really an early Battle of Britain, when the first modern taxation form, or *Domesday Book*, was being put together, it was noted that dozens of small towns and villages still lay derelict from William's wrath.

The few uprisings, like that of the Exeter uprising in 1068 or Swaine of Denmark and Hereward the Wake in 1070, were brutally put down. Though they never captured Hereward!

The north of England suffered the *Harrying of the North* that laid it to waste for decades. Bodies rotted where they were slain, famine and pestilence followed.

Lady Godiva made her naked ride through Coventry in opposition to heavy taxes. She was one of the only Anglo-Saxon women to retain large land-holdings under the Normans. Her lands are mentioned in the Domesday Book and although her ride had no effect she did become immortal. Her statue still stands in Coventry.

Let me tell you I think she was an old woman when she did her ride. Now I've spoilt it for the men!

Back on the battlefield near Hastings, Harold's finest warriors the Housecarls had fallen around his banners, the fighting man and golden dragon of Wessex. Along with Harold and his brothers half the nobility of England, nearly 3,000 lords or thanes, had also been wiped out in a single battle. Never before or since has such carnage taken place amongst the nobility. Their mutilated bodies were stripped of their chainmail, weapons, clothing and possessions and left to rot.

The Normans only buried their own dead, leaving there enemy where they lay.

They named the crossing on the ridge near Hastings, where the London road was marked by an old twisted apple tree and where England fell, Senlac, or lake-of-blood.

As promised, William had plans drawn up for a superb abbey to mark the spot of his most famous victory.

A victorious William holds up the model for a new abbey to be built at Senlac Ridge, now Battle.

In the same way that the bodies were stripped, the country was plundered so that William could pay his debts to his knights. William kept half of England for himself, gave a quarter to the church and the rest to his noblemen.

The country was split into manors, it was a true feudal system. The new rulers, in turn, became the rich gentry of their captured country. Astoundingly one fifth of England is still owned by their desendants.

For example William De Warenne was granted 43 lordships. Tvrold the dwarf, William's jester, prospered. He was small but bold and danced in front of Harold's army, before the battle, taunting the Saxons to come down from the ridge to fight.

Robert le Bigod was another, a poor Knight who had fought with great gallantry at Hastings. Some say that after Hastings he was granted land in East Anglia and endowed with the estates of the Earl of Norfolk. Along with more Norman estates he became a powerful warlord.

His family prospered over the coming generations and became entwined with the royal household.

In 1553 Framlingham Castle, their seat of power, was given to Mary Tudor, later to become the infamous Bloody Mary, whose reign led to the foul deaths of so many in her attempts at religious purification. During her five-year reign, one of the last of the Catholic rulers of England burnt her way into the history books forever.

In 1701 the Act of Settlement was passed, stopping a catholic ever again becoming monarch of England.

One nobleman, Richard De Clare, had even taken the precaution of measuring the area of his lands in Normandy with rope, to make sure that William gave him similar size lands in England. That must have been some rope!

William's half-brother Robert, count of Mortain, who saved William when one of his horses was cut down in the battle, became the second largest land-owner in England besides William.

The Norman Nobles did not get it all their own way. As William was dishing out the rewards at Westminster, a strange thing happened that started a legend and was later acclaimed a miracle.

Bishop Wulfstan of Worcester was ordered by William to relinquish his bishopric so that he could hand it out as a prize to one of his followers.

Incensed by what Bishop Wulfstan saw as a great injustice, he strode over to the new stone tomb of Edward the Confessor and thrust his staff of office or crozier into the stone. The very same crozier that Edward had given him!

All who tried failed to remove the crozier, including Lanfranc the Archbishop of Canterbury and Bishop Gundulf of Rochester. Only Wulfstan, later to become Saint Wulfstan, had the miraculous power to remove the crozier.

William, ever the superstitious man, took this as a sign from God and allowed Wulfstan to remain Bishop, just in case!

It was the act of pulling the crozier from the stone that some say inspired the great legend of Arthur as a boy of 15 pulling Excalibur from the stone.

**Bishop Wulfstan of Worcester inspiring the Arthurian legend.**

Edward the Confessor was dead but not yet finished. He was to become immortal. Miracles were seen, even the touch of his tomb brought about miraculous cures and healing. Eventually Edward was made a saint and became the patron saint of the Plantagenets.

His body now lies in Westminster Abbey, one of the many abbeys and churches that he rebuilt.

In truth, the whole of English history, and in consequence the whole of the world's, changed because of two things— family squabbles and the wind.

All principal parties involved in the battles for England were related. It was one of Harold's brothers, the treacherous Tostig, who was instrumental in helping the Norse or Viking army. William, Duke of Normandy, also had family ties and a strong claim to the throne of England.

Harold, in fact, had the weakest claim. The biggest culprit was really the dead king, Edward the Confessor.

Much more into religion than leadership, he was a poor decision maker and a weak leader, more of a puppet king. He would appease rather than confront, which is fine at home but not running a feuding kingdom. The childless king became known as 'the confessor' because of his constant praying and meditation.

Edward, a direct descendant of one of our greatest kings, Alfred the Great, was in fact almost more Norman than English. He had a Norman mother and spent most of his first 30 years growing up in Normandy.

To pacify his constantly feuding warlords he seemed to have promised the throne to just about everyone. His wife was Harold's sister so you can imagine the ear-bending poor old Edward was getting. And Harold was basically the strongest warlord in England. Should he wish he could have taken the country by force, his father had tried before and almost succeeded.

As all waited for Edward's death, he supposedly woke on his deathbed, after conveniently losing the power of speech earlier, to miraculously regain it, reach out and offer the crown to Harold, then snuffed it! Convenient for Harold or what?

Most upsetting for the heir apparent Edgar Aetheling and, of course, the ambitious William! With at least three people promised the crown, only war could follow.

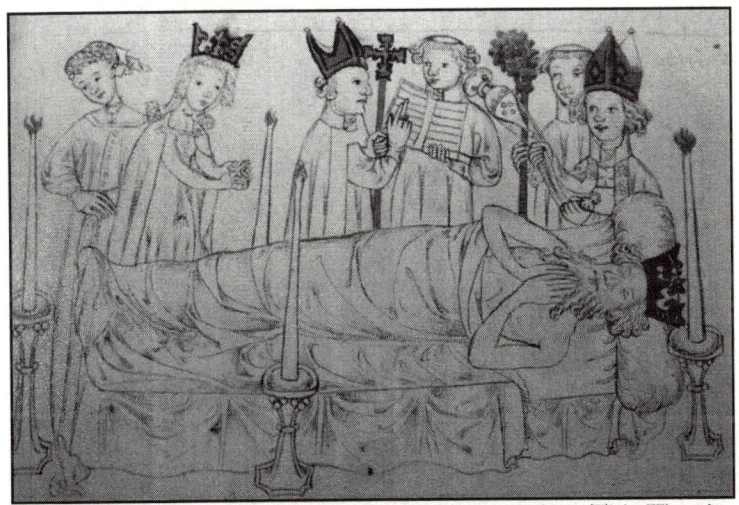

Edward's death as depicted in this early engraving. This King is dead long live the King!

Harold made sure that as soon as the king was buried he was crowned. In fact his coronation was on the same day. Burial in the morning, coronation in the afternoon, not even waiting for relatives to turn up! What sort of coronation was that?

By grabbing the crown Harold became the second Harold to be King of England, Harold II. He upset many of his relatives in the process. The powerful lord was a popular choice among the people after the weak Edward. Harold's years of fighting along the tough Welsh Borders had made him a feared and respected warrior that no one on English soil would challenge alone.

Harold was to have a short and tumultuous reign as predicted by the stargazers and fortune tellers of the day.

**Harold's rushed coronation 1066. Little did he know that he and most of his family would be dead in a few months!**

In the skies that April a comet had raced across the heavens. Priests squabbled and declared the omens were bad. It was a sign of foreboding and doom to all!

When William heard the news of Harold's coronation he flew into a violent rage. Ten years he had waited for the throne only to find that Harold had snatched it from under his nose. He swore that Harold *the oath breaker* would die by his hand!

In 1064, just two years previously, Harold had been captured by William while trying to rescue one of his brothers in

Normandy. Some say he was on a peace mission to see William. How or why he was in Normandy is obscure but while he was in Normandy and a *guest* of William he supposedly gave his oath of allegiance to the Norman duke. However true, it was, with other inducements, enough of an excuse to secure the Pope's blessing for an attack on England!

Now come on, if I was captured by someone like William, I would have said the same as Harold. It would be a simple choice, agree with his demands or meet an untimely demise!

Whatever the truth, as in a grand Shakespearian drama, the stage was set. Over the next few months of 1066 two great armies were created one to invade the shores of England and one to protect them.

William had forests felled and hundreds of ships built. Thousands of horses were rounded up and trained for war, some wealthy knights having several each. A fully-trained war-horse was the most expensive item of a nobleman's equipment costing as much as a house. Unlike the Anglo Saxons, who fought on foot, the Normans lives depended on their mounts and quick back-up if the horse went down. It was all part of the extensive training and preparation for war.

Blacksmiths worked day and night forging steel into arrowheads, lances and swords. Armour was beaten into shape that was to help win a nation.

In Scandinavia Vikings drank and sang great songs and readied themselves for battle. In England men were rallied from their homes and farms to pay their yearly dues and serve the King.

Both the Norman and Norse armies were really instigated by William who was playing a deadly game of winner-take-all, offering his Norwegian allies anything they wanted to attack. They were false promises; William wanted to play one against the other to weaken both armies. It worked.

I also believe that long before, William's father Robert, had drawn up plans to conquer England, and William grew up with that dream. Although Robert had died on a crusade to the Holy Land when William was only eight, the seeds had been sewn.

William grew into the most powerful duke in Normandy, slaying his rivals one after another and as his power grew he wanted England! A direct descendant of Viking blood, he became strong, bold and violent.

By July William was ready in Normandy—but he had no favourable wind. If the wind blew from the south William could sail. If the wind blew from the east the Norse army, under Hardrada and Harold's brother Tostig, could sail.

Either way Harold was in trouble. William had skilfully planned this double-pronged attack, promising Hardrada the world. Hardrada had a terrible reputation, his name even meaning tyrant!

Harold's men had been waiting months for invasion and were restless to get back to their families and to their harvests. But they had to wait week after week for either the Normans or the Norse to invade. Scouts scoured the seas and cliffs for signs, but none came.

In that strange way that fate has of working, soon after Harold had dismissed his main army of 13,400 men, known as the Feared, news reached him of a landing up north.

The soldiers, who had already served their two-month duty, had gone back to work the land and bring in the harvest that would see their families through winter. They had to be hurriedly recalled. Can you imagine a poor fellow, no sooner getting back to his family and land, having supper with his children, kissing his wife and feeding his animals only to be told to gear up and get back! I bet there were a few swear words in old English!

While the wind blew from the east for weeks, keeping William's fleet at bay, it had allowed the Norse to sail. Their longboats, with sails billowing, ploughed towards England. The course of history was set!

The Northern Earls were slaughtered at Fulford. Scarborough and York were laid waste in bloody violence by the marauding Vikings in search for land and power.

Harold had no choice but to leave the beaches of Sussex. He marched north at unbelievable speed, some say up to 45 miles a day. His men moved up the old Roman road toward York to meet Hardrada, and brother Tostig, at Stamford Bridge. Bye-the-way the Norwegian king also had a flimsy claim to the throne of England and it was first come first served.

However all the fierce war-songs and epic tales of the Norsemen were not going to save them from a surprise attack by Harold's swift army.

A great slaughter fell upon the unsuspecting Vikings. The Norsemen that had arrived with over 12,000 men in countless longboats crawled back in just a handful.

The infamous giant of a Norwegian king died, with an arrow in his throat, and Harold's brother was hacked to pieces with two-handed battle-axes.

Destroyed, the Scandinavian marauders were never to invade English soil again. There would be no more great songs of conquest sung over foaming beer and roaring fires, just one poignant saga of the defeated Norseman. Such was their defeat that the reign of the Viking in olden times was over.

It was an end to a chapter of our history and a beginning of another. But Harold's astounding victory was short lived.

The battle of Stamford Bridge would have been one of the greatest victories in our history but, because of what was to follow, it would be relegated to a minor footnote in our past.

Harold took a few moments after the battle to contemplate. He was once close to his brother Tostig, but family feuding and betrayal had left them bitter enemies. In death however all was forgiven.

Historians say it was this family rift in Anglo Saxon England that was the country's downfall. Had the family not fought but stayed strong together they would have beaten off any attack.

Harold was burying his brother in York Minster when news reached him of William's landing on the South Coast. What a blow! Little did he know that a few days later he and most of the nobility of England would be dead on a hillside in Sussex.

Had the wind stayed in the east for longer Harold would have had time to recuperate, gain fresh men and supplies and march south, gathering arms and archers along the way. When William arrived Harold would have been waiting.

In all likelihood a freshly prepared re-stocked army may have beaten William. But in that strange way that fate has of playing her hand, no sooner had Harold defeated the Norse than the wind turned and William's fleet sailed from the River Dives in Normandy.

Our history was to be changed forever by the wind.

Poor Harold was forced to march, ill-equipped and already suffering huge losses, to meet William near Hastings, at the opposite end of his realm. As he moved south he passed through his realm, through the villages and towns of Saxon England. It was a world that he had sworn to protect and a world that was all about to end on a bloodied mound near the South Coast.

I have written in detail about the Battle of Hastings before and we all know what happened. You only have to visit the abbey to see and hear the tales. That's if you can get by the French students, who are ferried over almost daily to see the site of their greatest victory.

Battle Abbey today is an imposing site

William out-manoeuvred Harold and over a fierce day of blood and guts took England. Harold had died fighting on the highest part of the ridge. The Normans had worked mercilessly upward all day to that point and Harold's death.

Harold, or what was left of him, after the Normans had cut him to pieces, was said to have been buried on the shore at Hastings and later moved by his family to Waltham Abbey where he was secretly interned. Or was he?

In the north of England, near Chester, an old tale is told to this day. It is of a one-eyed Saxon knight who, after being hit in his right eye and surviving a great battle near Hastings, lived out his life in the woods as a hermit. Who really knows?

I remember Spike Milligan witnessing an accident with several other people. They all saw the same event and all gave completely different statements. Spike said that he would never believe a history book again!

The Abbey Seal showing the front entrance.

What we do know is that King William, the first true king of all England, reigned for many years, building such great castles as the Tower of London, Dover Castle and countless others.

At Warwick Castle the original Motte & Bailey mound of 1068 is still visible!

Not since Roman times had such a building frenzy happened. He brought feudalism to England and from then on the King owned everything, granting land and favours to whoever he liked.

A great meeting of all the nobles gathered on Lamus Day at his palace, built on the Iron Age remains of Old Sarum near Salisbury.

Here the new nobility of England swore an oath of loyalty to William and witnessed the handing over of the almost complete, and dreaded Domesday Book, so called as its findings were as final as the Last Judgement! Dom is old-English for judgement.

According to several beliefs on Judgement Day all the good and bad deeds that you have done during your life will be weighed and judged by God. He will pass the Last Judgement on your soul. You had better be good! How about a quick pilgrimage to touch a few old Saints bones at cathedrals around the country? We could take a coach tour and all tell stories along the way like a modern Canterbury Tales. That would be fun.

One point of interest in the Domesday Book was that one tenth of the population of England were slaves! Provisions for a female slave were noted: Eight pounds of corn, one sheep, one sester of beans (don't ask me what a sester is), One penny in the summer but two pence in winter, food at Christmas and harvest time.

The Domesday Book, Document Number One in the Public Records Office, now lives at the National Archives in Kew.

William died, shortly after the completion of the Domesday Book, in 1087. He was suppressing an uprising in his native land later the same year. After burning the town, he was surveying the carnage, treading on hot ashes his beast reared up, throwing William and bursting his stomach on the pommel of his saddle. The injury that he sustained led to a slow and painful death. He was 60.

William was not fondly remembered, one obituary simply declared: *"He built castles and oppressed men."*

Another stated *"Wretched men starved, the land laid waste while Christ slept."*

In death William was treated with the same distain that he had treated others. While his sons and nobles scrambled to gain power, his body was stripped of all finery and dumped. His obese, swollen corpse was later stuffed into an undersized coffin and buried amidst the stench of rotting flesh.

He is, to my knowledge, one of the few kings of England not to be buried on English soil.

**Battle Abbey is run by English Heritage and still has a school inside its walls.**

His second son and successor, William II—nick-named Rufus due to his red-faced complexion, died instantly in 1100, being shot through the chest out hunting in the New Forest.

The debate still continues—whether it was an accident or not—but let me just say that his hunting party included a man who had already tried to overthrow him and his younger brother Henry, who shot to Winchester and seized the Royal Treasury.

William's direct descendants ruled for nearly a century and it was full of bloody in-fighting, brothers feuding and suspicious deaths.

The supreme Norman rule came to an end in 1154 with the death of King Stephen, William's grandson.

Blood descendants, including one of our greatest kings, Henry II, and his sons John and Richard the Lion Heart, were all distant relations. However as I have said many times in my scribbling, that is a whole different story. Now back to our journey.

I was about to spend an hour at a most annoying customer's house. It all started at the door.

**"Identification?"**

Taken aback I handed her my card with a forced smile.

"You are ten minutes late! What have you to say for yourself?"

Wow! I was being interrogated from the start. "I am so sorry Mrs Hill, traffic has been appalling and what with all the snow and ice!"

I was cut off with a wave of the hand, instructed to remove my shoes and was taken to the machine in a back washroom. But once I started to work on the machine she was at it again. It was like the Gestapo quizzing me.

"Exactly what are your qualifications?" she stared down her nose at me like a dried prune of a teacher. "I'd like to know before I allow you to touch my machine." Then her equally obnoxious husband came in and asked if my car leaked oil as it was on his drive!

By now I was silently bubbling, wondering why I bothered to get out of bed on such a cold and miserable day. I had spent a lifetime in the rag-trade and it was not her asking, so much, as the loathsome manner in which she did it. My choice was either to pack up my tools and walk out or grovel to the lady of the house so that she would let me work on her machine.

Seeing as how work meant money, in true self-employed spirit, I took the middle road.

I felt like Clint Eastwood in one of those *Spaghetti Westerns* where he rides into town and is abused by strangers. He gets off his mule and walks over to the men, his piercing eyes hidden below the rim of his hat, gun hand ready. He talks out of the side of his mouth while puffing on the stub of a cigar.

"My mule don't like people laughin' at him. Now if ya apologise like I know you're gonna." Laughter—gunfire—silence. A whisp of smoke as Clint walks away.

With spurs jangling and trigger-finger twitching I looked straight at my customer, "Look, Mrs Hill, it is very simple, would you like your machine working or not?"

Throwing a direct question at her took her aback—but only for a second. She threw me such a filthy look I thought I was going to have to run to a sink and wash it off!

Obviously she was used to giving orders and not accustomed to any lip from the tradesmen!

However, she needed her machine fixed and I was the man to get it working. She reluctantly agreed—and left me. No need to imagine what I was thinking as she left!

I repaired her machine just as fast as my cold little fingers could work, and hit the road without so much as a backward glance.

I left in the sure knowledge that had I sprinkled the machine with rose petals and bathed it in scented ass's milk she would still have moaned.

I had learnt, many years ago, that you can never please everyone. No matter how hard you try it is simply an impossible task. Another fact I had learned on my travels is that we all have problems. Every one of us.

They may be as different and numerous as the stars above, but each day we are confronted with them. I have always thought that they don't even disappear after you die. You just become someone else's problem. How they are going to bury you, your relatives, your money or whatever.

We all just have to get on with life the best we can.

My next customer was little better, a real beauty. She did not have an attitude—or, as far as I could discover, a brain! I had started cleaning and repairing her filthy machine when she announced in a loud squeaky voice that it had hardly been used and probably only needed the belt tightening or something simple like that!

She reminded me of a demented parrot squawking in a temper in her cage. I was not bothered if she had used it or not. I was still going to fix it for her. That was my trade. I wondered if she ever ended up on an operating table if she would instruct the surgeon on what to do?

Quite often customers think that if they say that it has hardly been used, then there can't be too much wrong with it, as if the words are enough to convince the machine and the engineer to ignore all of the facts. It was obvious, from the state that it was in, that it had been hammered. Her "*I know better*" manner was biting into me.

I prayed for silence but found myself retaliating. "If you have not used it, why are the bearings so worn?" I asked, raising my eyebrows.

"Dunno," came her vacant reply.

"Where'd all this muck and fluff come from then? It is only produced by sewing!"

"Dunno!"

"Have you had the machine from new?"

"Yeah."

"Then someone must have been using it!"

Silence...

"Look at all these scratches on the bed and the chips in the paint!"

"Nah, not me."

"What about these large dents?"

"Well I dun hit it didn't I!"

"Why?"

"It was playing me up so I whacked it wiv' the stick—twice."

"Did it help?" I asked in utter astonishment.

"Nah."

What a woman! I simply could not get a truthful answer out of her. I wondered if she could even lie straight in bed!

She picked up the stick that had been resting in the corner of the room, to show me. At the very same moment the dog who had been sleeping soundly in the corner quietly skulked out of the room!

I gave up disagreeing with her. All the lights were on but it seemed that no one was home.

I had no stamina left, and dealing with such a woman was proving too much. All she did was moan, moan, moan. She moaned more than an old people's home after the residents had been told dinner was cancelled and the heating was being turned off.

When I returned from the car after getting a part, I noticed her walk smartly away from my toolbox. I looked down into it and saw that my last three packets of needles were gone.

*My God*, I thought, *the cheeky mare has sticky fingers! She's helped herself to a five-fingered discount.* I said nothing, but later I added the needles to her bill.

When I gave her the bill she looked as if she was going into anaphylactic shock. I didn't bother to mention that I had not put my charges up for over four years and that she had just helped herself to a few freebies!

Everything else in the last few years had shot up—especially fuel which had doubled—but my prices stayed the same. As new machines became ever-cheaper, putting my charges up was not an option. Otherwise, people would just throw their old machines away and buy a new piece of plastic.

Boy was I glad to escape! I left as if the place was on fire. As I drove off she shouted to me. "Don't wanna' see you again—know what I mean? No offence like."

*That made two of us*, I thought, as the Land Rover bumped up and down along the lane. If I never saw her again it would be a day too soon!

Driving away from my customer I was feeling as depressed as the winter weather. People had even been complaining about me being early! I stopped at the end of the lane and parked-up for a moment.

I ran my hands through my hair and rubbed my burning eyes. My breathing was slow and heavy. I knew from bitter experience that more than a handful of bad customers in a row and I would be depressed all day. One more like her and I would shoot myself. Only in the foot as I would need to carry on working!

One problem with getting older is that you get more cynical, something that I hated happening to me. Oh where were my mad eccentric customers when I needed a laugh, not here, not today!

*Time waits for no man* I thought as I turned the ignition key, *unlike the grim reaper who had been waiting for me for over 50 years and was hopefully getting bored.* The car sprang to life and I pulled up to the junction. As I turned onto the main Rye road I had to laugh out loud, the road sign reminded me of where I was, *Dumb Woman Lane*. How positively perfect!

It had been a miserable start to the year. I was loosing my favourite customers at the convent after the remaining nuns had decided to join another group and would soon be moving. They had rattled around in the big manor for far too long and when they had to have walkie-talkies to keep in contact with each other, the decision was made to move. Without consulting me, I might add!

The vicar and his wife in Ashdown Forest had moved to Salisbury, and so I had lost my favourite drive down their old pony road, through the great ancient woodland. A large factory that I had helped set up closed its doors and headed for Eastern Europe, where they could get the same goods manufactured at a fraction of the price. Fanny Lulu's Café in Newhaven had closed, depriving me of the best bacon buttie this side of Brighton.

Frank Richardson, the old upholsterer who ran Hannams in Cavendish Place had decided to retire, twenty years late. No more would he tut, tut, tut, picking up bits of thread I had dropped while he carefully wound them around an old spool to use again.

"Lads of today," he would mutter, "don't know they're born."

He was still driving around Eastbourne in the same old green 1950s van he'd had since I was a kid.

To top it all off, two of my favourite customers had died. Jenny Skinner, who was a keen machinist, had left to join her quilting group in the sky. I remember once laughing so hard at her attempts to show me an old dance that I could not stand up. I was crying with laughter, tears running down my face and having trouble breathing, when she agreed to stop, purely for my health.

Then my oldest customer had popped her clogs at the tender age of 98! Maud had promised me to make it to 100 but never quite managed. I thought about a letter of complaint to St Peter!

The weather was drab, real brass-monkey stuff. The snow that had covered East Sussex had turned into dirty grey mush. Broken ice lay in puddles like shattered mirrors. Buildings that, for a short while, had been turned into diamond-encrusted palaces from a fairytale had returned to their normal sombre attire.

For two days I had driven through another world of ice queens and dramatic landscapes. The snow had covered the South East in a diamond-white blanket. The crisp, powder-blue skies, and brilliant white had made all of the ordinary seem extraordinary.

Kids ran home from their schools, throwing snowballs, their fingers burning. Then rushing up the sugar-coated hills, wrapped in thick coats and scarves with their sledges tugged on bits of old string with their breath trailing like little fire dragons. There footprints were closely followed by puffing adults of all shapes and sizes crunching through the snow.

Snow has that magical ability to bring the child out in all of us, well most, there are always the moaners!

The hardy Sussex sheep carried on, oblivious in their thickest winter coat, layered with an extra covering of snow. They pawed the ground before nibbling at the grass beneath and ignored the screaming kids rushing past.

As each breath of wind shook the trees they dropped showers of sparkling snowflakes from their laden branches. The snow silently fell, muffled by the all-enveloping softness. It was inspiring, beautiful and, sadly, now all gone.

I passed Rye Pottery, noticing a row of clay pigs on display. The old pottery clings to life on the thread of a few passing tourists. I am sure its days are numbered as tourists seek thrills and spills, not ancient traditions.

The little clay pigs come from an old tradition in these parts. A long time ago, when life revolved around small hamlets, the Sussex Pig ruled supreme. He was a mighty pig, proud and fat, the envy of the land.

The reason for the pig's health and weight was the lush grazing lands to the south and the deep, rich, forests to the north of the county, and the time-honoured tradition of Pannage.

Pigs spent months on the fertile farms of Sussex but, come autumn, they were in for a treat. The farmers would march the pigs up to the ancient Wealden forests. Here they fattened on acorns and chestnuts, moss, forest fruits and even truffles.

All the bounty of nature was there for the snuffling.

This tradition of pig fattening went on in this area for so many centuries that the pig-paths became tracks and, eventually, roads. If you could travel back in time to the earliest human farmers in our area, you would have found them marching pigs into the forests in autumn. Domesday records show that in 1086 over 150,000 pigs were being driven into the lush forests for fattening.

If you travel on a small road, around my area, that leads directly from the coast into the forest, you may well be travelling on an old pig-path. If you examine a map of this area closely, you will see many of these types of road. They don't lead to villages or towns, as most normal roads would, instead they travel straight up to where once rich forests flourished.

Some give themselves away by being deeply furrowed from centuries of pigs marching to and from the ancient Sussex woodlands of Anderida.

In-between the great North and South Downs lies the area know as the Weald, Saxson for forest. The sunken pig-lanes, that were once so plentiful, ran into the Weald. Over the centuries of pig migration, the pigs would clear the woodland under the trees so thoroughly that clearings were made.

These clearings, known as dens, became the perfect place for humans to settle, so the first human settlements in the weald followed.

Today, many of the towns and villages that end in *den*, such as Tenterden, Cowden, Newenden and many others were originally from these humble pig-clearings in the ancient woodlands. At one time there were dozens of such villages but most have now disappeared. The only mark left an old pig-road that leads nowhere. Funnily some of these pig-lanes are now rat-runs, or shortcuts that cars race through, a bit of a difference!

Pigs were so important to a family, and to the community—for food and bartering—, that one of the best presents at a wedding was a live pig. Thus a Sussex pig became a traditional wedding present.

As time rolled by, in the annoying way it does, many of the rural hamlets that survived became villages—then towns. The largest is Benenden.

It became a little impractical to give a live pig as a wedding present when you lived in a row of terraced houses! Mind you, they made a comeback during times of war and deprivation, when many a back-yard held a jolly pig or two.

In the New Forest the age-old tradition of Pannage still survives for a few commoners. They have the Right of Mast to allow their pigs to feed for 60 days on the forest fruits. This works well. The pigs love green acorns and waffle them with joy. The green acorns are poisonous to the ponies, so all benefit, fat pigs and healthy ponies.

A traditional family loo & pig-hut

With the pig's demise, the tradition continued in the form of a little clay pig, rather than a real one, given as a present. Rye Pottery, at present, still makes them. Sweet little critters they are too. I have one on my dining-room sideboard, smiling at me every evening.

Keeping a pig and killing a pig are two different things.

While all the family could take scraps and chuck them to the beast, only an expert could despatch it humanely. When the time came for the pig to be used to provide for the family and keep them fed through the bitter winter months, the slaughter-man would be called.

I won't go into detail but the old saying *kicking the bucket* probably comes from the tying up and despatching of the family pig. The bucket, used to catch the precious blood that made pig's or black pudding, was often kicked in the struggle.

The pig that was fed on waste throughout the year and slaughtered in autumn, provided for the whole family.

Besides all the normal cuts of meat there was also kidneys, bacon, ham, black pudding, sausages (intestines for the skins), brawn, liver, cured meats, sweetbreads, brains, trotters boiled and pickled. No part was wasted. The pig skin was superb for gloves and patching, the bristles for brushes and needles, even the bladder was blown up and kicked around the yard by the kids.

I have said before that no part of the pig was wasted—except the squeak and, later, even that was found a use. It was sold to British Leyland in the 1960's, for their brakes!

The saying *going the whole hog* comes from the time it was much cheaper to buy the whole beast from the butcher than just parts of it—, just thought I would pop that in.

I parked in Rye town centre and walked up Turkey Cock Lane noting that even Rye, one of the most picturesque small towns in all England, looked fed up.

The old cobbled streets were strewn with litter that could not be cleared while the snow covered the ground. The ancient houses that lined the narrow streets looked frozen. Normally the buildings leaning toward each other reminded me of fishwives gossiping over the garden fence. However, today, they were silent save for the biting wind whistling through the crooked alleys.

People rushed by, heads down, clutching hats and collars, in the cold easterly breeze that rushed up the river estuary from a leaden and menacing sea. Its' icy fingers searching for the slightest gap in their winter clothing.

Out in the Channel the breeze was rising sharply with a storm riding its tail, chasing it all the way from Scandinavia. The ancient gods of the Norse people were arguing in the heavens. Loki and Odin were tussling in the firmament, causing all simple mortals below to suffer their wrath.

Jim Sutton would be down on the shorefront looking at the darkening horizon. Jim's family had been in the same business for a thousand years. They use funnel nets, hardly changed through the centuries, placed at low tide to catch fish. Mentioned in the Domesday Book, his family business is quite possibly the oldest family business in the world.

The weird name of Turkey Cock Lane supposedly came from a monk, whose ghost is said to still haunt the old cobbles of Rye. As punishment, after trying to elope with a young woman, the monk was said to have been bricked up alive somewhere near the lane. As he slowly starved he went mad and gobbled like a turkey, hence the name!

There are many ghost stories around Rye and some may have a foundation in truth. When the railway came to this area two skeletons were unearthed, clutching each other in an eternal embrace. They added substance to the old stories of Cantator and Amanda, another unfortunate young man from the priesthood, and his lover, buried alive after trying to flee across the marshes!

I stood on my next customer's doorstep, took a deep breath and knocked on the door. I steeled myself for another negative onslaught.

"Alex! How lovely to see you my dear. Do come in. Let me take your coat. The fire's on and the kettle's hot. How did you manage to get through? I was expecting a call saying you couldn't make it because of the weather!"

How welcoming her warm words were on such a day. I smiled for the first time. I thought to myself, *isn't it funny how easy it is to please someone and how seldom we do.*

"Takes more than a few inches of snow and a bit of ice to stop my old Land Rover Letty! What is that gorgeous smell?"

"Fresh bread. Fancy a slice?"

I thought I must have died and gone to heaven. I had completely forgotten that Letty was a little jewel.

What a difference one person with a happy countenance can make to a day. I wish that I had at least one *Letty* in every part of East Sussex, so that I could call on her every day during my rounds.

"Letty, I would love a slice—if it tastes half as good as it smells it will be delicious."

"I've bought a new machine that makes the bread all in one. Just pop all the ingredients in and press the button. A few hours later—bingo! Hubby has put on six pounds since we bought it, so now he is rationed to two slices a day. And then only if he has been good!"

"Alex, would you be so kind as to get the Singer out from under the table? I find it a job to lift at my age."

"I thought you told me you were only 37!" I laughed.

"Just because I reverse my age doesn't mean it's true Alex." We were both smiling now.

"Oo'h, it's been a long time since a man has got down on his knees to me," she giggled.

"Letty, don't make me laugh," I groaned, hoisting the old beast onto her table. "If I pull something in my back you'll have to carry my tools to the car!"

"There's many a good tune still played on an old fiddle you know Alex!"

"Letty, I must tell you that it is a pleasure to be here. I have had an awful day—nothing but moans from my customers."

"Oh, you don't want to worry about pleasing everyone Alex! You'll never do it even if you lived to be a thousand. You'll always meet a WOMBAT or two in life."

"Wombat?" I enquired wondering what a squat, chubby, buck-toothed Australian marsupial had anything to do with my previous moaning customers—except looks.

"**W**aste **O**f **M**y **B**rains **A**nd **T**ime, WOMBAT!" She shouted back to me as she headed off to her kitchen.

*How absolutely perfect* I thought. One word that summed up how to react to the depressing- moaning customers or anyone who was that way inclined. I made a mental note to silently refer to the next moaner as a WOMBAT. I was feeling better already.

Letty brought my elevenses while I was still smiling at her last remark. She was so right because today I had met more than my fare share of WOMBATS. Normally they are diluted amongst the thousands of customers but today they were all together.

"That'll put the roses back in your cheeks my dear."

I settled down to servicing her old sewing machine, with a pot of coffee and a plate of soft bread and jam by my side.

The roaring fire danced away in the hearth below the old smoke-seasoned timbers and Letty charmingly chatted about all the things she had made on her machine since I had last called. The warmth of the old house wrapped itself around me and comforted me, like a friend massaging my shoulders.

A calm came over me—as if all the troubles in the world were irrelevant—as if just this room, just here and now, was all that mattered.

I was at peace, pampered by the sweetest old dear—whose ability in life was to make someone feel needed. To make me feel like an important part of her life. What a welcome change from my previous customers! Isn't it always the way that the smallest things in life can often give us the most joy?

As I left her home she pulled my collar up around my chin and said, "Alex just remember—sing like nobody's listening—dance like nobody's watching—love like you've never been hurt and always work like you don't need the money."

With my mood lifting I started to notice the outside world. I had visited Doreen, my next customer, many times before. She is one of the more colourful characters of Rye who, though in her late seventies still sews daily for the local drycleaners. With her husband, Jim, they buzz around Rye carrying out alterations and repairs. They are known locally as the A-team.

Doreen would often tell me of her early days in London as a theatre-costume maker.

Doreen, from the East End, started work at 14 in 1945 and worked for a Russian Lady in the West End of London. Katya Krassen was to teach Doreen the fine craft of dressmaking in her Saville Row shop.

In London there were several companies specializing in television, film and theatre costumes. Among the best known was the Burmans Company, and another called Angels, run by the three Angel brothers.

The one Doreen worked for was Blacks in Shaftsbury Avenue. George and Alfred Black had taken over the theatre costume business from their father. With a huge warehouse in Wimbledon they fitted everyone from Tony Hancock to Charlie Chester and the Tiller Girls.

In her house she still had a few pictures of famous dancers and performers of yesteryear, clothed in spectacular gowns— all made by her fair hand.

A superb photo stood out. Miss Blackpool in a costume so stunning that it would stop the show.

**Doreen making adjustments to Miss Blackpool's dress**

"I remember my favourite dress was for a gawky, bucktoothed, girl who became a beauty. I am sure from my memory that she was living in a small flat near a horsemeat-butcher's in London," reminisced Doreen as I worked on her industrial machine.

"She had the voice of an angel and perfect pitch, that girl—it was so clear and pure. She used to sing at her aunt's dance school. But later I saw her go into a studio in Hanover Square. You could hear her beautiful voice float all the way down the road. Although she was a child she had the power and range of a gifted adult, very rare."

"One day I was asked to make a very special dress for her because she was to be the youngest ever performer in front of the King and Queen at the London Palladium.

"It was beautiful with huge ruffled open-capped sleeves and pleated neck. At the Royal Command Variety Performance, alongside Danny Kaye, she sang God Save The King and another song that rhymed with mayonnaise but for the life of me its name is gone. I'm sure she was hardly twelve! After the show she was presented to Her Majesty the Queen and Princess Elizabeth. King George was unfortunately ill. I read all about it in the fish & chips paper a few days later. She went on to star in some of the most successful films of all time."

"Doreen, don't keep me in suspense. Who was it?"

"A'vent you guessed me dear… It was the pigtail prodigy herself, Mary Poppins— Julie Andrews!"

"Wow! Now I'm impressed," I said, astonished.

"Oh yes, people think she had it easy, but she had to work, that girl. I think from memory that she used to be Julie Wells but it would make no matter what her name she was a star. Her stepdad, who she always called pop, trained her. He was a super performer called Ted Andrews. Give him a guitar and an audience and he was away. A friend told me once that during the Blitz he would perform down the tubes in the underground with bombs falling all around. People would cheer over the sounds of the debris falling. Now that's an entertainer!

I was as proud as a parent every time we went to the flicks to see her latest film. I ain't laughed and cried so much in all me life as when we went to see the Sound of Music. Best film ever made—mark me words!"

Julie Andrews singing her heart out at the Palladium in **1948**.

*Life is full of surprises,* I thought as I drove from Rye along the twisting Sussex Lanes and left the ghosts of the past to fade into the story books of the future.

I passed the place where the old town of Winchelsea was lost in several great storms in the 13$^{th}$ century. A swollen red October moon was a foreboding sign of the coming tempests.

The town was rebuilt, by permission of the Edward I, on a hill nearby called Iham. Winchelsea was one of the first towns to be built on the modern grid-system used today in so many cities, with the addition of strong fortified walls to keep invaders out, though the Spanish and French both succeeded in sacking the town.

Besides all the hidden secrets there like Spike Milligan's grave and the Methodist leader John Wesley's last open-air sermon in 1790, there are three amazing facts about the mini-town that astound me and show what a busy place it once was.

Firstly the king once sent 25,000 archers for training at Winchelsea, wow. Just billeting them would be a huge feat. Then it was the largest importers of wine outside of London.

In its heyday around three quarters of a million gallons of wine each year flowed from Burgundy to the busy port, some 40 million bottles a year!

Where was it housed? Well the final fact is that Winchelsea still has the second largest cellars in England. Today they are all hidden under pretty chocolate box cottages.

Royal visits from the Virgin Queen, great armadas setting sail for battle, murder, religion, smuggling and intrigue. The sleepy little town is bursting with hidden history.

I decided that one day I must write more about the fascinating place so proudly standing on Iham Hill.

At Hastings I passed the ancient Hastings Castle standing eerily on guard against its only modern foe, the elements.

Hastings Castle was the first proper castle built by King William on English soil. One of hundreds that would help stretch his iron-clad fist across our land. He had brought several wooden prefabricated castle parts with him from Normandy. A sort of early Ikea flat-pack.

They say that Hastings was the first real Motte & Bailey castle. I doubt that, and wonder if there was not some sort of castle on the high ground long before the Normans came. It is too perfect a place not to have a castle.

Hastings was a natural harbour and the shortest route from Normandy across the sea. I bet the Romans did not miss that, what with Pevensey Castle, their stronghold, just down the road.

A cormorant or, as the French call these jet-black birds, *raven of the sea*, was perched on one of the battered walls. Fat fingers of moss stretched over the cracks like giant hands clutching the walls. Ferns, gripping precariously in nooks shook angrily at the wind. The cormorant had its wings outstretched and head snobbishly raised as if posing for some heraldic shield. Even in the coldest of times they have to dry their feathers which have evolved to allow air to escape as they chase fish through the water.

The scene was perfect. At the dark end of the year the winter sea crashed against the shoreline, beneath a brooding sky and the whole world seemed to have forgotten the warm days of summer.

On a day like this the sight of the ancient walls—soaked with the bloody history of invasion, conquest and domination— would wrap a chill around the strongest heart. Legend tells that the ghost of Thomas à Beckett haunts the early Norman fortress.

Mind you, he is a busy ghost and does a lot of haunting from Hastings to Canterbury and even the Deanery in Lewes. Henry II's chancellor was butchered after celebrating Christmas in 1170 at Canterbury, when Henry's unfortunate words fell on the wrong ears. Thomas, once Henry's closest friend, had become a thorn in his side. He died on his knees in a pool of blood, praying, and took his first steps to sainthood.

Hastings Castle in its prime was once one of the mighty castles of the land, its boundaries stretching many times the size of its remains today. There were large enclosed jousting fields where William's beautiful daughter would host great tournaments and feast in its huge banqueting halls. The castle was visited not only by William but also by his son, William II, and many other kings, including John, such was its importance.

Great storms in the 13<sup>th</sup> century, similar to those that had destroyed Winchelsea, also took their toll on Hastings, sending part of the outer defences crashing into the boiling sea below.

I wonder if they blamed that terrible period on global warming? I doubt it— just Mother Nature at her worst.

As the castle fell into disrepair more was destroyed or removed for other building, until what was left was just a shadow of its former glory.

Strangely, after the death of Beckett at Canterbury, his ghost would appear at the castle! Henry, the barrel-chested Plantagenet, one of the most powerful of all our Kings, whose lands stretched from the Pyrenees to Scotland, paid penance for the rest of his life for his foolish-loose-words.

Thomas à Beckett had been Dean of the church at Hastings and his ghost is said to roam the castle precincts on wild and foul nights.

There are other ghosts that roam abroad on eerie nights around the castle. A nurse from the First World War is said to search for her wounded soldiers amongst the rubble. In the 1960's a tourist caught one of the ghosts on film, a nun serenely gazing towards the old altar.

The Ghost Club, founded by Charles Dickens in 1862, would have had a field day at the ruins. Although Dickens had seen the darker side of human nature and had a consuming hatred of the legal profession, he had great expectations of the human spirit and knew that good usually won over evil.

His belief in the purity of the eternal spirit led him to look for it in many places. He would have loved Hastings Castle, when the wild sea-banshee clawed their way up over the icy cliffs and raced through the arches and passages of the grey stone relic. Norman ghosts, who rode to bloody victory near here nearly a thousand years ago, still echo in every windswept stone.

* * * * *

Down below on the Shore the entire Hastings fishing fleet was beached. Hastings still has the largest shore-based fishing fleet in Europe, but today was no day to be out at sea. The Stade, where they are based, is a shingle beach with a shallow rise—making it possible for some of the larger boats to be hauled up the beach.

Stade is an old Saxon word for *landing place* and boats have been based there since at least the ninth century. It is a timeless and enduring trade that has passed through history into our age.

Paul Joy, one of the Hastings fishermen, launches his craft using a tractor to push it into the sea and to haul it up again. Boats are pushed to the water, and back, over greased wooden blocks called Troes.

Paul would know of the fisherman's tale that, on some mist-laden days out at sea, the old castle ruins magically appear rebuilt, shining like Camelot on the hill.

Hastings Fishermen were once known as *Chopbacks* because of an old feud between the Hastings and Rye boatmen. The story goes that during a fight over smuggling revenue, the Hastings men only used the backs of their axes to avoid too much damage to their rivals, and from then on the name stuck.

Fishing is a hard but rewarding life for the tough Hastings men whose distant relatives would have watched, with dismay, William's massive fleet landing at Pevensey in 1066. They would have witnessed his scorched earth march as he moved the 16 miles to a ridge above Hastings where he would become King in a day.

It would have been the Hastings Shoremen who had also seen the Great Eastern on her maiden voyage. The ship, six times larger than any vessel ever built at that point, made her way along the coast, passing Hastings on her way to Holyhead at 6pm on the ninth of September 1859.

What a sight she must have been. The jinxed leviathan moving like a great black shadow across the horizon. The ship had already claimed the lives of several men and was about to take more!

The press on board were temporarily jubilant, "*The mistress of the ocean held sway as she met the rolling waves and foaming surf.*" Little did they know disaster was looming!

The Great Eastern was six times larger than the largest ship ever built at that time.

The mood onboard the ship, that was later to lay the first transatlantic cable, was soon to turn from triumph to terror!

Isambard Kingdom Brunel was not onboard for her maiden voyage. He had collapsed on the deck of the luxury liner just days before.

As he lay clinging to life in his London home, a huge explosion erupted from the forward funnel of the liner. Five more men died in steam and flame.

The ship had been plagued with problems right from the start. One hundred thousand people turned up at the Isle of Dogs to see the launch of the luxury liner, which was able to transport over 4,000 people across the Seven Seas in sumptuous comfort. It was a disaster.

The monster failed to drop down the slipway, taking a further 90 days to get into the water, forced into its new element with huge hydraulic ramps. It was like a beast refusing to go, killing another workman on its way. Eventually the largest weight ever moved by man slipped into the water.

Isambard had been constantly hounded and ridiculed by aggressive tabloid hacks. He tried to take no notice of the papers that overlooked his revolutionary and inspirational skills, just to make cheap copy. He pushed his weak body to its limit to perfect his engineering brilliance and forge a new empire. Bridges, tunnels, ships, railways—the genius designed and built them all.

Worn out from a lifetime of overwork, stress and negative publicity he fell to the deck of his last fantastic engineering feat.

This photo was taken just hours before he collapsed, aged 53!

The photo taken just hours before his collapse shows a man far older than his age, withered by stress and overwork.

As he lay dying, he clung on to life, hoping for positive news of his last triumph. His friends were reluctant to tell him of the liner's disaster, but when he was eventually told it was his death knell.

Six days after the accident, his family divulged the truth about the men killed on the Great Eastern's maiden voyage. Isambard closed his eyes, groaned, rolled over and died. He was only 53!

The greatest engineer the world had ever seen died a sad pitiful death filled with failure and remorse. Only then did the press of the day change their tune, and praise the man for his amazing accomplishments, many of which still stand today.

The Great Eastern was an engineering masterpiece that changed the shape of all future ships. However it was also a financial disaster. It never reached its potential and never fulfilled Isambard's last dream. The jinxed monster was scrapped in 1889 with one more morbid tale to reveal.

When they were tearing the beast apart they found two more bodies between the plates of the hull. Riveters left to die inside the belly of the steel monster.

A tormented Isambard Kingdom Brunel, our greatest engineer. Looking older than his picture of him taken at just 48.

On a lighter note, did you know that in 1851 the Duke of Brunswick became the first *wanted* man in history to escape by air! He escaped by balloon to France, from Queens Road in Hastings, landing in Boulogne. Amazing. Often when I stroll down the road I think about where he might have taken off. How exciting our history can be if you look for it.

I could not help but wonder about Letty as I left Hastings to its icy winds and eerie ghosts. She was just such a dear.

I recalled her words as I left her home, "Alex just remember— sing like nobody's listening—dance like nobody's watching—love like you've never been hurt and always work like you don't need the money."

I had almost kissed her.

The Land Rover's engine rhythmically rumbled along by the Delaware Pavilion in Bexhill, now looking resplendent since its lottery grant spit-and-polish.

It was a true gift that Letty had—to always look on the bright side of life. Was she born with it? Had she learnt it through years of hardship on her long journey? I could only guess. But her talent to make people feel welcome and enjoy the simplest things was truly priceless. It reminded me how important it is to make people feel welcome and, in reality, how simple it is to do.

I had left Letty's little place in Rye full of enthusiasm for the day. Full of hope and with the sure knowledge that things were not that bad after all. Even if I did have to put up with the occasional pain in the butt or WOMBAT.

I had to agree with Charles Dickens too—when all around seems dark the human spirit will always shine.

As I drove, with the windscreen wipers hypnotically working in their rhythmical motion, all I could think was that if I had my way Letty, my angel in Rye, would live forever.

And as for my silly customer living in *Dumb Woman Lane?* Well, wasn't she just in the perfect place! Hitting her sewing machine with a stick! Whatever will I come across next?

I laughed, dropped the car into fifth gear and purred home.

# The End

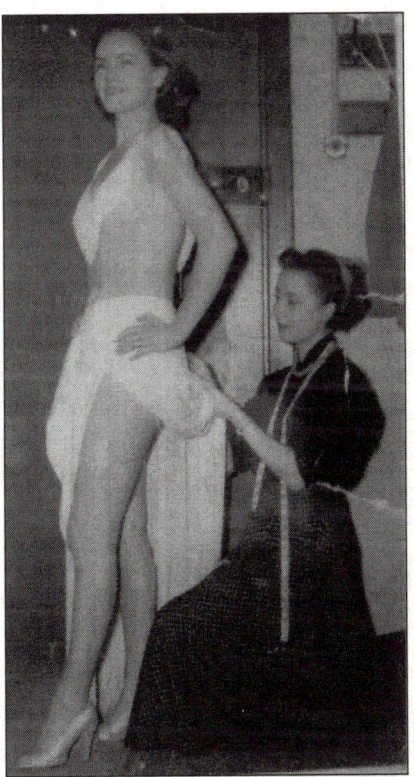

Doreen putting her magic touches on another dazzling outfit

## Onset

The mellow season's fading fast
Autumn old is chased away
While winters bitter blast is
Slicing through the ricks of hay.
Skies turn bleak and overcast
While the squirrel lines his dray.
Summer sighs and breathes her last
As hoary beard is tugged astray.
Crows caw for the summer lost
While the robin puffs in the bay.
The White Witch blows her kiss of frost
And winter's chill comes to play.

Alex I Askaroff

# The Last Cockney

The day was moving fast and I needed to get my wagon wheels a-rollin'.

As I drove to my second customer of the morning in Uckfield, the sun lifted over the fields, low and bright, pouring yellow fluidly through the thick trees and throwing a barcode of shadows across the road. I took the back lane cutting through Rotherfield.

The word Rother is an old Anglo-Saxon word for cattle. The word Rother pops up all over the country. Rotherfield, in my area of East Sussex, was once an old cattle market where farmers would meet and sell their goods. The Rother cattle were long-horned, fleshy beasts prized for their meat, milk, hide and horn. Many of today's breeds have a little of the ancient Rother beef in them.

I was calling just off Uckfield High Street, down a twitten opposite the church near Pudding Cake Lane. There was no parking, so I tramped up the twitten with my tools, fresh-faced and red-cheeked against the morning's bite.

I was hoping my customer's husband was in. On my last call he had made me giggle so much I could not work properly.

He was a Londoner with the thickest Cockney accent I had ever come across and just a dream to listen to. Harry, or 'Arry, was a professional cockney. Born and bred in Cheapside, East London, just a few streets from St Mary-le-Bow and the sound of Bow bells. Although Dick Whittington said the bells could be heard as far away as Highgate, Harry told me that now you were lucky to hear them two streets away, what with all the London din! So the area of the true Cockney had diminished, but not Harry's accent.

He spoke in rough rhymes that made little sense to me, a sort of pigeon English that had been used for centuries. Luckily, Aggie, his better half, was usually on hand to translate. Harry called her an assortment of names, *Lover, Pearly Queen, Trouble 'n' Strife* or *Duchess* but hardly ever by her actual name. They were an inseparable couple, totally devoted to each other.

I knocked on the door, fingers crossed.

"Hello Aggie, how are you?"

"Been better, been worse, I haven't dropped off the perch yet, so mustn't grumble, mustn't grumble. Old age is not for sissies Alex!"

"Is Harry here today?" I asked enthusiastically.

"He'll be back shortly, my dear. He's just popped up to get his linen, oh sorry dear I mean his paper. I have been listening to his cockney for so long some of it has stuck. I have his breakfast almost ready, and he's a man who needs feeding. Come in, the machine is ready for you."

The cottage was filled with that irresistible smell of an English breakfast in full swing. I almost dragged myself in by my nose. One day I would get one of those breakfasts out of Aggie. Perhaps she would offer one today? Anyway, smelling it was almost as good as actually eating it, with far less calories. Mind you, if she offered, who was I to refuse? Such an insult would not fall from my lips!

I have always found that a house that has been lived in for any amount of time tells the character of its inhabitants, Aggie's was no different. There was a warm and welcoming feel to the place and I was happy to be there.

Aggie saw me looking around. "Don't mind the dust. A house is not a real home until you can write your name in it somewhere. Anyway I always tell people it protects the wood!"

I smiled and got stuck into Aggie's machine. No sooner had I started than the door flew open. In strode Harry, dapper as usual in his trilby and camel Crombie.

"Aggie," he shouted. "I'm so 'ungry me stummik finks me frotes' bin cut. I'm bleedin' 'Ank Marvin. Bring me a cup of rosy over lover and put a smile on your chevy."

He carefully hooked up his coat, or 'weasel' as he called it, placed his hat lovingly over the peg with an extra stroke and marched like a penguin to the table. He threw his *News of the World* on the table and pulled out a chair. "I need to get me bleedin' daisy roots orf, me plates are killing me!"

Harry sat with a heavy thump and started to remove his shoes. As the first one came off there was a deep sigh of pleasure and a wiggle of chubby toes. Harry looked up to see me sitting opposite, smiling back at him.

"Blimey 'o 'Riley, if it ain't me old china! I see me Pearly Queen as got yer to fix that runner bean of hers. She has bin swearing sumfink rotten. Women and machinery eh! 'Ow did we ever win the war!"

*Harry was cruisin' for a bruisin','* I thought.

"One more swear-word out of her," he continued, "and I would 'ave to leave and find lodgin's down the docks where they speak the Queen's English wiv' out her colour. I kept tellin' me lover it takes twice as many muscles to frown as it does to smile but she said her face needed the exercise!

"I see you're still alive and wriggling then Harry?" I threw across to him.

"Yep, still 'ere and still causing trouble. When I go I want to go peaceful in my sleep, like me dear old Da—not screaming like his passengers!"

"You can still tell them like the best Harry?" I said laughing.

"Bought that on the strap we did," said Harry, nodding in the direction of the machine while removing his other shoe. "Eight bob a week every week for a year. Every Saturday after I 'ad me greengage from work I used to pop down to the shop on me old bike to settle up and get the Singer book stamped. Cost the same as a week's burton for our flat that did."

"Don't listen to him," shouted Aggie coming across the room, "there's nothing but broken biscuits in that silly sod's bonce!"

Aggie set before him a plate of heaven. "He's been losing about an inch in height a year these last few years and now waddles around on his stumps like he is looking for the South Pole! That's why I need the machine working to take his trousers up... again! If he keeps shrinking and waddling when he walks I am going to rename him Pingu!"

She disappeared and returned with a side-plate of buttered bread, cut diagonally, and a cup of steaming tea. Harry paused for a moment surveying his kingly meal.

"Let's 'ave a butchers at this then. Nothin' better than a fry-up on the old Cain 'n' Able to make your juices flow eh! Makes the jam-tart pump. Yeah we'll 'ave some of that," he sighed in approval rubbing his hands together. "I'd pay a Pavarotti for one of these back up the Smoke, but it was never as good as me pearly queen made. The only food that'll beat a fry-up is eel pie and mash wiv gravy, eaten out of a paper tub under the Embankment on a rainy night. That'll put blood in your boat race."

"There was a time boy when every self respecting fish 'n' chip shop in the East End sold jellied eel!"

Aggie smiled with satisfaction at Harry's kind words, wiped her hands on her apron. She quietly explained that slang was a living language that changed with the times, a secret language once only used by the London Costermongers, originally apple sellers, and then Barrow Boys. It was used in the fruit markets so that no outsiders knew what they were up to. The market tongue. Slang was actually short for **s-**ecret **lang-**uage and it was very local.

A *Pavarotti* in rhyming slang was a tenor–tenner–ten pound note. It used to be a chicken & hen but Cockney slang had moved with the times and became a Pavarotti. Some was more obscure. A tin was a suit! Tin whistle, whistle and flute—suit. In parts of London slang ruled. Those that learnt the language were always thought of as one of the lads!

It was much the same as the Pearly Kings & Queens. Once, to signify a market king or queen, there were just three buttons on each lapel of their blazer in a flash, hence the sayings *flash git* or *flash Harry*. However, what with Cockneys loving to wear their wealth and compete, there was hardly a spot on their entire suits that was not eventually plastered in pearl buttons as each market tried to outdo the other. The suits weighed a ton and rattled as the Pearly Kings and Queens walked.

I had to smile to myself looking over at Harry, he was a man who would never waste one word when three would do! He was just so opposite to the old Sussex folk that I was used to. He loved the sound of his own voice and had the habit of answering his own questions, which made for a perfect one-man conversation. I bet he happily chatted to himself when Aggie was out!

It was pure pleasure to listen to his banter. I remembered Aggie telling me about Harry when they first met. It took her months to get used to his accent and rhyming slang. At first she couldn't understand most of it, but he had the gift of the gab, a cheeky smile and a motorbike. What else could a girl want!

As I worked, Harry put the world to rights. Complaining about all the things that annoyed him, and the useless politicians and worse footballers. By the time I had found the problem Harry was polishing off his food.

"Harry, I wonder if we could use your shed. I need to drill out a peg and replace it, to get the winder working! It is a two man job if you feel up to it!"

"No problem me old china One more sip of me rosy and I'll be wiv ya."

I looked on with envy as Harry finished off his breakfast. Shadowing his meal like a large-eyed vulture. He wiped his last corner of buttered bread around the plate in a circular motion, cleaning it perfectly with a practised sweep. If he had wiped any harder he would have taken the pattern off as well! He dropped the concoction into his gawping mouth, poured some tea from his tea cup into his saucer, blew on it, and slurped it down with a satisfied grin.

"Right me old China, let's get to work."

As Harry rose, pushing up on both arms of his chair, he passed an embarrassing ripple of wind. Harry looked over his shoulder with a quizzical expression, "Eh! Who's let little Jimmy out'a prison!"

"Harry where's your manners you dirty old man!" Admonished Aggie with her hands on her aproned hips.

"Calm down Lover, don't get your knickers in a twist, it was just a little backfire! I couldn't help it. Anyway, better out than in," he grinned wickedly.

"And, Lover, you know there ain't nothing easier to break than wind and harder to break than a bad 'abbit."

"Well you have enough of those for all of us. When I married Mr Right I didn't realise his first name was Always!" said Aggie flicking him on his bum with her tea towel. Harry yelped. "Now get off with you and help Alex get my machine working or you won't get your trousers turned up—short arse!"

Harry made for the door rubbing his bum as he waddled along.

We both left in a rush, Harry laughing and pushing me so that he could get away from Aggie's pin-point tea-towel.

Harry had a great laugh. A deep bear's laugh like my dad. It rose up from his toes, churned around his huge belly and came out of his mouth in a roar. You could not help but love him.

Like a couple of naughty school kids we made our way down the garden, through the long damp grass, to his workshop. Harry started to hiccup. "Now look what me Pearly Queen's gone and done! She's given me the Wild Bill's!"

The cold workshop flickered into life with buzzing fluorescent lights. Tools lay around on the workbench and Harry cleared a spot next to his vice for me to work.

Idly gazing out of the dirty window I noticed an old outside brick built loo at the end of the garden. "Don't see many of those anymore." I nodded to Harry.

"No-me old China, not many left now. When I was a lad there was one of those down every yard. Before we had running water the *Thunderbox* was a place to avoid at all costs. It smelt something 'orrid. We used to 'av a *Jimmy* or a *pony* and cover it with ash from the fire.

"In the summer we never stayed in there any longer than we could hold our breath! No reading the arsewipes like we did other times. See, besides the smell, there was always a chance of a bluebottle buzzin up ye backside trying to escape. Nasty feeling that!

"It was emptied by Joe, the Corporation man. We called 'im '*Oilskin Joe*' 'cause of his clothes. He was covered in a huge leather apron to protect him. He worked mainly at night using a back-hatch from the bog leading onto our alley.

"He would load it onto his cart with his long-handled shovel, one bog after another. It was a well paid job but no one but Joe wanted it!

The *Muck Man* had the smelliest job in the world and we all 'ad a song about him, let me see now. It was sung in tune with *my old man's a dustman*. Now 'ow did it go…

"*The Corporation muck cart, was full up to the brim…, The Muck Man fell in backwards, and found he couldn't swim…! He sank right to the bottom…, just like a heavy stone…, and as he sank he gurgled…There's no place like 'ome.*"

"When water and flushing bog's came they froze in winter, being outside like. So we left a candle stub under the cistern on cold nights so we could flush. Mind it was a trip we never made unless we 'ad to! We didn't have an inside bog until 1969. What a luxury. I used to use it just to see it work!"

"Harry you are so full of stories you could work in a museum!"

"I've 'ad me working days me old cocker, all I want to do now is stop shrinking and relax."

"Well we had better fix Aggie's machine then." I said. "That will make her smile and help you relax as well."

We had to drill out a seized piece of the winder and replace it with a new one. Then we had to modify the new one to work, as it was from a later model machine.

Things went well until I asked Harry to hold the winder while I made a punch mark which would allow the drill to go through. Harry was holding the winder on the vice and I was lining up the centre-punch to the pin.

Just as I went to hit the punch Harry hiccupped! The result was that the winder moved and I missed the punch. The small pin-hammer came down on his thumb!

Harry howled, dropped the winder and started to dance around his workshop like a Red Indian. What a dance, first one foot then the other, all the time Harry blowing onto his injured thumb. *There's never a fiddle around when you need one* I thought. What a tune I could have played as he danced. I knew I had not hit him hard, it was just a glancing blow, but what a performance.

Harry could have been the opening act at the Palladium.

"Harry, I am so sorry," I said trying to muffle my laugh. "You moved! Let me have a look."

"Bleedin' armchairs!" he hissed halfway through his little jig around the workshop kicking up dust. What he was talking about I didn't have a clue.

After Harry calmed down we both looked at his thumb with great concern, examining at every wrinkle. "I can't even see a mark," I exclaimed in a professional doctor's tone.

"I need to sit down, I feel a bit Tom & Dick, I've come over all ginger!" Harry sighed as he dropped heavily onto a stool. "I'm bleeding cream crackered and I've got dust in me mince pie! Cor blimey me old cocker whatever next!"

Harry sat looking exhausted, rubbing an eye with a fat wrinkled old knuckle. "Let me have a look Harry." I stared into his squinting eye. Staring back at me was a lifetime of wicked laughter but no dust.

"Can't see anything Harry, probably just the shock."

"Shock—shock! You need a kick up the Khyber! Takes more than a whack with that little pin-hammer to send me into shock me old china. I'll be right in a sixpence—just get me breath back."

Harry licked his thumb, then blew on it for a minute or two and made a miraculous recovery. Grabbing the hammer off the workbench, he said, "Right! It's my turn to use the hammer and your turn to hold!"

I had no choice but to allow Harry to make the mark. Shaking and with my eyes closed I held the winder on the vice and waited for retribution. Silence... Whack...! No pain.

I opened my eyes to see a perfect mark in the centre of the shaft that now only needed drilling. I sighed in great relief.

"That's how it's done me old china but you will need a bit of Donald Duck to make the new parts fit," nodding at the pieces on the table.

"Leave that to me Harry, I'm the expert."

"Some expert! If you fell down a well you wouldn't hit water."

Laughing, we worked on the bobbin winder together and before long it was running like new.

Back at the machine in the house, Harry had to retell his ordeal with graphic details, not missing out his hilarious dance, which by now had taken on the magical qualities of Fred Astaire in full swing!

'He 'it me so 'ard I felt it right down to me cobblers! What I had to go through, me lover, to get your machine back, you'll never know—the pain, the agony."

"The bull," Aggie finished off. "Come here you big old fool," said Aggie, pulling Harry to her. She gave him a big kiss. "What would I do without you to listen to all day, eh?"

For a few seconds their two bodies melted into one. A lifetime of familiarity left no molecule of air between them. I could not help but notice two people deeply in love. I knew once one of them departed this world the other was sure to follow closely behind. A phrase from my old Scripture Union days sprung to mind from Mr Verrall's patient bible teachings. *Happy is the husband of a good wife for his days are doubled.*

Harry pecked Aggie once more on the neck before bursting into song as he strode cockily back to his chair. Chest out, shoulders back. "Anytime you're Lambeth way, any ev'nin', any day... you'll find us all... doin' the Lambeth Walk."

He leaned back on his chair flicking open his paper. "Just not appreciated," he whispered under his breath.

*Back to his cocky self,* I thought. Aggie smiled at me behind his back. "I saw that," floated Harry's words through the paper. "Pay the man his bread 'n' honey me lover and make sure it's a kite!"

"Kite?" I exclaimed.

"Yeah, kite," said Harry folding down his paper as if he had to explain to the village idiot once more.

"See—there are two kinds of Gregory Pecks, ones that bounce and ones that fly. And you don't want a rubber one do you! Cor blimey, lads of today don't know their arse from their elbow. Raw as green tomatoes," he added flicking his paper back up.

I couldn't help but notice that his thumb had gone quite red, but I was not about to tell him in case he flew into another of his melodramatic episodes before I got to the door.

I left Harry and Aggie throwing their usual banter back and forth. I never did figure out who wore the trousers in their house, but I had a sneaky feeling he thought he did and she knew she did!

I meandered back down the twitten towards my car, already longing for a return visit, cockney lessons included.

And, although the thought of eel pie was not too appealing, Aggie still had not made me a breakfast! So there were at least two good reasons to re-visit the *Pearly King and Queen of Uckfield*.

# The End

Brian & Margaret Hemsley are two of my customers and carry on the tradition of London Pearly King & Queens.

# Haunted House

Twenty-five years! It just did not seem possible—but it was. I had been a married man for a quarter of a century. The years had passed in a blink of an eye. A mixture of memories and images that had been my married life.

It seemed like only yesterday that I had used up nearly two tanks-full of fuel in my Puch Maxi trying to bump into my future wife. Purely by accident of course!

For 18 months I went everywhere on my 49 cc powerhouse. That little red devil took the flat roads in its stride and, at a push, would even attempt hills. The Austrian manufacturers, ever thoughtful, had been so kind as to include a set of pedals to help the gutless donkey gasping between my legs. Climbing hills we would wheeze in tune as I, in my most manly teenage fashion, peddled as fast as I could to stop the beast grinding to a halt. Youth and enthusiasm took me everywhere.

Things got even more interesting as, with a double seat bolted on and a set of foot-pegs drilled into the back struts, the little marvel coped with my new girlfriend clinging on for dear life at a dazzling 25mph. Yana had a full car license so we were legally allowed to travel on my little Puch. With my passenger holding on tight the little red devil took two of us on long happy journeys, avoiding hills as much as possible.

Aah, the blissful joys of youth, mixing the fuel with oil at the petrol stations. Spending hours idling the time away and arriving home with my ears ringing, bum aching and stinking of two-stroke fumes.

The Puch Maxi, more bicycle than motorcycle. The pedals were useful for the hills!

My mind was a blur. For 25 years of putting up with me, I should plan something special for Yana, but what? Getting married, as we had, in bleak midwinter had been strange. There was no unexpected baby due and no father-in-law with a shotgun waiting for me around the back of the barn. It just worked out that way.

There must have been a reason to get married in January, but the whys and wherefores were lost in the back of my fading mind.

I subconsciously checked the age of the kids but they were way too young. Maybe we were just desperate to get married. We were young and our blood was hot! What I did know was that we had survived a quarter of a century together through thick and thin and a good celebration was in order.

When we had set a date we were teenagers and it seemed fine, but January was definitely not the best time for a honeymoon in England. Back in the 1970's trips abroad were way out of our limited budget. Freddie Laker and cheap air flights were only just getting started.

We ended up taking my works van down to the West Country and spent a wonderful week in a country pub on snowy Dartmoor.

Browsing through endless holiday brochures, I accidentally dropped one. As I picked it up I thought providence had played a hand in our celebrations.

The brochure was all about an old hunting lodge used by King Henry VIII on his wild boar and stag sorties into Ashdown Forest. Everything about it looked great. It had the second largest fireplace in England, old banqueting tables and in the best room was a 400-year-old four-poster bed.

My mind was made up as images of roaring fires and hearty cooked breakfasts sprang to mind. I rushed for the phone and booked the best room in the lodge for two nights. Though expensive, it would be a real treat and worth every penny.

Yana was delighted.

As our anniversary drew closer, we pawed over the leaflets and re-read all the great things we were to enjoy during our stay. The warm welcome by the *Lord of the Manor* who had contacted us via e-mail to say he would welcome us personally, the walks in Ashdown Forest where *A A Milne* scrawled his fabulous *Winnie the Pooh* tales, the *Great Hall*, the food, it all sounded fantastic.

Thoughts of old ghosts and roast boar in front of huge fires sprung to mind. Minstrels played and the dogs rollicked under huge tables gnawing on the discarded bones that I had aimlessly tossed to them. Okay, so I was letting my imagination run away a little, but there was no harm in that, as the brochure stated...

*Set in a stunningly beautiful location on a 30 acre estate away from main roads and noise, where pheasant and deer roam the meadows and woodlands. A fantastic evening of entertainment and feasting at a 500-yr-old castle.*

You know what they say, it is not just the getting there but enjoying the journey as well.

It is hard to beat a great old manor in the English countryside. I should know, I have visited so many of them over the years and have never been disappointed. I was delighted they were open for business in January. It all sounded like the perfect anniversary celebration.

Too good to be true? You bet your life it was!

Things went wrong from the very start. We got lost in Ashdown Forest and we could not find the castle. Strangely, no one seemed to have heard of it. As the cold January afternoon started to ease into an early night we were still wandering along dirt tracks and down deserted back roads.

Eventually we spotted an old man wandering in the woods with his dog. I stopped once more and asked for help. He pointed across the woods with his pipe and ominous words followed rolled in smoke.

"Never met no one from there, don't go down that part of the forest but that's where it be!"

As the winter's night slowly stole away the views over a cold bleak forest, the Land Rover's lights picked out the old castle, throwing eerie shadows up the high walls. The car turned nosily on the gravel drive in front of Henry's old hunting lodge.

At last we had arrived at the castle. It lay there among the forest trees, dormant, like some great sleeping beast, black and ominous in the dark.

I peeked out of my car window up at the daunting sight. Old creeper that had died over the winter months clung to the high walls, gripping the building, smothering it with great wrinkled hands. No lights shining from the windows. No human noises. Nothing but the howling wind cutting through the barren forest.

The lake that was probably so appealing in summer was frozen and dead. A few reeds poked out like lifeless fingers. The ice lay like dirty shattered glass on the surface. The whole place looked bleak and sullen with some cracked windows and mess everywhere. It was as if it had been vandalised by a band of wandering gypsies who had left in a hurry.

We stood silently at the large oak door sunken deep into the thick stone. I knocked hard. A small flurry of snow circled around our feet and I shivered.

I had a disturbing feeling creep over me but kept a smile on my face. I did not want Yana to suspect that I was worried. It was a desolate place, no other people, no cars or guests. Where was the *Lord of the Manor* to warmly greet us and take us to the roaring fire for dinner?

My thoughts were broken when the huge door slowly creaked open. A tall bearded man wearing an old stained shirt stood before us.

"I have been expecting you," he said in a broken accent. "The Lord is away but he has told me you were coming. You need to pay me... Now!"

I was taken aback at his sudden and abrasive approach but kept my composure. We were on holiday after all!

"Do you take credit cards as we have not brought our cheque book," I asked smiling politely at the stranger, hiding a tinge of annoyance at his abruptness.

"No..., no cards..., you will have to pay cash. Have you the money?"

Once again trying to keep everything upbeat and happy, I reluctantly parted with our shopping money for the following day and settled our bill, two nights, in cash, in advance, and we had not even seen the room!

On checking the payment, he took us up a large and ornately carved oak stairway, then along old wiggly passages that had wood panelling and large beamed ceilings.

We were taken to the furthest room in the desolate castle. He unlocked the door and gave us two keys, one for our room and one for the front door, explaining that there was no one but him staying at the place. "Someone will be in to make breakfast." He muttered.

So much for our cheerful lord's greeting!

I placed our cases in the room and turned to tip him but he was gone! I peered back up the long passageway but there was no sign of him!

Yana and I walked into the enormous room where an old four-poster bed sat in the far corner. The stained carpet looked as if it had seen many better days. I walked around the room, found the kettle and put it on for a cuppa. If there is one thing that cheers me up it is a nice cup of tea. I peeked into the bathroom.

"Yana I am not too happy about this at all." I said, running the hot tap. "There is no hot water and what's coming out of the tap is brown! The towels are filthy and the carpet is disgusting."

"Bed looks nice though!" Yana perked up in her usual positive mood.

"Yeah at least that looks a bit like the brochure, but this is so weird. There are no other guests and no noise, just the opposite to a normal hotel where something is always happening. No chatting or passing people in the corridors, no cutlery or china clinking in the restaurant, no barmen or porters, check-in or waiters...no life! This is just a dark bleak place.

Have you seen the views? It is so drab, look over there." I pointed out of one of the dirty, diamond-leaded, windows toward the dark forest. "We are all alone in this big old place and its bloody freezing. We're inside and I can see my breath! And where's the sauna that is supposed to be in the room? It had a big mention in the brochure! But it certainly ain't here!"

By now I was fuming—in a very cold sort of way.

"I can't see King Henry putting up with this, so why should we? If he courted Anne Boleyn here they would have both died of frost bite! Where's the roaring log fires and central heating eh! Not exactly the romantic anniversary I had in mind. I can't even take my coat off!"

"Alex, don't be such a misery," laughed Yana. "He told us he would put the heating on and look, there is a little electric heater as well," she said pointing at a miserable contraption that I had turned on the instant I spotted it.

The poor thing was almost bursting its guts trying to pour some warmth into the large room—, and failing miserably.

"You will feel much better when you have had a good meal inside you, and the room has warmed up."

"Suppose so. If the place had no guests why in God's name didn't he say? He didn't need to take our booking, we could have stayed at The Mermaid in Rye, where you wanted to stay in the first place!

"They could have told us it would be deserted and freezing here. Big log fire, my arse! No wonder he took our money at the door! The other thing is…, have you noticed how really creepy it is here? I have never seen a place like it and we don't know where this other door leads," I grunted shaking it vigorously.

"And it's locked from the other side–plus the windows won't fasten at all. See?" I said, waving the catch up and down.

"Anyone or anything could get in! And listen when I open this big one… it's silent! Not a whisper, not a creak or squeak, nothing! What's that all about! All windows make some noise. Anyone could get in and we would hear nothing… till it's too late, that is, and I wake up with two holes in my neck and a big fat bat flapping around the room with a satisfied grin!

"What sort of maintenance man leaves the place looking like a dump, but oils all the windows! This place really gives me the willies, and those stains on the carpet! Washed out blood I expect!"

"Alex, stop it! You're rambling on like an old woman! Come on let's get some good pub grub and see what it is like when we get back."

I quickly agreed. We creaked our way along the rickety dark corridors back to the ground floor, where a single light threw scary shadows up into the dusty corners of the high hallway entrance.

I was glad to get back into the familiar surrounding of my trusty Land Rover, and happily followed a fox down the bumpy pot-holed gravel drive with my car headlights.

We had a great meal at a superb country pub called *The Hay Wagon* in Hartfield. It is amazing how a good meal and a local beer can lift the mood. We sat beside an open fire eating, drinking and laughing about the strange and scary place that we had booked into.

However, laughing about the place when you are somewhere else, and laughing about it when you had to go back was very different altogether. I delayed as long as possible in the pub but closing time soon came and we departed for our accommodation for the next two nights.

Reluctantly and very slowly I drove back to the lodge. We rolled back up the drive, the headlights lighting the barren trees that were clawing at the car in the bitter night wind.

"I'd like to see a pheasant or deer around here!" I quipped quoting the brochure once more. "I bet they've all been shot!"

The ominous feeling return as I parked the car below the stark castle walls. I deliberately backed the Land Rover up to the main door of the lodge. Yana looked at me quizzically. "It's just in case we need a quick getaway!" I explained in earnest. "There is no one else here so no one will complain... except maybe that strange old butler."

Yana was giggling, rather the worse for wear, as I unlocked the huge front door and tried to find a light switch in the hall. I had turned on the tiny light on my key ring, and was hopelessly looking for anything that might light up the ghostly place.

I followed the panelled wall around with my hand, feeling in vain. I screamed like a girl as I touched a suit of armour.

I gave up searching the hall. "I can't find a bloody switch anywhere, we will just have to try and find our room in the dark. Hold my hand."

"Why are you whispering?"

"I don't know, I've never stayed in an abandoned castle before. Is this place, scary or what? The hairs on the back of my neck are not only standing on end they are doing a good impression of a hedgehog on speed!"

We slowly crept up the creaky old stairs that had looked almost charming earlier, but had now taken on an unnatural appearance in the darkness. The old castle seemed to be in its element, scaring me half to death. Never had I been in such a place. All the years that we had stayed in haunted houses and castles, none had come close to this. I was terrified.

It was as if we had been dropped straight into an old Hammer horror film, and, being the only guests, were obviously the victims!

We made our way along the corridors with the floors creaking and the howling wind laughing, as it tugged at the windows and whistled through the old hunting lodge.

"Here we are at last," I said, placing the key into the lock of our bedroom door. In vain I tried to unlock the door. "It locked okay, blasted thing, now it won't budge." After what seemed like an eternity of wiggling keys I gave up.

"Yana, you wait here. I will go and get that weird bloke who let us in. I saw his light on in the far corner of the castle as we came in. I should be able to find it, I won't be long. Don't move!"

As I walked away, pointing my tiny torch in vain, a sudden thought hit me. I slapped my forehead with the palm of my hand. *This is just like the horror films... they always split us up!*

I stopped and went back. "Better had come with me. I have seen those old movies, if we split up you won't be here when I get back!"

Hand-in-hand we made our way around the dark old building, up and down the stairways to where I had spotted the light, knocked and waited, knocked again... and again.

Eventually our host came and took us back to our room. He could not get the key to work either and went off to fetch a replacement. He returned with a whole bunch and between us we spent the next half an hour trying assorted keys.

Bent over the keyhole, fumbling in the dark, we found the correct one and we entered our chamber for the night. This time I kept an eye on our host just to see if he disappeared—or did actually walk down the corridor!

Things were not all bad. On the plus side we could no longer see our breath and the central heating had moved the room to just above freezing and the water was almost warm, brown but warm. There was just enough for Yana to have a bath while I busied myself with the essential job of jamming chairs under the handles of the doors. I then tied the window latches together with my shoelaces.

By the time Yana came out the room was secured. Anything trying to get me tonight was going to have a fight on their hands!

"I think I am going to have a bit of trouble sleeping." I said.

"Not after this you won't." Yana said, pushing a whole teacup full of port into my hand.

We wrapped ourselves in blankets and sipped port, sitting in front of the heater that was putting on a grand display. I leant over quietly and reached behind Yana's head then suddenly pulled out a hair. She yelped. "What on earth are you up to now?"

"DNA," I replied. "If we disappear and are never seen again we need to leave a trace of us behind!" I squeezed my hand down the back of the chair and placed the evidence with a knowing smirk! I nodded to myself with quiet satisfaction.

Before long the port started to work its magic and I felt more at ease. I jumped between the sheets of the four hundred-year-old bed only to find they were freezing.

Worse was to follow.

As I snuggled down, my feet pushed out of the end! **"Bleedin' Nora**! Can you believe it? I'll have to sleep with my socks on or I'll loose my toes through frostbite!"

"You know if I wasn't well over the legal limit for driving I would get up and go. This place has just about finished me. In fact I think I am going to sleep fully clothed just in case!"

Yana started to laugh, "In case of what you fool, ghosts going to get you are they?"

I looked at Yana and we both laughed. The only difference was that my laugh was touching on madness. I had gone past all rational behaviour and was about to spend my first night in the lunatic asylum. Our laughs echoed around the old room. My eyes, glazed in the reflected light of the heater, did a good impression of an inmate of Bedlam.

"You'll be fine dear. You know it is a genuine four hundred-year-old bed, and in those days many people only grew to about five feet tall, unless you were a well-fed king. At least you know it is not Henry's bed. He was a lot taller. Just get a good night's kip and things will look much better in the morning after our hearty castle breakfast. Night–night."

Yana rolled herself up into a little ball like a hibernating hedgehog, and slipped off to sleep as if she were in a cosy warm bed with angels serenading. Eventually, after staring at each-window in turn, I drifted into a fitful sleep.

I woke with a start.

I had been dreaming of someone trying to pull me out of bed by my feet. In the pitch-black dead of night I sat upright in the rickety bed. My feet were blocks of ice. No wonder they had made their way into my dream. I rubbed them, trying to get some warmth back into frozen toes.

Glancing at my watch, which I held up to moonlight, I could just make out that it was two hours past the witching hour. It was no good trying to get any more sleep. I was wide-awake. I clutched the bedclothes to my chin and stared at every corner of the room, my eyes like saucepans. Every noise made me jump, every creak and groan of the old building. Every rush of wind at the windows that howled through the bare forest made my eyes open even wider.

"What are you doing?" moaned Yana, half-asleep.

"Waiting for dawn!" I hissed back.

"Oh," she said, pulling up the blanket without the slightest interest.

It was up to me to keep watch! The moon cast eerie shadows over the curtains, and the castle howled in wicked pleasure at the torment it was providing.

Eventually dawn came on that longest of nights.

With a watery grey daybreak the cold January day brought with it a feeling of elation. I had survived a night in one of the strangest places I had ever been in my life. I rubbed my poor burning eyes and jumped out of bed.

By seven, I was washed and ready for my hearty castle breakfast, the one fit for a king! I replaced my shoelaces and removed the chain and chairs from the doors.

I explored the empty place and wandered around the huge banqueting rooms and great halls that had scared me so much the night before. Even the suit of armour looked interesting. I bravely lifted the visor and peeked in. Easy! The 15th century castle-come hunting lodge looked almost appealing in daylight. I made a mental note of where the light switches were for the forthcoming night.

By 7.30 we were waiting for signs of our cook. I was starving and we had a busy day of retail therapy ahead in Tunbridge Wells, on plastic now that our cash had gone!

We sat patiently at the table and waited, and waited… and waited. There was not even a paper to read. I paced the floor, checked for any signs of life in the kitchen and began to fester again. It was almost nine before I snapped. "That's it! I've had enough. Come on let's leave this dump."

We packed in a flash, threw it all in the car and pushed the keys back through the door. We were soon speeding up the drive. *Good riddance to bad rubbish* I thought as I pulled onto the Tunbridge Wells Road.

Yana was a bit upset that we had paid for two nights but were leaving after just one- horrendous one. I explained that there was no way I was going to stay in that place even if I had paid. It was pure torture. And while the ghosts had not managed to get me on the first night, surely they would not miss a second time!

We parked on a high spot and I got out of the car to clear my thoughts. I looked out at the grey dawn. As I was staring aimlessly, the wind that had kept me up all night, seemed to give a last great sigh and disappear as if it was all just too much effort.

The sun nudged a cloud and peeked down, throwing a shaft of gold down onto the distant graphite sea. The sea, in turn, rose to the occasion and painted a path of platinum to the shore. It was the perfect scene. All it needed was Jesus to walk over the stormy waters and calm them to be complete. That was when inspiration hit.

Far off in the distance Rye was glimmering, beckoning enticingly. The charming old port town was my deliverance. I went back to the car and got on the mobile. Within moments I was connected to *The Mermaid* in Rye. Seconds later we had the best room booked for that night.

They may have eleven ghosts, but even if they all arrived in my room together it was not going to be as scary as where we had been. I hung up and turned to Yana. She burst into tears.

"I have tried so hard to be cheerful but that was the most horrible place we have ever stayed in. Thank you so much for getting us out of there."

"What are husbands for?" I shrugged. "If not for getting us into trouble and then sorting it all out!"

I started the car and headed for a good breakfast and some serious retail therapy. The perfect cure-all.

By three in the afternoon, with satisfied faces, we were meandering down the Kent lanes towards Rye. The back of the car was full of shopping and our bellies full of good food, all paid for on the plastic!

*The Mermaid* was fantastic, as always. No, it was even better because of our previous night in the creepy castle. The contrast with the barren place where only ghosts seemed at home was so stark.

The evening meal at *The Mermaid* was a six-course affair starting with quail's eggs, beside an open fire. Coffee was brought to our room with silver service, and the old butler turned down our beds with pampered perfection.

As the windows rattled in the January night, not one of the many *Mermaid* ghosts managed to wake me from my blissful sleep.

The next morning, after a breakfast really fit for a king, we took the slow road home. Morning tea in Winchelsea, lunch in Hastings.

By the time we arrived home we were fully rested and recovered. All the frights had become funny, even hilarious, and my sleepless night at the scariest place in the world seemed like a million miles away.

All in all we had a roller-coaster of an adventure. We were disappointed, then scared to death. Sleep deprivation followed, then starvation, then perfection. It all ended well and we had a trip of a lifetime to remember, and an unforgettable 25th anniversary.

I guess the lord of the manor was not too bothered about the whole affair. We never did get a refund, phone call, letter or even an enquiry as to what happened to us!

We were the guests that disappeared after one night—never to be seen again. After all, he did get his money with very little effort. Besides getting someone to open the door and put the heating on, that was it.

I got a few extra grey hairs, the scare of a lifetime and a great story to tell friends round the dinner table, so I guess it was a deal!

I also learnt from then on to check my hotel room before paying, and have never been caught since.

Now every time we drive past the old place we laugh, but I always notice my laugh has an insecure tinge to it. Not once have I dared drive back up that old gravel drive. Just in case some of those old spooks recognised me as the one that got away!

# The End

# Gone Fishing

I retrace my childhood steps, as I have done countless times before, and head for Langney Point.

In years past the shingle, pot-holed, dirt track was hard work on my bicycle. Today, new roads and a car make the trip simple. I stand upon the rock-strewn shore, face the heavy pre-dawn waves, and breathe deep the untamed sea.

A warm wind flies through me from the wild tossing surge. Wind and wave, the ancients that were here to witness the first dawn of our world greet me.

The waves rise and fall in heaving sighs and spume flicks from the tips as if shaken from some sunken hand. The Royal Sovereign Lighthouse sweeps the waves towards the shore with her warning light.

My lure plunges the depths where silent silvered beasts stalk the darkness. My rod bends against the current as I feel for the slightest knock on the line. The simplest movement that foretells the electric energy that follows a take on the lure.

The sun breaks the dark. First winking at me beneath the churning troughs then, slowly, lighting the horizon.

Eastbourne rises, like Atlantis, from the depths of night. First the seafront hotels glow orange, then the church steeples of All Saints and St Saviours. South Cliff Towers rises amongst the thundering surf.

Behind the town lies the green softness of the Downs capped in gentle mist, contrasting the dark brooding sea nibbling at its base.

Cormorants shriek at the dawn. Terns spiral down into the emerald green, like javelins thrown by invading hoards. Up they come, their dying prey swallowed alive to face the dark death. No screams in that black, silent, gasping.

All creatures of the sea seem to prey on the helpless whitebait that huddle together, shoaling like silvered sunken clouds, only to be picked off from above and below.

Fishing boats rise and fall, throbbing out from their moorings at Sovereign Harbour. Sometimes just their mast lights showing as they pitch and roll.

They fight their way onward to their different fishing grounds. The low boulders of the Geenlands. The mud and pebbles of Shingle Bank. The sand and rock of Coppar Shoal where the Robin Huss, Cod and Turbot roam.

Some point towards the rocks of the Gullivers and the rough ground of the Bushes, where the Bull Huss and Skate feed. I see the *Clar Innis*, named after a tiny Scots Island, with her twin hull and long, low back, point toward the horizon. She ploughs her way to the deep grounds where sunken wrecks hide Tope and Conger eel.

The *Relentless*, originally out of Ramsgate, pauses over the sunken boiler stacks of the *SS Barnhill* that was bombed by Germans off Beachy Head in 1940. Its back broke off Langney Point as it was being towed to harbour.

Now only visible at low-tide, the black barnacled boiler stacks reach skyward through the surf like giant arms, but no rescue is to come for her. Silently she will lie in her sandy grave. Her brutal death lost to all but those few old men, who still string their yarns over pints of beer and puffs of smoke.

Fishermen brave the sea, as did their forefathers, in hope of food for table and pocket. The hard unforgiving life at which they labour–making a living–sometimes.

Not one of them would swap their precarious unforgiving toil to become a landlubber. Not one would change the slippery rolling deck, the lashing sea, the danger and the complete fulfilment of their souls, for a safe, warm office.

A bite! Sharp, electric, shuddering.

The rod bends and the line rises in the surf, slicing the sea like a cheese wire as it lifts, tightening from rod to fish. I scramble over the green weed-scattered rocks. Slipping ... pain!

Rod held high, bending, juddering, I regain my feet. I feel a throbbing down my leg. I know I am cut, but I am in a battle. An ancient battle between man and beast. Primeval instinct prevails. As the hunter-gatherer I fight on. As does my adversary.

I reach the shingle. Safe, loose footholds now. I wind and play the wild creature. It kicks and runs. First left, then right. Up and down. We battle, swords drawn against the great Cyclops now rising fast on the horizon.

I catch my first glimpse of the fish as it lifts from the surf. It is a beauty.

I back up the beach. The waves crashing down and spraying me. I feel my leg sting as the fresh salt-water bites into the new wound. My wrist that took the full force of the stumble, aches. But I fight on.

Now comes the most dangerous place to lose a fish… the surf. The backward surge of the surf acts as a lead weight on the fish.

I time the last long pull to coincide with the incoming wave that rises like a leaping beast, crashing down and greedily clawing back the gravel, like a gambler at a card table.

There he is. A perfect wild bass of around three pounds in weight. A king-in-waiting. Master of his environment. He lies on the shingle, gills gasping for life, exhausted. The unblinking wide-eye…, staring.

I grab my cloth and carefully wrap it around the bee-sting spines. I remove the hook. It fights once more, now in its foreign land of air and earth.

I watch its gills open and close, its mouth gasp. In its moment of attack the hunter became the hunted. Its prey, now captor, a shiny *Abu* pike lure.

We face each other. The conquered and the conqueror. Does it think? Does it know that I hold its life, this beauty of the wild oceans? Quickly I bring out my camera. One picture that is all I need and back to the sea.

As I move closer to the surf the bass feels its element and fights once more. I wait, counting the rollers and, after the seventh, always the largest, I throw it back into the receding wave. A slap of the tail and it is gone, back to the mysterious world I will never know.

As hunter-gatherer I no longer kill these beauties for food. I am surrounded by stores stuffed with more food that my ancestors could dream of.

Farmed fish from my local chippy on a Friday night, soaked in vinegar and sprinkled with salt, tastes as good as anything I have ever cooked.

Yet the primal urge to hunt still pounds in my old veins and draws me to the hunt.

I sit on the wet shingle and pull up my trouser leg to see the damage. Blood trickles down in three places. Bruises will follow, pain, stiffness and, finally…, just memories.

I stand and stretch. My neck hurts, my back hurts, my leg hurts and my swollen wrist won't make the smooth motion to wind the reel.

I decide it is time to head home. During the battle dawn has broken. Warmth from the sun dries the wet stones and bright colour fills every pore of my world. I scrape my way up the steep shingle bank, heavy, hard work that was once so easy in my youth.

One last time, breathing heavily from the toil, I stand as I had done so many times since a child, surveying the scene that only a god could make.

The great sea that surrounds our island pounds the shore as it does my veins. The sea that shaped our nation of seafaring islanders; that took us to the four corners of the earth in exploration and conquest is in my blood as sure as the air I breathe.

Eastbourne has risen, bright and busy. The sky is blue. The sea is green. All around there is movement. People walk, run, cycle. There are cars, buses and noise. Not the early, natural, noise of my primal dawn but man-made noise.

I walk awkwardly to the car, but I have to turn once more. I must have a last look, one last peek. One more picture to take with me to the old people's home for when I close my eyes in years to come. I breathe deep.

Home. I bathe my damaged limbs, eat. With my pain the battle returns, fresh to my mind. A smile follows.

How many times I have fallen, tripped, ripped and broken in my life? Would I change one single time? Never.

One more war wound, one more battle.

## *The End*

A calm sunrise at Langney Point

# TEARS OF A CHILD

*I rarely write fiction but this is a little story I started many years ago and have now finished. I hope you enjoy it.*

A troubled dawn threw shafts of uneasy light through the gap in the tatty curtains. I rose slowly, stretching to ease my knotted muscles. I'd had a broken night, sleeping propped against the dormitory door, covered by my old grey blanket.

My only chance of escape was now. The only window of opportunity was the few short minutes between the release of the door locks and the time when Big Bert, with his stale fag-beer breath, made his early rounds.

Although watches were not allowed at the school, I had learned to count my heartbeats in time with the main clock in the assembly hall. The clock was perched below a wooden plaque that pronounced to all that entered **THE WAGES OF SIN ARE PAID BY THE DEVIL!**

This was supposed to be a reminder of why we were all here. At fifteen, I had already spent four hard years at the place— four years too long. They had taught me to read and write but the price was paid and the cost was high.

I had worked out that 80 of my heartbeats made 60 seconds and, from that, I could calculate the three minutes I needed from the first *clank* of the automatic locks until Big Bert got to the dormitories. Three minutes were all I needed to make it to the outer fence and freedom.

I knew my route. Lying in bed night after night, I had planned it a thousand times. Today the Bermondsey School for Wayward Boys was going to lose one of its inmates.

Lying on the lumpy old horsehair mattress I shared with several other creatures, I had planned my escape down to the last detail. I had left nothing to chance. God knows I'd had enough time to plan it. Now all my possessions were in a tightly rolled bundle tied with my mate Jimmy's shoelaces. It was tucked under my arm waiting for the right time.

I could just imagine his face when he went to put his shoes on later, but I knew Jimmy wouldn't mind—he was a special mate.

Jimmy was a watcher. A boy of few words. When I'd first arrived at the school he'd spent a week observing me from the corners, saying nothing. I'd been aware of him, but like a new fish in the pond I'd spent my days examining my new surroundings, finding out where I could and couldn't go.

Jimmy was full of complex emotions. Hard as nails on the outside, soft as putty on the inside. Though he was younger than me, he was tough. As he walked he swaggered, an instant message to leave him alone and keep your distance. His hands were rough and calloused from work. His nose was stubby and crooked from countless scraps.

After a lifetime of borstals or *secure schooling* as they called it, his feelings were hidden under a thick skin. Sharp glances from his electric-blue eyes told you all you needed to know. Jimmy was nicknamed Sledgehammer because, if he hit you, you rarely got up.

He was the only boy in that hellhole that the school bully left alone.

A few days after I'd arrived, I came across Jimmy in one of the changing rooms. I'd heard strange noises on my way from the loo and come to investigate. Jimmy was sitting slumped forward on a bench. The summer sun was streaming through the window, lighting him in a beam. He was sobbing his heart out. As I cautiously approached him, huge gulps of breath shuddered out of his body. I wondered what had happened.

"What's up, mate?" I asked hesitantly.

He slowly opened his hand. There lay the remains of a butterfly, bits of its delicate wing scales all over his palm. "I tried to let it out," he gasped through his tears. "But when I went to catch it, I killed it."

Jimmy wanted his own freedom so much that the death of the tiny fragile creature he had tried to set free was too much. A lifetime of pain poured out of him that sunny morning.

We sat in silence, my hand on his shoulder, the only gesture of comfort I knew. From that moment, though we never talked of the incident, he became my guardian angel. We were mates.

Around my neck now hung the shoes sent to me two years earlier by my hated stepfather. A short note inside had read, "You may want these. I don't!" It had been an unusual offering from a hard, violent, man. He'd probably had no one else to give them to and couldn't bear the thought of wasting them. They were already worn and too large for me.

I took great pride in polishing them, using everything from candle wax to pork rind. As my feet grew they pressed at the ends and my big toes pushing up two shiny lumps on the brown leather, which looked like conkers. I often playfully passed the time by pretending to have conker matches, clicking my feet together. I didn't care how they looked. Now they fitted like a glove and they were mine—all mine.

A tear-stained letter from an aunt telling me of the death of the little brother I had never met had finally spurred me into action. Pete had lived for less than three years. The letter was short and painful to read—the opposite of how happy I'd been when I'd heard I had a baby brother. I'd kept the letter and read it over and over. I knew Mum couldn't write, so it was up to others to let me know. I examined the envelope that had been redirected to three other schools before finding its way to me.

So many times I'd dreamed of what Pete and I would do together. So many plans. We were going to rule the world. Now it was all over—bought to an end in a fit of rage by a sod who'd drunk away the wages he'd been paid for working in the pit.

I knew Mum needed me now and I was ready and willing. Over the years at the school I'd grown from a scared cowering child to a hard resourceful fighter. The tears for my brother had turned to hate. Hate for the man who had taken from me everything I'd held dear after my real dad's death.

The time was right and my plan to escape was now in action. I slipped out the door and crept along the corridor, keeping to the side of the smooth maple floor. Thousands of children over a hundred years had polished the wooden surface that roared when we all thundered down to breakfast. Now, at dawn, the only sounds were the slumber of one hundred and thirty-six forgotten children—and the boards gently creaking under my feet.

At the stairs I spread my feet wide to reduce the creaking of the boards. My worn grey socks pushed into the edges of the skirting board as I made my way to the first landing. My lumpy socks had been darned many times. It was always a race to get the least mended and most comfortable pair after washday.

I passed the spot where I'd gotten a huge splinter in my first week, and suddenly thought of Matron. Known as Busty and the butt of most of our gutter humour, Matron was the only nice person in the dump. She had shown me a few moments of tenderness in an otherwise hostile world. She'd pulled the offending item from my heel and I'd felt like a wounded lion saved from an agonising fate. I was infatuated. From then on we'd always exchange cheerful smiles when passing her doorway. I'd often wondered if she had any kids of her own, or if we had become her family. She sometimes wore a sad, distant, smile as if she had another life somewhere in her past.

Once on the landing, my next task was to get past the masters' quarters and into the laundry room.

The night before I had jammed all the bits of used chewing gum I could collect into the lock. My favourite place to find old gum was the main sink in the downstairs loo, where nearly every time I checked I would find a piece or two stuck to the enamel under the drinking fountain. I held my breath and slowly turned the handle downward. Everything rested on the door being open. If the chewing gum had not done its work I would be trapped.

It opened with a gratifying click. I slithered past the masters' rooms, then along the great hall where the ghosts of old teachers stared down disapprovingly from their gilt frames. They seemed to be frowning more than usual and I took silent pleasure in this.

When I got to the laundry shaft I climbed into the wooden box, pulled the doors closed and untied the rope.

Fate has a strange way of showing its hand. I knew I could get to the ground floor from the laundry shaft because of the school bully, Brainless Basher Billy.

Billy and his gang had cornered me one day on the way to lunch and dared me to climb down the laundry shaft—or else. I had to do it. Everyone at school knew Basher got huge pleasure from putting kids' fingers under the sash windows and smashing them to pulp. No one had ever ratted on him. No one.

Revenge by that mindless thug was far worse than the most severe beating by the teachers.

On that, my first trip down the laundry chute, I'd arrived at the washroom with a thump and heard deputy head Mr. Simmonds call, "Who's there?" Yeah right! As if anyone would be stupid enough to answer! But as hard as I'd pulled on the ropes, I'd been unable to lift the box back up, so I'd taken a gamble, bolting from the small box and running for the main stairs. I'd taken them at full speed, three at a time, and had been back to my floor before Simmonds had a chance to see me. That dare had given me the escape idea. Little did Brainless Basher Billy know I had something to thank him for!

This time I slowly lowered myself down the chute, hand over hand in the dark, cold shaft. The only noise was the squeaking of the pulley as the rope rolled over it. Then, my worst nightmare! The precious bundle around my back caught in the gap between the shaft and the laundry box, jamming it solid.

I let go of the rope. Nothing moved. I tried to pull my jammed bundle but it wouldn't budge. I started to shake and whimper nervously. I remembered the last time, when I'd found I couldn't pull myself up. All my plans were doomed!

I slumped in the corner of the laundry box halfway down the chute, overcome by visions of the teachers pulling me out and marching me off to the evil headmaster. His cane swung before me in the darkness as tears rolled down my face.

Suddenly another feeling came over me: I must not, could not, fail. This was for my brother! I got up, determined to continue. I made one last desperate attempt to pull the box up enough to loosen the bundle. The rope twisted around my left hand, snakelike, gripping into my flesh. My right hand pulled so hard that I felt every muscle in my chest strain.

"Please, God, just this once!" I whispered, face contorted, eyes squeezed tight.

With a jolt the bundle shot out. No time to rest! The weight of the box pulled downward, the rope burning my arm as I dropped down the chute. I fought for control and made my way to the bottom, where I dropped, panting. I almost smiled at how my plans to count the magical three minutes with my heartbeat had been blown apart. My heart was racing like a steam train on the London Express.

I was blowing on my arm and hands to ease the pain when I suddenly became aware of a strip of light coming through the crack in the chute doors. Surely no one was here at this time of day? Horrified, I moved closer to the doors. A shadow passed by and I fell back with a thud. Wide-eyed with one hand over my mouth to hold in a gasp I froze. After a moment I crept forward again and put one eye against the crack.

I could feel the cool air rush past me up the shaft as I focused on a large shape. It was Cook. Big, fat Cook, who made Bert look positively waiflike. His grubby white apron swung from his enormous girth as he shuffled about. I hadn't counted on this. It had never dawned on me that he would be here this early. I watched silently, a rat in a cage, as he threw off his dirty apron and tried to tie a new one around his belly. Flapping around like an oversized chicken, he was fighting a losing battle, his fat fingers stretching uselessly around.

Suddenly he stopped, as if remembering he twisted the apron and tied the knot to his side, and slipped the apron around until it was snug, hanging like a huge canopy from his frame. He slapped his head with his palm and walked off, a satisfied grin on his big fat face.

I had a soft spot for Cook. His food was always hot and there was plenty of it, as long as you held your nose when he dished up Tuesday's hotpot. "Get your laughing gear round that," he would chuckle, slopping it into our bowls.

I waited, praying he would go. After what seemed a lifetime he waddled off and I made straight for the laundry room window. The wonderful scent of fresh washing rose from the laundry. It reminded me how great it was to get those fresh clothes each week. Then toward the light of the windows, past the wicker baskets that routinely rattled up and down the corridors to collect smelly clothes. I made it to the window and eased it open and slid alligator-like over the sill to the playground below.

As I closed the window I heard footsteps in the distance. Bert must have started his slow, heavy plod up the stairs to unlock the main hall doors and check the dorms. The wood creaking under his weight signalling his progress. I knew his stink would be trailing behind him, as it always did. It would hang in the air for ages after he had unlocked all the doors and made his way down to see Cook for breakfast and another of his endless fags.

I slipped on my shoes and tied them really tight then looked about. All was quiet. Dawn was breaking and the run across the grounds that was supposed to have happened in the early light was about to take place in bright sunshine. In front of me were the playground and 300 yards of playing fields. Beyond lay the fence and that beautiful thing I so longed for—freedom.

There was no time to waste. Fag-breath would soon notice I was gone, and I was way behind schedule. A quick look about; left, right. I crouched like a hundred-yard sprinter, took one last look and was away.

I ran like a startled rabbit. Bounding across the playground and the fields. Each stride brought me closer to my goal. I could see the bush where I needed to stop. I could feel my bundle banging against my back, urging me on. My feet were digging into the soft soil as I ran. I was fit. Years of physical training, stodgy food and scrapping make a child fit. Years of running around the field in endless circles with Mr Gregory, the ex-paratrooper at the centre, shouting at us like only a gym teacher can. He would have no slackers. I remembered the day Jimmy had fallen and cut both his knees. He'd made Jimmy run around the field another ten times in the rain, blood trickling down his aching legs as the rest of us watched in horrified silence.

I slid to the bush and rolled over to see if I'd been spotted. A hedge sparrow, startled by my sudden appearance, shot away chattering its annoyance. Otherwise nothing moved, nothing stirred.

Opposite the fence was Mabel Baker's place. I used to watch the wrinkled old girl through the fence as she tended her small patch of garden. Death had been a patient bystander with Mabel Baker. He had called five times, once for each of her husbands and for two of her seven children, but had let her be. In the school dorms there were ghost stories late at night about how she'd made a pact with the Devil. I'd envied her so much as she toiled over her little patch of ground on sunny afternoons, free to come and go as she pleased.

Now it was my turn. My heart was pounding. I gulped down air. I was by the fence. The outside was shouting to me. I was so close now that I could smell the sweet, free, air.

I moved to the spot in the fence where I'd spent the last weeks digging. I'd hidden my work with some dead brambles. I removed them and shovelled away the loose earth, my fingernails clawing frantically at the soil. Then I started pulling at the wire. Within seconds there was almost enough room for me to squeeze under.

On the last day I'd been digging by the fence, Jimmy had crept up and asked what I was doing. It was hard to lie to him, but I had to. This was a one-boy escape. One boy with one purpose—to get home and help Mum. Jimmy was my closest mate and I knew I'd probably never see him again. If I was caught and stopped I'd be sent to a higher-security establishment, not back here. From bitter experience I knew to keep my mouth shut. It was difficult enough trying to get close to the fence on the short breaks without being spotted.

When he surprised me I told him I was burying a blackbird. He helped me mark the spot with a few bits of bramble. Then, typical Jimmy, he insisted on saying a few words over the fake grave, including the only part of *Who Killed Cock Robin?* that he could remember. As hard as I tried, I couldn't stop laughing at his rendition. I think I was the only boy in the school who could get away with laughing at Jimmy.

After some wild digging on my knees I decided there was enough room and wriggled under the fence. I caught my sweater on a twist in the wire. I panicked. It was as if a teacher were pulling at me, trying to stop me. I struggled to get free, ripping the sweater and leaving part of it on the wire.

As I got to my feet I heard a commotion in the distance. I looked back toward the school to see figures rushing around behind the windows.

There was a second's more silence, then the still morning air was split with the howling alarm.

They were too late! I was up and running. No money, no way to get home—but I was free!

I sprang over old Mabel Baker's flowerbed. Would she ever wonder at the footprints left in her soil? Where they had come from? How they'd been paid for in blood.

I began to run toward the town where I knew I could disappear in the early rush-hour crowd. Finding me would be as hard as finding a needle in a haystack—a moving needle, at that.

I was in my element in the back streets of a town. Growing up a street urchin, as I had, I could easily blend into the morning scene and then make my way home. I heard the sparrow that I had startled earlier, chattering in annoyance again.

I started my run for the town. I thought about how the evil headmaster, Splinter Harris, would never again whack his cane across my palms with that twisted, piercing look of pleasure as I screamed. Never again would I lick my hands and hold them out the window to catch a breeze to cool the welts.

The terrifying prelude to the pain he lashed out was watching Harris whack the cane across his desk to get it just right. He'd earned his nickname from preferring to whack with a split or splintered cane. Harris was a small skinny man with thin pale lips who held the school in a grip of terror.

The sound of the swish as the cane cut through the air made me run faster. This time I was cutting through the air! I was the swish of the cane. I ran with the sound of the free wind in my ears and the air rushing into my eyes.

Tears of joy welled up as I ran through the cold morning. The only time I would ever feel them again would be when I held my first child, whom I christened after a little lost soul I had so longed to meet. Behind me lay everything I despised and hated, in front of me only dreams.

At last I was out! My feet lifted up on cushions of air as I flew toward the town. This was it! Freedom! A different taste, a flavour only the once-caged can truly understand.

On turning the corner of Blackferry Street I leapt into the air and threw my bundle into the sky, announcing to all that I was coming. I shouted, "YES!" and punched the laughing sky. My journey from now was still fraught with danger but, as before, I would try to overcome.

I wiped the tears from my face. I knew that whatever the future held—however many times I was caught, however many times they would try to break my spirit—this was the best escape. The one I would always remember. The one that would mean the most to me. This was my greatest escape and the beginning of my hardest journey.

"Going somewhere without me, mate?"

I jumped out of my skin and shot round to see Jimmy standing behind me wearing the biggest grin I'd ever seen.

"Bloody hell, Jimmy, how did, what—why?"

"Never mind now, mate. We'd better scarper before they get onto us. Where we going, anyway?"

"To the railway station to catch any train away from here! Once we're out of the area we can plan what to do."

"I see you've thought about it," Jimmy panted as we raced toward the centre of town.

"All I thought about was escaping and getting home. The bit in between we'll have to work out later. Hey, nice shoelaces!" I puffed as I glanced down at the bits of string holding Jimmy's shoes onto his feet.

"Yeah, some bugger nicked mine. Just wait till I get him!" he laughed.

We made straight for the railway station and went around to the back yard by the coal bunkers. "We need to get into a baggage truck. It's easier to hide there than in the compartments," Jimmy shouted.

"Sounds like you've done this before."

"You don't grow up in the East End without learning a few tricks, mate. Never paid for a ticket in me life! Look, there's one—let's make a run for it!"

We bolted across the railway yard, leaping the tracks until we came to the baggage compartment of the last train on the track. "She should be going soon as the engine is fully steamed up," Jimmy said. "They only get a head of steam like that when they're about to leave."

I slid open the side door to the baggage compartment and heaved my bundle in. I hopped on board and pulled Jimmy up, sliding the door closed behind.

"Let's get comfortable under the sacks before we're spotted," Jimmy whispered, moving the empty post sacks from the corner and piling them up around some boxes.

We moved one of the boxes and startled the chickens inside. They made a right racket but they settled down once they were covered again.

Within a few minutes there was a bump and a judder then a whistle blew. "We're away, mate!" Jimmy announced.

The train let out a mighty blast and slid away from the station. "I reckon we'll be safe for a while now." Jimmy settled into his corner and made himself comfy on the bags.

"How on earth did you know I was going to escape?" I asked.

"How thick do you think I am? I saw you digging at the fence that day you made up that pathetic story up about the dead blackbird. Mind you, it was fun pretending to bury it. Ain't laughed so much in years."

"Yeah, but how did you know it was today I was making my escape?"

"Just a matter of watching you. When you nicked my shoelaces last night, I figured you were ready to go. That was a neat trick with the chewing gum, by the way. I was a bit worried you'd lost your marbles when you started collecting the old gum in the bogs. Still, it all made sense last night when I saw what you did with it. You ain't so dumb as you look. I spent years in that dump thinking about escaping but, if truth be known, there was not much on the outside for me to go back to, so I was just sitting tight. It was only when I saw you going that I thought it would be a good time to see how the outside world had changed. So here I am. Free! Great feelin', ain't it?"

"You sure got that right Jimmy, there's nothing to touch it!" I leaned my head against the sacks as the train grunted along the tracks to an unknown destination. Within moments the pressure of the restless night and the escape caught up with me and I slipped into a dreamless sleep.

"Sam, Sam, time to wake up!" Jimmy said, shaking me. I rubbed my eyes and for a moment couldn't understand where I was. As it dawned on me that I was free and running away from my hellhole, I grinned. Jimmy handed me a chunk of bread and a slab of cheese.

"Where did that come from?"

"Cook was busy picking his nose when I went through the kitchen so I grabbed what I could. I saw you go under the fence just as I got out the window, then a bleedin' sparrow scared me half to death as I ran across the field it came up out of the grass like a bullet when I nearly trod on it. Anyway, I reckon I have enough food for about two days if we eat careful like. Then we'll need to find something. But first things first. What's the big plan?"

"Look, Jimmy, I don't want to drag you into this," I said. "I'm on my way home to Burnley to help my mum and get even with that bloody stepfather of mine for killing my brother. I'm going to settle the score with him that he started the day he walked in on me and Mum."

"Sounds good to me, mate. Nothing I like more than settling old scores. Bit of revenge always makes you feel satisfied like. I knew from what you told me he was a bad sod, but your mum won't take kindly to you mushing him up like, will she?"

"I'll worry about that when we get there. My first job is to see that she's all right. My mum, how can three little letters mean so much? She is my whole world, she is everything now. Sorting my stepdad out is just a bonus. That is, if you still want to come?"

"I ain't got nothing better to do this week—but let me jus' check me diary." Jimmy leafed through his imaginary diary. "Yep—thought so. I can just squeeze in an escape and beating before the end of the month. Oh, just one question. Where's Burnley? I ain't never been out of London except for a day to the seaside before me Mum died."

"It's way up north in a place called Lanku'sheere, I think. It's all full of mills and mines. The only good thing there was the football. Still, I ain't been there for a few years. Don't reckon much will have changed. When we get a map I'll show you. Not much of a place, mind." What a mate, I thought. Who'd have ever guessed we'd end up running away together?

"Right, mate." Jimmy munched on his bread. "We need a plan. Sooner or later this train is going to stop, and we're going to have to act fast."

"Let's see where we end up first. Then we need a map to see where we need to go and probably some shelter for the night."

"Sounds good to me. Plan sorted. Wake me when we stop." With that Jimmy brushed some crumbs off his jumper, rolled over, scratched his bum and went to sleep as if he were in his own bed.

I got out of the sacks, stood and watched the countryside pass by. I kept breathing big, deep breaths and looking at the fields and animals. How fantastic it all looked, how different from where I'd spent the last few years. I could only imagine what was going on back at the school. Splinter would be whacking his cane in anger. Bert would be scratching his bonce, looking stupid, as he always did, and all those silly paintings along the hall would be turning in their graves. I could have bet all the other kids would be cheering at our escape. We'd all talked and dreamed about it and now Jimmy and I had actually gone and done it.

Suddenly the brakes screeched and a shudder went through the train. Jimmy was by my side in an instant. "I think it's a regular stop. We seem to be heading straight into the Smoke!" he reassured me. "I know this end of London and I know a place we can spend the night, too. We'll have to make a jump for it as we get down by the river."

The train screeched again as it lurched around a bend. Jimmy slid the door open and grabbed his bundle. "Get ready mate, we're going to have to work fast!" With that Jimmy threw his bundle from the train and shouted, "Follow me!" I chucked my bundle out, closed my eyes and leapt. The world spun and I rolled around and around and all went black.

"Sam, you're still alive! Christ, you hit the dirt so hard I thought you were a goner for sure! You nutter, you're supposed to look where you land! You made a bloody bomb crater of a hole where you landed. Stay still and catch your breath—we're safe here."

I tried to focus on Jimmy but he seemed distant and blurred. I went to speak but it all turned black again. When I awoke it was dark. Jimmy was by my side. "How long have I been out?"

"All bleedin' day mate, and you've got a corker on your bonce the size of a football. You must have hit something mighty hard when you tried to fly earlier. Here, sit up and drink this. It's some cold tea I nicked it from a workman's hut down the line. Here, look what else I found in the hut—a map and a train timetable. I been lookin' at Burnley. It's on the other side of the world! We sure have got a trip on our hands. I reckon we need to head for Euston Station to get a train to Burnley. Can you stand?"

I shakily rose to my feet as Jimmy helped me. I brushed some coal dust off my ripped jumper. "That's seen better days," he laughed. "I saw you left some of it on the wire fence back at that hole we escaped from. How do you feel now?"

"Bit wobbly, but nothing seems to be broken. Lucky I have thick skull, eh?"

"Down the road about a mile is a shed we can stay in for the night," said Jimmy. "Let's go and see how you feel in the morning. We're going to have to start early if we want to go north tomorrow."

The walk to the shed was hard and my footsteps were clumsy, but we made it. Exhausted, I drifted back to sleep.

The next morning I felt a lot better—dizzy but stronger, and I could walk. We made for the river and into London. By midday we'd made it all the way to Euston Station.

"Blimey, Sam, we only got thrown off two undergrounds and one tram. That's got to be a record! Lucky we didn't have to run, 'cause I don't think you would have made it," Jimmy said. "Still, that big black woman who let us stay on the bus probably only did so 'cause she felt so sorry for you. Time for a spot of lunch." Jimmy handed me another chunk of bread. "Tonight we'll see if we can catch a train up north, eh, mate?"

"Jimmy, I couldn't have got this far without you. I seem to be muzzy still. I'm sure I'll be a bit better tomorrow."

"No worries, mate. You leave it all up to Jimmy. He'll look after you, all right."

By nightfall we were looking for a back way into the station. "Here it is, Sam, a nice hole made just for us." Jimmy pulled up the fence and I slipped under it. Jimmy followed and supported me as we sneaked over the tracks. Before long Jimmy had lifted me onto another baggage train, where bewildered I hit the sacks with a thud. The last thing I heard as I fell asleep was, "Don't you worry, mate, get some rest. I'll look after you."

The next morning when I awoke I was still dizzy and couldn't stand too well. "It's probably the train," Jimmy said. "You'll be better when we're off it. We've made a dozen stops, and I reckon another three and we're there!"

"Where?" I asked.

"Burnley, dummy! Home!"

Home. My mind couldn't get around the word. It seemed so unreal. Could I really be nearly home after all these years? The dream was coming true!

Filled with renewed purpose, and some food, I felt a little stronger and not having to jump off a moving train when we arrived was a real plus. We crept out of the railway yard and headed out of town to the small suburb of Rose Hill. I kept giving Jimmy directions as we walked the last few miles to the road where I'd been born. Every step I took brought me closer to the mother I loved and the man I hated.

As we turned into Berry Lane I pulled on Jimmy's arm. "Jimmy, we need another plan."

"Another plan, mate! You and your plans. Look, you knock on the door and if it's a man I'll punch his lights out. How does that sound?"

"Well it is a plan—of sorts. And I don't feel up to doing anything but sleeping so we'll have to go with that."

"Always knew I was a genius, mate. Jimmy the genius—that's me."

At the front door I hadn't seen for nearly five years I hesitated. "Jimmy, whatever happens, always know that you are the best mate anyone could ever ask for. I owe you everything."

"Aw, shut it, you're making me go all mush and I need to be ready to fight," he replied. "Can't fight with tears in me eyes, can I dummy? You ready?"

"Yeah, let's do it!"

Jimmy knocked on the door and we waited. "I'll have to let you go for a mo' if I'm gonna crack your stepdad on the nut," he whispered. "You ready to stand up on your own?"

"I'll manage."

The handle turned and the door creaked open a tiny bit. I felt a surge of energy as I got ready but the door didn't open further. We could hear someone trying to tug the door but whoever it was couldn't pull hard enough. Then around the corner of the frame peered two large eyes. "Hello," came a sweet little voice. "My name is Emily! What's yours?"

"Oh!" I exclaimed. "My name is Sam, and this is my friend Jimmy. Could you tell me who lives here?"

"I live here, silly!"

"Yes, but who else?"

"My mum!"

"What's your mum's name?"

"Sylvia, silly."

"Sylvia?"

"Yes."

My mind was in turmoil. How could there be two Sylvias living in my house? Who was the girl? Where was the evil stepfather we had travelled hundreds of miles to whack?

I turned to see a bemused Jimmy looking at me. I turned back and felt my legs shake and all went black.

Slowly my eyes opened. The blurred view contained moving white shapes. I felt warm and comfortable.

I heard a familiar voice. "Come back to the land of the living, then, mate?"

"Jimmy, that you?"

"Sure is, and there's someone else here to see you as well. But keep your voice down. Here I'm called Frank."

"Frank?"

"Yeah, don't ask. It's me *nom-de-plum* in hiding. I'll explain later. Now come and sit up."

I felt Jimmy lift me and place pillows under me for support. "Don't worry about that bandage on your head," he advised. "You've been asleep for two days, pretending you have concussion jus' to get some sympathy. Now I would like you to meet someone. Remember on the train how you told me about those three little letters that meant so much!"

I turned my head and as my eyes started to clear I saw a face I had not seen for so many years. "Mum! Mum, is that you?"

"Yes, dear, it's me." She reached down and hugged me. I cried, she cried, we all cried. I even noticed the nurse at the end of my bed with a tissue. Jimmy looked at the ceiling as if he were examining the light, blinking continuously.

"I don't understand, Mum. Where's my stepfather?"

"He's gone," she said. "Took a boat to Australia to find his fortune. Walked out on us. Good riddance to bad rubbish!"

I looked over Mum's shoulder to see Jimmy pulling a face and smacking one fisted hand into the palm of the other. Then he shrugged and smiled. "Best laid plans, eh, mate!" he laughed. I smiled and hugged Mum even harder.

"Look, Sam," Mum began. "I've made a lot of mistakes. The biggest was listening to him and sending you away after that trouble with the police. Looking back on it, I know we could have worked it out, but you were so angry, and he was so mad. If I could turn back the clock I would do it in a second!"

"There hasn't been a night that I haven't prayed for you, not a day that you haven't been in my thoughts. It was only after that miserable man left that I tried to find where you had been moved to, but I had no luck. I searched and searched, and not being able to write, all I could do was keep asking people to help and have faith that someday we'd meet again."

"I know this is all going to be hard for you to understand but we're back together now. A family once more. And, I promise, I'll never hurt you again!" Mum clasped my face in her hands and kissed me.

"I have another little surprise, as well. When auntie May wrote to tell you about Pete and his death." She paused a little to catch her breath as the weight of her sad words brought a heaviness to her. "We never told you about Emily, she is Pete's twin sister. We kept her birth quiet as we thought she would never survive. She was so frail and underweight, the doctors told us she only had a slim chance of survival. I did not want you to worry about her. But as you can see she is a fighter, just like her brother and now she is fine."

Without pausing, Mum turned to Jimmy, who picked up something from the floor between them. She turned back. "This is your little sister, Emily."

"Hello again, funny man," said Emily, why do you have a towel on your head?" She said pointing with a puzzled look.

"Hello, Emily," I answered in total confusion. "I've had a bit of a bump. Where did you spring from?"

"The postman brought me, so Mummy says when I'm naughty. She sometimes says she'll send me back— but I know she's only kidding."

"Well, Emily, I'm your brother and I never knew you existed until we met at the front door and then I didn't know who you were. But now I know I have a little sister, I'll be the best brother you'll ever have!"

"Mum, Mum, I've got a brother!" Emily squealed excitedly. "It must be a silly postman that brought him here instead of home and he must have dropped him on his head. I would complain!"

We all laughed. I felt my energy return and it filled not only my body but also my soul. A happiness I hadn't felt for a long time poured into me. I heard myself laughing louder and louder. Laughter was falling out of my mouth. I had no control over it, and looking up at Jimmy I saw that he hadn't, either.

"Got a job already!" he wheezed out between peels of laughter. Your mum got it for me yesterday. I'm a shop assistant on ten bob a week. Beat that! And what's more, I'm sleeping in the big bedroom. You're in with your sister. I got dibs on it, 'cause you were out cold. That'll teach yer!"

Three days later, Jimmy, Mum, Emily and I walked out of the hospital and caught the bus. We walked up Berry Lane toward home. I felt my heart lift as if I had finally made it. My impossible dream had come true. I looked over at Jimmy, who was carrying Emily on his shoulders. He was laughing as she tickled his ears. Beside me walked Mum, her arm wrapped around mine. I held her tightly.

When we got to the front garden and walked up the path, I noticed a paper sign on the door. It had little handprints in different colours around its edge.

"I made that," piped up Emily. "Well, me and Aunt May dunnit, but it was mum's idea," she beamed.

It simply read…**Welcome home Sam. No more tears!**

## *The End*

## Days End at Combe Hill

*At the end of another busy day when the last drops of heat from a dying sun fall lightly upon the earth. When the hectic day breathes a deep sigh and softly leans toward night. How sweet the gently exhale of spent hours that welcomes evening with outstretched arms.*

*The scents and sounds of nature's evensong are so pleasant to nose and ear. This is the time that the small creatures whose tiny noises are lost in the midday hum come to the fore.*

*Sounds, lifted by the lateness of the hour float easily over the light mists of angles breath gathering in the low places. I see the spires and turrets of our ancient land reach above the fading landscape.*

*Life slows to the pace of the night and the stars that once shone upon the pharaoh's upturned faces rise once more to sprinkle our galaxy with fascination.*

*Oh this land, the land from which I grew, my glorious land.*

*How great it is to be alive, to breathe, to see, to feel this wonder.*

**Alex I Askaroff**

# Wakes Week

Dawn was still a long hour away as my Land Rover rumbled along the damp lanes. The deep-purple winter night was veiled by a most delicate sheet of wafer-thin cloud. I stopped to take a closer look.

Every now and then nature has that amazing way of tapping you on the shoulder and for a few moments you connect with her on an emotional level, in awe at her constant marvels. It was one of those special moments.

An unusually bright winter moon was lightening the thin sheet of cloud into the palest translucent white. It was a *tinkers* or *poachers* moon, clear and bright. No trout or pheasant would have been safe in olden days on a night like this. The cloud was silently gliding through the sky, like an old battle-torn sail pot-marked with cannon-holes. Through the holes stars sparkled in the midnight blue. It was a serenely beautiful sight.

The horizon had started to lighten into a paler blue with a wafer thin strip of orange propped up by a black sea. Venus, the Morning Star, brightest of all the stars, was slowly pulling up the sun from its nightly slumber.

Back in my car the headlights picked out the trees as I passed, instantly freezing them with a ghost-like glow. The tarmac was a shinning ribbon of black lace, wet from the mist and winter road-salt. Lamp-posts-lights hovered over the road like invading beings from outer-space, shining their yellow ray-guns through the mist down upon the unsuspecting motorists who raced between the rays and escaped into the darkness.

The haze that hung in the air was a sure sign that we were going to have a calm dawn.

Amazingly some of the trees still had their leaves on and a multi-coloured display of autumn hung between their branches.

One of the warmest summers on record had produced the perfect Indian summer. Britain in autumn has to be one of the most beautiful places. But as always the greatest show on earth was followed by the grim reckoning of winter, which, though late, had arrived full force.

Deep midwinter is when Britain is lashed by rain and beaten by storms. The darkest season was upon us with hardly eight hours of light in every 24. The sun, like a welcome old friend, only makes fleeting visits. It is, strangely enough, the season that a lot of Brits who have emigrated miss the most. I always long for December 21$^{st}$ when the sun turns and starts its slow climb back towards spring.

The South Downs take on a different hue in winter. They become dark and mysterious, like an ancient land lost in the mists of time. The hills, often shrouded in cloud for days, seemingly appear and disappear at will.

The valleys become wild and untamed. Their hearts are the pumping rivers, arteries of life swollen to full flood. They roll topsy-turvy to the sea, swirling and seething in muddy torrents.

Midwinter is the time when nature becomes the all-powerful lady of the long nights—and short, sharp days. The winds howl, the trees shake and the land shivers.

Ancient Britons survived these hard times huddled around their fires in caves and thatched wattle-and-daub dwellings, praying for the sun, for warmth and for spring to come. How glad they would have been to have our warm winters these last few years.

On the morning radio was yet more bad news.

In days gone by the news would always finish off with a lighter topic to soften our often-harsh world—but not anymore, bad, bad, bad.

The radio was announcing that two million Brits had left the country for good, and many were still leaving daily. A massive exodus was taking place, on a biblical scale.

England was being taxed at one of the highest levels in history, with more than 100 *New Labour* taxes, and all our complaining from years ago had come back to haunt us.

*Born free, taxed to death* they used to laugh! Now it was true. Every pensioner's pound was stretched to breaking point.

I reached for the button and silenced the radio's depressing news. Never had our country been more prosperous and never had people been so miserable. A strange paradox.

I breathed a deep sigh and drove on in silence. Just the low rumble of the Land Rover's engine to soothe my aching brain.

I met a wonderful old character once who told me that she had not seen everything in this world but had not missed much either in her 95 years. She said that there were two ways to go through life, happy or sad, and why would anyone choose to go through life sad!

I snapped out of pondering on life as the traffic ground to a halt on the main Lewes Road. A cow was ambling along the highway as nonchalantly as if on a picnic. Cars were stuck both ways as it came to a halt at a gate. It stood there looking at the field, waiting for someone to open it.

A few cars pulled around the cow but no one got out to open the gate. Farmer Harmer had his cattle in this area and it was probably one of his. I pulled up onto the verge and opened the gate and gave the beast a slap on a clean part of its arse. "Walk on," I shouted manfully. The cow, with hardly a sideways glance, lumbered nonchalantly into the field and started nibbling grass, as if to say *it was about time!*

I had no idea if it was allowed into the field but it was a lot safer than on the A27 with cars racing by. I look like an old farmer, what with my Land Rover and all, so I get away with doing these silly things! In fact if I had my life again a farmer I would be for better or worse.

Traffic ground to a halt again two miles before the road works to the new bridge over the railway line at Beddingham. I looked across to the entrance to Firle Place, one of the outstanding manors of my area and a beautiful example of early architecture.

The Gage family is now remembered for the greengage fruit but it was Sir John Gage that was the real gem of the family. He lived through one of the most exciting times in our history.

**Firle Place, one of the outstanding houses in my area.**

Sir John was a friend to a young and impetuous king, Henry VIII. He witnesses Henry's outrageous actions and more importantly flourished alongside the egomaniac. For his faithful service Sir John was well rewarded and built his grand house in Sussex where he lived along with forty retainers in full livery!

Sir John became Constable of the Tower of London but still found time to command an army to march North to defeat King James V of Scotland at Solway Moss in 1542.

Henry was so fond of Sir John he even left him money in his will. Things got a bit tricky for him as Henry's son, Edward VI, was a staunch protestant and Sir John would not give up his Roman Catholic beliefs. However he hung on to his position at the Tower. It was to there that poor Lady Jane Grey, queen for just a few days, was brought after Henry's daughter, Mary, wrenched the throne from her.

Lady Jane Grey, the first true Queen of England, went to the scaffold last, after witnessing her family's execution. Sir John was there to hold her shaking hand as she walked her final steps on Tower Green.

Delaroche's depiction of the final moments of Lady Jane Grey, a 16yr old said to be the brightest star of her age. She was Queen for just nine days! Her last words were, "Lord into thy hands I commend my spirit."

Sir John was responsible for the preparations for execution of Elizabeth, Mary's illegitimate half-sister and daughter of executed Anne Boleyn. Sir John treated her harshly knowing that to form any fondness toward the young girl would make her death all the more painful. For a year he looked after her knowing that she would follow the same fate as her falsely accused mother.

Elizabeth was just three when the French swordsman, hired by her philandering father, arrived to remove her mother's head.

Luckily, as history shows, Elizabeth wriggled out of her execution by young cunning and charm. She went on to be one of our most glorious rulers.

Her reign will always be the height of the Tudors, a true golden age, but few realise that she had over 700 people executed during her long reign, over twice as many as Mary who will forever be remembered as Bloody Mary.

Sir John died before Elizabeth became queen but left enormous wealth, lands and Firle Place, which has been looked after by the Gage Family ever since.

I knew I would sit in traffic for an hour edging forward inch by inch along the Beddingham Road. I decided to slip off a side road to Ringmer and drop down to Lewes from there.

I drove through the beautiful village of Glynde still fast asleep in the dark hours, then up the hill passing Glynde Place and onward to Glyndebourne, home of the world famous Glyndebourne Opera House.

Glyndebourne Opera was built for love and it always gives me a little thrill when I pass.

Old Etonian and lord of the manor so to speak was John Christie. The eligible bachelor used to pass the time at his estate by holding events around the country calendar. He loved music and in his 80-foot Organ Room he had one of the largest organs in Britain outside of a cathedral.

During one of the musical evenings a young singer caught his eye. Besotted, Christie followed Audrey Mildmay on her tour around the country showering her with gifts. His dogged persistence paid off, for he won her heart.

Within a short period the lovers wed and designs were soon afoot to build a magnificent opera house. On May 28th 1934 the 300 seat Glyndebourne Opera House opened with Audrey performing in Figaro. A special train was commissioned to run from London Victoria to Lewes.

It was a perfect love story. Only curtailed briefly by the war when children from London were evacuated to Glyndebourne. Glyndebourne now has seating for over 1,200 people.

Before long I had made my way to Lewes and my first call of the morning.

As I got out of the car the cool air was layered with the sweet smell of barley wine. Thick and smooth, like treacle on fresh bread. It was drifting over from the old Lewes brewery, *Harveys*.

It was their traditional mixture of freshly-ground malt and barley called Christmas Ale. The scent of the hot liquor from the mash tuns was gently wafting through the winter's air, coating it with its heady aroma. Sussex's oldest brewery was doing a fine job of continuing their special ales, and promoting the festive season in their own time-honoured way.

I parked under a large sprawling oak tree. In the shadowy half-light it looked ominous and overbearing. Large gawky limbs stretched awkwardly into the blackness. Its leaves were rustling and branches were pointing finger-like in the midwinter dawn—as if to shoo me away.

I hurriedly made for the door where a light shone through the small glass centre, and reached for the brass knocker.

The darkest time of year is often when holidays are on everyone's minds. And my customer was no different. When we got around to talking about our future holidays, some wonderful old ones came to life. I was introduced to a Northern specialty, in a full Lancashire dialect, the wonders of the long-forgotten Wakes Week.

When I first wrote this story I wrote as I heard her speak, if that makes any sense. However trying to translate the thick Lancashire accent into writing that was easy to follow proved too difficult and awkward. Even I had trouble reading it and I wrote the thing!

After much debate I tore up thousands of words and started again from scratch. I rewrote the whole of Penny's story with just a touch of her accent. I hope you like it.

Penny was 97 and still living independently in her own home. A small lady no more than five feet and a fag paper tall with fading eyes set deep behind a wrinkled smile. She had a crystal clear memory and such enthusiasm for her old holidays that when she told me about Wakes Week it was if I had been there with her.

"Wakes Week were the best week of the year when I were a child and the best holidays of me life," said Penny excitedly. Glad to talk and have someone to listen. "I remember them holidays as the happiest of times. I was born into a Lowry

Landscape in Oldham, Lancashire, when milk was still delivered in pail by horse n' cart and collected on doorstep with jug.

"Horses droppins were like gold to them with gardens or allotments—but there were rules.

"In our street droppins belonged to the house nearest where they plopped. If you wanted them you had to ask permission from house nearest, then 'oik em off with bucket'n'spade.

"Many a-time Pa would come back with a smile and a bucket of droppin's for his veg'. Them were the days. Simple things that pleased. We used to say you get owt for nowt! And a good bucket of droppins made sure you got the best veg possible.

"Oldham were a mill town in centre of cotton industry. The world centre!

"Largest producer of cotton in world when I were a kid. Long gone now, but in my youth it were industrial heartland of large mills that darkened skies on our way to school.

"Great brick buildings swallowed up thousands of workers every morning and spat them out exhausted every night, full of dust and fluff. When Lowry painted the Lancashire Mills and people he caught a bit of the atmosphere but his paintings were too moody for me. In reality it weren't all doom and gloom, everyone just got on with there jobs and daily life in the mill towns. There were jobs for all.

"Pa told me once that there were mills for every day of year in Oldham. Working day and night.

"Let me see, there were Hartford Mill, Glebe, Heron, Durban and Devon—and more. Hundreds of them there were. Must have been tens of thousands of workers spinning and weaving cotton for whole world. The thirties were bad, what with recession an' all. It hit mills hard. But there were good times as well.

"After the Second World War we had workers from all over the world come to Oldham. Street next to us didn't have two families in row from same country. We were real multicultural.

"We all got on great in early days. It were only when work started to run out that trouble came.

"I doubt there's one mill left still running today. Most of them have been knocked down, made into units for storage or office space.

"Mind you they were ugly beasts. They had chimneys like great ocean liners, and huge factory gates of iron and wood, and a million bricks that made the whole colour of the town different.

"Both Ma 'n' Pa worked at' mill as a weaver and winder, as did their kin before them. They were both brill at sign language and superb lip-readers. Specially Ma who could have a conversation across a noisy factory without a word spoke. I was too young to work in mill—but I did get the benefit of Wakes Week and it were great," she bubbled.

"Wakes Week were the one special week of year that factories closed in Oldham. They used to close mills down town by town, all on different weeks, so that mill production and output would not be affected.

"Wakes Week were an old tradition steeped in history. Story was that long time ago there were a great drought across the North of England. Cattle died, people starved but in Lancashire and Derbyshire the wells never ran dry and so the people were saved.

"To thank God there were a well blessing. The well were all dressed up and the local priest would give thanks to God once a year—every year. That practice went all around the towns and villages, week by week from March till September.

"They still follow the tradition today in many towns and villages in Derbyshire. Each town celebrated Wakes Week finishing on Saturday with carnival like. The tradition stuck.

"Now, our holidays weren't paid, like. Times were different then and it weren't all good. We would have a few days at Christmas and then one week unpaid for the whole year. Can you imagine that today?

"We would all save the whole year to afford our special trip. And special it were too, for it were the only time of year that we got away from the smoke and grime of our mill-town home.

"Ma 'n' Pa would put all their money into an old biscuit tin under the floorboards in their bedroom. The chamber pot was always on top of it so no one would steal it!

"Money were money in them days, hard earned and carefully spent. It was always kept at home as banks were not to be trusted!

"It were such a big do, Wakes Week, and a whole year's savings went in the pot. Ma would sew special clothes for us to look smart like on holiday.

"I had two brothers and they would always squabble over who got to wear the newly made clothes and who had last year's hand-me-downs.

"It were most exciting time as we got close to our break. All neighbours gossiped over the washing lines in street and kids chatted about where they were going, Bridlington, Llandudno, Morecombe or Scarborough. Some went as far as the *Paris of the North*, Southport.

"But there was only one place for us, the *Holy Grail, Shangri-La*... **Blackpool**. The best place to have a week's holiday in Britain come rain or shine and the most popular holiday resort Britain ever had.

"When the final factory hooters blew on the last work day there were stampede out factory gates. Everyone were in such high spirits, even the grumpy old men who wouldn't smile for love-nor-money all year, would almost grin that day.

"It were great, bundlin' on to trains, Pa would drag the old suitcase on from platform. We were packed like smoked kippers but we knew just about everyone on the train so we all chatted and swapped sandwiches.

"When we were at Blackpool we would bump into so many folk from Oldham. It were as if the whole town went to same place.

"It were strange really. Many of the families worked together, lived in the same few streets, holidayed at the same place at the same time every year.

"It were really like home from home. The atmosphere were grand. I'll remember those days till my last gasp leaves me. Did I say it were grand?"

We both laughed. She was in full swing and loving every second, as was I. She continued...

"Blackpool were always heaving. They couldn't have got more people in the place with a shoe horn. After breakfast at the hotel, which were always the *full English*—better than we ever ate at home—we would run to beach and play till lunchtime, then back to hotel again for a great lunch. All paid for from our Wakes Week club savings. We watched our pennies but everything cost money. We even paid for the cruet at the hotel, salt and pepper were extra like.

"Pa would carry his deck chair all the way back to hotel as he weren't going to pay for it twice! Often, when it were sunny, you couldn't see a free spot on the beach and even when it were raining the donkeys still went up and down for sixpence.

If you were a good rider they'd let the old things, with their straw hats, ears poking through, break in to a canter.

"I came a cropper several times. If you fell it were only soft sand. My little brother fell off once and cried for an hour. He only shut up when Pa bought him the best ice cream Blackpool pier had to offer.

"Some days when sun shone you could not see the sand at all, just a million people all having fun and what a noise. You could have landed a jumbo jet and no one would have heard it! Ma made my swimsuit, it were knitted from wool, like many of them were in those days. When it got wet it just sagged all out of shape and looked bloody silly. Still we all looked silly so it did not matter. Many just tucked their skirts into their knickers and paddled!

"Pa never had a swimsuit in all years we went there. He would just roll up trousers to his knees and plonk himself down in chair, slip his cap over his head and snooze, in his jacket too!

"Pa's holiday was doing as little as possible for as long as possible. I suppose just the opposite of his usual hard working day at the mill. He would get stuck into the odd sandcastle now and again but usually he concentrated on his deckchair.

"Even when the wind blew and the rain came we went to beach. In our Mac's and Wellies armed with bucket and spade we built sandcastles and channels for the sea to rush into. We collected shells and searched for sea monsters which often turned out to be crabs with legs missing.

"Ma was mostly the one who took us out. Some evenings we would sit on the sand eating fish'n'chips out of old newspapers folded like upside-down hats, drowned in vinegar and salt. Taste were pure perfection.

"Of course in those days fish'n'chips and mushy peas were good for you. Food fit for a king. And fish'n'chips eaten on the beach, by the sea, with the fresh salt air blowin' in yer face, better yet. Any leftovers were thrown to gulls that would gobble them up in an instant.

"People thought that the sea water would cure anything—and some folk even took it home in bottles, daft sods. Made me sick, just a mouthful. Now we would shudder at thought of drinking any of that filthy stuff and, believe me, it were worse in years gone by than today. Mind you I have to admit I saw a saltwater nasal spray in Boots the Chemist last week so there may be some truth in it after all!

"At night you could see lots of girls and boys kissing'n'cuddlin' under the girders of the piers. Ma would tell us not to look but we would peep through our fingers, giggling at them, on our way to amusements.

"Were another world to the grime of Oldham. The air smelt of sea and candyfloss and the lights twinkled along the sand like a magical kingdom. It really were a place of dreams.

" View from North Pier to Tower were like a different world… the Pleasure Beach and the Golden Mile stretching along the coast would shine at night like a million stars fallen from heaven.

"Blackpool's Giant Wheel at the Pleasure Beach was so scary we just had to ride it over and over. Screaming all the way of course!

"With the lights at night it were like Christmas every day. Blackpool were where I had my first drink of Tizer. We only had the occasional bit of squash at home see, nothing with bubbles. I took a gobful and it exploded. The orange fizz went straight up me nose and felt like it were going to burst out of me ears! I must have looked a treat because the rest of the family laughed so much they cried.

The roller coasters took my breath away, made my eyes run and scared me to death, but we just had to go on them. Time after time, till pocket money run out and we couldn't beg more.

"You had to keep an eye out for the trams mind! They were up and down all day and most of the night. Ting, ting, they would go rattling along tracks, all posh and polished. You could put your hand out and jump on board.

"Pony and traps would run along the seafront taking people to and fro, from the huge Blackpool Tower or Fairyland to their hotels or fun-fairs.

"I remember one year my brother broke a tooth on a stick of Blackpool rock. He cried so much that sweet-seller gave him a whole new stick. That soon stopped him, but he never shared it, little git!

"Then there was the Roller Rink where we bolted on the fibre roller-skates to our shoes and off we went free as birds floating across the rink. It were like flying till you hit someone, which was most of the time when it were busy. Then we would fall into a huge bundle of arms and legs laughing out heads off.

"Our savings soon dwindled with all our fun. A year's money was going in a week but what-a-week. Blackpool were our week of dreams that kept us alive all year.

"It were the thought of Wakes Week and Blackpool that kept us going when times were hard and times were often hard for mill families. Fifty-one weeks of work for one week of heaven!

"Only once in the week's holiday would we go to ballroom. Tower Ballroom were superb, like.

"With giant Wurlitzer's rising from the floor, being played as they rose. It were the most beautiful place I'd ever seen. It burnt down once but they rebuilt it even better than before. It were like some French King's palace. We would sit for the afternoon like royalty, eating cakes and drinking squash while couples danced.

"We would watch as Ma 'n' Pa tried to dance to the different tunes on the sprung dance floor. Watching them was so funny, but they didn't care. They could dance as well as the next couple.

"After dancing they would hobble back to hotel to soak their sore feet. We used to copy their walk all the way back, giggling behind.

"We always knew when week was coming to an end as Pa's fingernails were clean as a whistle from not working at mill but playing in the sand.

"Aah, when I think back now that week each year were pure magic. Train ride home were not so noisy as we knew it would be another year to wait… but we would start saving as soon as we got back.

"All in all it were the perfect holiday from start to finish. I have had nothing to touch it for 50 years!

"One year, we needed money for doctor so we couldn't afford the trip to Blackpool. We all cried, even Pa. But times were hard and we had to make the best with what we had. We stayed put that year. When the train whistle blew with everyone leaving you could have heard a ghost walk across our room.

"Pa just poked the cold fireplace with the fire tongs and lit up his pipe while Ma peeled spuds silently crying into the bowl. I hugged my doll tight and said nothing. That were a hard day for us.

"Oldham were like ghost town. No working mills, no noise, no people. Well there were a few—but not like normal—and they all went to same place for treat.

"Down centre of town were market called Tommyfields. It were named after Tommy the pig breeder but that were where the travelling fair stayed.

"The fair went round to all mill towns one by one, it were real treat to see them arrive in procession down street. There were always a drummer in front leading the way. There were another park, Alexandra Park, up in Glodwick but the fair never went there.

It were Tommyfields where all the action were.

"All rides were penny a-go and, if you smiled nicely at some of young fairground workers, you could get ride for free! It were not as great as Blackpool, like. But a lot of fun all the same. Cheap n' cheerful.

"The Oldham Brass Band would parade down the streets with symbols bashing and drums rolling. We would line up and cheer. There be nothing like a brass band to whip you up when you are down. When they played Land of Hope and Glory you would have a lump the size of an apple in your throat. William Tell would make your blood rush it was such a great tune and Danny Boy, played on that polished brass, so soft and mellow, would make a grown man reach for his hankie.

"By the 1960s it were all coming to an end.

"Mills closed. Workers striked. Families quarrelled. All of a sudden sides were taken as last jobs at mills were being fought over.

"Blackpool also suffered—as did all the holiday towns that catered for Wakes Week. No work meant no money and no money meant no holiday!

"Lucky for me, my future was down in London, so I missed worst of the riots. Foreign competition took its toll and best mill town in the world crumbled into despair.

"Only now is it sorting itself out, but not in cotton any more. We don't produce anything anymore except rubbish mountains!

"Funny now, when you see Blackpool all quiet and sedate, like. There were times when you could have shouted at top of your voice and someone a few yards away would not hear you. That crowded it were. A million happy people all in one place for one thing… **holiday**!

"They were the glory days, all gone now. I'm glad to have been alive to have seen it. The like will probably never come again.

"Well, I should never say never. Blackpool still gets millions of visitors. There's even talk Blackpool may get a giant casino licence that will really put her back on the map again. Las Vegas of the North! That would be grand.

"The old Blackpool ballroom would be full again! Now that would be something to see!

"So there we have it, Wakes Week, just a memory now for the few folk that has them. All gone now the mills, the way of life, the community spirit, friends in every street.

"Mind you, you can take the way of life–but you can't take the memories. There will always be a bit of my heart in Blackpool.

"While I breathe those days will put a smile on my face.

"Well young man now that's what I call a holiday—, Wakes Week."

I had been working away on my customer's machine and travelling with her through a fascinating period of our social history while daybreak snuck up.

Out of the window the low sun was under-lighting the clouds in a bubbling Satsuma sunrise.

The clouds were playing catch-up in the virgin sky. To excite the imagination they were forming the shapes of faces, spectacles, eyes, ships, trains—and countless other patterns as they folded into each other in that great pudding bowl high above the earth.

And even above them, in the lightest blue of heaven, strings of pure white knitted the atmosphere where passenger jets were taking excited holiday makers to their dream destinations.

The huge oak, under which I had parked, had changed from dark pyjamas into a resplendent suit of brown and gold. He had performed a Jekyll and Hyde on me.

Earlier he had looked so menacing in the darkness, but now was cutting an imposing figure.

There are short periods each day, as the sun rises and, again, when it rolls lazily over the horizon after a hard day's toil that is sometimes magical.

The light is completely different to the rest of the day and, just for a few fleeting moments, the world is soft and beautiful. Even great, ugly, sprawling cities can look stunning in the light. Today was no different.

It is the time that film-makers used to wait for, just to get that perfect love scene when all seemed right with the world.

The mighty oak stood proud like an *Admiral of the Fleet* trimmed in sky-blue. The base of the tree was pushing through a blanket of flame-kissed autumn leaves the colours of a fruit shop display. The wet bark, caught in the first rays of the sun, glittered in sparkling ribbons. The bronze oak-leaves, covered in droplets of dew, shimmered in the sharp dawn breeze sparkling like medals with pearls of bright light on them.

Gulls floated high above. Silently circling, searching for scraps along the River Ouse that was in full flood. I felt like standing to attention and saluting the proud old tree. I restrain myself from these sudden urges to save spending years in an asylum!

As I drove to my next customer a fox ran through a field to my right, scaring up a bright male pheasant and his harem. Their panicked rasping-warning hic-ups were lost against the rumble of rush-hour traffic. Soon their portraits would be proudly portrayed on Christmas cards all over the country as part of our British celebrations, and yet funnily they are not *British* at all, being imported probably by the Normans.

So what! They look stunning, especially the male in his vivid plumage. The daft birds that I occasionally chase down country lanes, often too lazy to fly, are part of our colourful countryside.

I noticed some mistletoe on one of the bare old fruit trees. As Christmas drew close it would be picked and hung in rooms up and down the country for the cunning purpose of stealing kisses.

The local name for mistletoe is much more fun. Anyone who has squeezed one of the ripe white seeds will instantly understand why its nickname is *Christmas Bogey*! Never has a seed been surrounded by a more sticky mass of gooey snot.

Holly shone from the hedgerows with red berries bright in the new light. The decorating of homes with holly at Christmas was one of the pagan rituals adapted by Christianity. Christians were only too happy to use holly as the prickly leaves were a reminder of the Crown of Thorns that the Son of God wore and the red berries signified his blood. Pre-Christians originally used to decorate there homes with holly to appease ancient gods and to stop lightning striking their dwellings. Hey! It may work!

As I rolled forever onward, to my endless customers, I pondered on life's up's and down's and the current state of affairs.

The exodus that was going on all over the country would just have to go on without me.

Our world is ever-changing. Like the elements all around. I had long ago decided that I would be in my little corner of the world to watch it all happen.

In the ebb and flow of our history, would this turbulent time be remembered years from now?

As I live through it, the feeling amongst the people is real and palpable. However I believe in the circle of life and the balance it brings.

I am quietly confident that Great Britain, our kingdom, as she had done for centuries, will sort her self out. We have faced many challenges, many enemies from sea and air. With determination and courage we have won through. Our history is full of sound and fury, of cannon shot and battle cries and our spirits have never dulled.

We will stand proud once more amongst the great nations of our world and I will be there gladly waving her flag.

Anyway, I was having way too much fun to go anywhere and there were so many more stories to write.

## *The End*

# Epilogue

Rolly ran in front of me along the ridge of Butts Brow. My faithful hound stopped to smell the wet grass with her usual interest. She turned to look at me. Her eyes were bright but the once jet-black hair around her face had turned grey with age. She almost smiled at me as droplets of water fell from around her mouth. For twelve years the old girl and I had walked the highways and byways of my beloved county. How many miles, how many paths?

I knew, at best, that we would only have a few more years together. The thought alone brought a tear close. I rubbed her flank and patted her as she ran off once more to discover new scents. Dogs seem to be forever filled with enthusiasm. I often wished that I had more of what they had but I would soon get arrested for smelling people! I re-called the phone call when Shelly Froggatt first rang, "I have your puppy here!"

My mind had gone into overdrive. I had remembered saying what a lovely dog she had and how I would adore a dog just like that. Over a year had passed since my visit to fix her sewing machine and the idle thought had soon slipped from my mind. Now I was confronted by a decision. I had never owned a dog. What to do? Reluctantly I went to pick up the little mutt with Yana, not realising how the bundle of fluff would chew my furniture, pee on the carpet and add pure joy to my life.

I had gone for a walk with a purpose, to get away from the phone and business and to think of how to finish my book. I had so many more stories to write. There was gorgeous Joan Godfrey who, as a young girl, had driven ambulances around

London during the Blitz. One time her ambulance heaved up into the air as explosions lifted the road.

The hilarious Sid Day who used to get the Wrens drunk and take them skinny-dipping along Eastbourne Seafront, after cutting his way through the barbed wire with borrowed clippers. Then there was old chap who, as an evacuee, went to pee on a haystack on his way to his new school in Bexhill, only to be shouted at by the Home Guard hiding inside! A shock he remembered all his life.

I had hundreds of stories still to write. The Hawker who made umbrellas and sold them along Oxford Street whose faithful dog waited by the bus stop for him every day, even after he never came home.

Then my old mate Ron Saunders who was turned down for military service as he was a land worker of high importance, *reserved occupation*. He reluctantly watched his mates go off to war. One evening at a local dance a girl handed him a matchbox. Inside was a white feather, it broke his heart.

There was Dan, who, as a kid witnessed the bombing of a margarine factory and saw a billion peanuts fly into the air only to be scooped up by eager locals with buckets and wheelbarrows. And the ghost of Sir Arthur Conan Doyle that stalks the back lanes of Crowborough searching for his grave, moved in the early dawn many miles away from his chosen spot at Windelsham Manor.

Sad stories, funny stories, I have them all. Piles of notes scribbled at customers' houses over the last four years as I had been writing Tales from the Coast. Chadwick the suppressor man who stalked the streets of Eastbourne during the 1950's and 1960's tracking down radio interference with his antenna looking like some mad professor.

Albert Blake, who, without a second thought for his own life, saved Eastbourne by jumping into an ammunition train and racing it out of town under heavy aircraft fire.

All books must come to an end but the stories go on. The time had come to draw a line under one book and hopefully start another. It was a hard decision to say goodbye to all the years of hard work and close the last page but it had to be done.

As Rolly ran out of sight along the soft green of our sensuous South Downs she, like this book, was flying away. I would have to close the last page and say goodbye.

And so, my dear readers, Book Four comes to a reluctant end. I have loved writing every word. I do hope you have enjoyed my journey, our journey, and should I be spared a few more years I shall soon start on our next great adventure.

Now, as the curtain lowers on my performance, I take my bow. Farewell.

# *Alex I Askaroff*

An Eastbourne lad born and bred.

*I have learnt many things on my journey. One of the more important ones that this messy life has taught me is that I'd rather be laughing on my bike than crying in a Bentley.*

Alex Askaroff

Alex's previous **Random Threads Trilogy** of books, packed full of more short stories, are available from all bookshops by quoting the ISBN details below.

**By phone** Tel: **01323 509874.**

By Internet: www.sewalot.com

**Alex Askaroff**

| | |
|---|---|
| PATCHES OF HEAVEN | ISBN 0-9539410-4-3 |
| SKYLARK COUNTRY | ISBN 0-9539410-2-7 |
| HIGH STREETS & HEDGEROWS | ISBN 0-9539410-3-5 |

# Tales from the Coast

Inspiring stories from fascinating people

By

**Alex Askaroff.**

**148 WILLINGDON PARK DRIVE**

**EASTBOURNE BN22 0DG**

**UNITED KINGDOM**

Order by phone UK: **01323 509874**

International: **00441323 509874**

UK ISBN: 978-0-9539410-5-6

**Other stories are available free online by visiting: www.sewalot.com**

Back cover: Eastbourne seafront towards the Pier by Alex Askaroff and the author with a winter cod at Langney Point by Gary Moore